The Darker Side of Death

After twenty-six outstanding crime novels, Martin Russell turns his attention to the short story—with equal success. The talent for neat plotting, sharp characterization and smart dialogue which has stood him in such good stead in his novels is here skilfully deployed in shorter compass. Whether he is dealing with skulduggery at the local golf club (*A Slice of Justice*), a disturbed mental state (*Hard to Live With*), friction between neighbours (*Kill Before Publication*), or the rivalries in an old people's home (*Paula's People*), his ability to chill the blood even as the hand mesmerically turns the page is never in doubt.

The short story, often considered one of the most difficult art forms, is safe in Martin Russell's hands. They are those of a master.

by the same author

CENSOR
A DOMESTIC AFFAIR
THE SEARCH FOR SARA
ALL PART OF THE SERVICE
RAINBLAST
BACKLASH
CATSPAW
DEATH FUSE
TOUCHDOWN
A DANGEROUS PLACE TO DWELL
DAYLIGHT ROBBERY
DIAL DEATH
MR T
DOUBLE DEAL
MURDER BY THE MILE
THE CLIENT
PHANTOM HOLIDAY
CRIME WAVE
DOUBLE HIT
CONCRETE EVIDENCE
ADVISORY SERVICE
DEADLINE
HUNT TO A KILL
DANGER MONEY
NO RETURN TICKET
NO THROUGH ROAD

MARTIN RUSSELL

The Darker Side of Death

SHORT STORIES

THE CRIME CLUB

COLLINS, 8 GRAFTON STREET, LONDON W1

William Collins Sons & Co. Ltd
London · Glasgow · Sydney · Auckland
Toronto · Johannesburg

First published 1985

British Library Cataloguing in Publication Data

Russell, Martin
The darker side of death.—(Crime Club)
I. Title
823'.914[F]   PR6068.U86

ISBN 0 00 231985 3

Photoset in Linotron Baskerville by
Rowland Phototypesetting Ltd
Bury St Edmunds, Suffolk
Printed in Great Britain by
William Collins Sons & Co. Ltd, Glasgow

Contents

A Slice of Justice

'That's him,' nodded Captain Stevens. 'Coming in now.'

'The little bloke in the wine-coloured anorak?'

'With the dark-haired woman,' confirmed the Captain dispassionately.

'Is she a member, too?'

'Has been for years. Her husband used to play here, off a nine handicap. Died in 'seventy-six, poor old Bob.'

'She hasn't remarried?'

'Not yet.' The Captain gazed ruminatively across the rim of his tankard. 'From the look of things, though, she may be having new thoughts on the situation.' Swallowing the remnant of his pint of bitter, he dabbed his mouth fastidiously with the back of his left wrist. '*Chacun a son goût*,' he concluded on a note of faint humour, and turned back to face the bar.

Squinting across the clubhouse, I saw what he presumably meant. The pair who had just arrived from the course had an ill-assorted air about them. I was reminded of an amateur production of *The Student Prince* I had once endured, in which the reasonably presentable heroine had been partnered by a Prince of such lumbering ugliness that they seemed to have arrived on the same stage by accident, giving an impression of total unreality to the performance. Similarly, the attraction of the dark-haired woman's escort was lost upon the casual observer. Evidently she saw something in him. Unless they had teamed up by chance this morning at the first tee and agreed upon a round together. From the way the Captain had spoken, however, I had to infer that this was by no means a first and only occasion.

While he was rapping instructions to the bartender, I gave consideration to the possibility that what lurked behind the Captain's mildly astringent observations were his own secret hopes in respect of the widow, with whose late husband he appeared to have been on good terms. On the surface, he was anything but a frustrated suitor. Nursing designs of his own, I guessed, he would have been alongside the pair of them in a trice, buying drinks and dominating the conversation. His detached assessment of the affair for my benefit smacked more of a military situation report, lacking personal involvement.

Thoughtfully I kept the improbable couple in view as they conferred at the far end of the bar. Now that he had been pointed out to me, I remembered the small, overweight, practically hairless male constituent quite well. On my second visit to the clubhouse after becoming a member early in the summer, I had somehow fallen into conversation with him. Details of our exchange were vague, but the impression I had, looking back, was that most of them had originated with him. Something about a fantastic new job . . . Echoes of five-figure salaries drifted in my subconscious. A choice of two jobs . . . That was it. Faced with the dilemma, he had opted, he told me, for the post that gave him responsibility, challenge, the chance to work with people, help mould their careers. I recalled thinking that to be moulded by such a garrulous little squirt would have spelt humiliation for most people, and had seized the earliest opportunity to break away from his vicinity. Observing him now, I wondered how his marvellous new position had worked out.

What it seemed to have done was to have consolidated his ability to handle women. The widow, who although not physically overwhelming had a reasonably striking personality and, as far as I could see, good teeth, was clearly hanging upon his words, laughing unrestrainedly at intervals and downing with enjoyment what looked like a large Scotch and soda. In the hubbub the little man's voice was inaudible to me, but evidently he was employing it to maximum effect. Accepting a fresh drink from the Captain, I exchanged a few more polite words with him before wandering off to navigate closer to the pair of them.

From closer range, I was able discreetly to take stock. The widow—her name, the Captain had informed me, was Miriam Parfett—wore an autumnal outfit of thick-knit scarlet jersey and beige trousers, and looked to be about fifty or a little under. Of medium height, she dwarfed her attentive friend, whose elbow was forced upwards at an excruciating angle when he tried to lean upon the bar. His height I judged to be less than five feet, and apart from this handicap and his surplus poundage he carried some facial geometry that ought to have attracted some kind of Government improvement grant on the grounds of creative neglect. His age was indeterminate. He could have been five years her senior: equally, if someone had declared him to be in his early forties I should not have felt disposed to argue. A sizeable vacant area, I noticed, had formed about them. As I watched, to my chagrin the little man spotted me, gave me a beaming smile and waved me over. To ignore him would have been too pointed. Making the best of it, I joined them.

Miriam Parfett seemed none too pleased. She had been happy, I suspected, with the status quo. Her companion, for his part, greeted me as though I were the person he had been waiting for since daybreak. 'That was a great round of yours,' he declaimed, without preamble. His voice was unexpectedly full-bodied. 'Beautiful drive off at the sixteenth. Treat to watch.'

'Thanks.' I hadn't been aware of an audience. 'It's nice when it happens. Doesn't often.' I turned a look of friendly inquiry upon Miriam. 'Did the ball run for you?'

Before she could shrug a non-reply, he interposed deftly. 'Malcolm, isn't it? Malcolm Hooper? Saw you enter your name on the tournament list. I'm Adrian Whitechapel.' A white, soft hand came at me: grasping it was like putting my fingers around a ball of suet. 'Like you to meet Mrs Parfett . . . Miriam. Now that we know each other,' he went on at dizzying speed, 'how about another noggin all round? Malcolm?'

I mentioned a small lager. Lobbing the order over his shoulder and adding to it a dry martini and another Scotch, Adrian went on talking as fluently and with as much enthusiasm as if we had grown up together and kept in touch since adolescence. 'What d'you think of the greens over on the far side? Cash well spent, in my opinion. That stuff they used on 'em last year . . .' He sucked in a breath, shook his head with his eyes half-closed. 'Scorched the living daylights out of the turf. But they seem to have cracked it this time. Found 'em pretty fast, didn't you, my dear?'

Miriam simpered. 'That's a flattering way of putting it. What you mean is, I overshot the flag every time.'

'The ball,' he said seriously, 'was running on.' He sounded like a TV commentator excusing the occasional lapse on the part of an ex-Open champion. 'Your approach shots, now they were going like a dream. Nobody can do much about excessive pace on the greens. Right, Malcolm? They'll settle down, though. A week or two and they'll bed out. You'll see.'

I wasn't sure if he was talking science or gibberish. He sounded completely authentic, as if he had studied greenkeeping to thesis-level. I said dutifully, 'What sort of a round did you have, yourself?'

Again he shook his head. 'Had to opt out. Pulled a pectoral last month and it's still giving trouble. Sick of the sight of doctors' waiting-rooms, to tell you the truth. No, Miriam was in the driving seat this morning. I caddied. Every bit as pleasurable.' They swapped confiding smiles.

I caught myself wondering whether Adrian had ever actually handled a seven-iron in his life. I made a note to ask Captain Stevens. It seemed more likely to me that his golfing activities were confined chiefly to patronage of the nineteenth hole . . . and largely at other people's expense. Our drinks had arrived, and Adrian was making vague gestures of a hand in the region of his breast-pocket while failing to achieve contact. On the point of producing my own wallet, I was forestalled by Miriam, who whipped a couple of banknotes from her purse and slid them to the hovering bartender behind Adrian's back. Poker-faced, the man retired to his till. Adrian, with barely a break, talked on.

'Just before you happened along, Malcolm, I was seeking Miriam's advice. I'm in a quandary, you see. Had a very nice job offer last week—several thousand above what I'm getting now, great people, good prospects: the works. But now what? I'm being wooed by my present crowd, would you believe? They want to promote me. It's as if they *knew*. They might, of course. Word does tend to get around on the grapevine, as you probably find yourself. Question is, what do I do? Stall? It's a problem, I don't mind saying. Miriam feels I should be frank, clear the air on both sides, leave 'em to fight it out between 'em . . . and she could well be right. What's your view? The new situation would mean a fair old bit of travel, and although naturally they'd provide a wagon . . .'

I listened spellbound. His style was mesmeric: I could understand why mature females hung on his words and paid cheerfully for his drinks. The ease, the sheer flow of his delivery was matched only by the tantalizing content, offering glimpses of a mode of existence aspired to by the masses but attained only by the elite. At the same time, he had the gift of making his listener feel appealed to, a vital factor in the discussion, an irreplaceable sounding-board. Against my will and judgment, I found that I was starting to be impressed.

This didn't prevent me, when I was able to insert a question, from making it a rather unfair one. 'What exactly is it you do, Adrian? Accountancy, did you say?'

I knew that no profession had been mentioned during our previous exchange, which he had plainly forgotten; and it was obvious that he had no intention of alluding to one now. He took me up smoothly. 'Now there's a line to avoid, old son. Tell you something. Pal of mine, a pretty big noise in electronics, he dabbled for six months in company business —six months—and it damn near ruined his career. No kidding. They're out to get you and if they can, they will.' He paused impressively. I had no idea what he was talking about, but found myself nodding wisely. 'So I'm keeping out of it. Safest plan. Malcolm, here, has the right idea,' he informed Miriam, who greeted the news with muted rapture. 'A media man. An observer of events. Keeps his finger enjoyably on the pulse *and* gets paid for it. That's what I call having your cake and licking the cream.'

I wondered how he could have known. Had he been compiling dossiers on the membership? Not that it mattered. My Press connections were no dark secret, and if Adrian chose to present them to others in the most theatrical of terms, who was I to object? As for his own occupation, or lack of one, I remained none the wiser. Later, having engineered my withdrawal—to the manifest relief of Miriam, who had shown signs of increasing impatience with my interruption of their privacy—I made inquiries of the Membership Secretary, Miss Barton, who pursed her lips and looked coy.

'I imagine,' she said carefully, 'he Dabbles. Actually I did ask him once, myself, and he hinted at some kind of confidential work in telecommunications . . . which between you and me, Mr Hooper, I took to mean that what he did was to send out customer phone bills, because it later emerged that someone had spotted him in the accounts department at Telephone House with a file in one hand and a beaker of tea in the other. But I've an idea he was made redundant. I wonder if he's had much in the way of steady employment, since. He seems to spend quite a lot of time here.'

'Good for bar profits,' I suggested.

'Yes; though frankly . . .' Miss Barton hesitated, before deciding that the chances of my publicizing her remarks nationwide were perhaps too slim to signify. 'It's the people he's with who tend to provide most of the support. He does seem to have quite a knack of inspiring generosity in others . . .'

Her thinly-veiled comments made me chortle on the way home: after that, Adrian Whitechapel went out of my mind. As did thoughts of golf, until on the Wednesday of the ensuing week, finding myself with a free morning at the end of an assignment, I decided to visit the club for a relaxing nine holes, with or without a partner. The clubhouse was almost deserted. Coming through the bar on my way to the first tee, I noticed a figure seated in a basket-chair by the main window overlooking the course. It was Miriam Parfett. A cup of coffee stood at her elbow and she was immersed in the *Guardian.* Hearing my footsteps, she glanced up. I gave her a guarded grin.

'Had your exercise for the morning?'

'Not stirred my stumps,' she replied languidly. 'I was hoping someone might turn up. I hate going around alone.'

'I'm about to embark. Care to join me?'

Slightly to my surprise, she rose with some alacrity and made for her clubs, waiting in a wheeled bag just inside the bar annexe. 'I'll be a bit of a passenger for you,' she said defensively. 'My drives are feeble at the best of times, and I'm not on my game at the moment.'

'Suits me,' I assured her. 'I'm not here to set a course record.'

She proved to be right about her lack of power. However, her strokes were straight and consistent, and we got to the third hole in a brisker fashion than I had envisaged. By then, we had begun to barter a few remarks other than golfing platitudes. She was, she explained, deputy head teacher of a local primary school which had taken a week off for half-term: she liked to keep active, but unfortunately none of her staff colleagues was a golfer, and her immediate circle of friends was likewise deficient. I said helpfully, 'What about Captain Stevens? He's generally on call, they tell me.'

Her mouth contorted a little. 'He's a bit out of my class, wouldn't you say? I'd hate to cramp his style.'

Seemingly oblivious of the backhander she had just dealt me, she set off down the fairway. Catching up, I added casually, 'And then of course there's your friend, Adrian Whitechapel. Not available this morning?'

'Working,' she replied briefly.

She executed a flighted drop on to the green. Joining her an extra stroke later, I made my putt and stood watching as she lined up her own fifteen-footer. Before unleashing the shot, she glanced up.

'You were asking about Adrian,' she said, in an oddly

tight manner. 'The truth is, he plays such a dire game of golf that I'm afraid I avoid going round with him if I possibly can. I don't like to hurt his feelings. He's sensitive about it.'

'I see.' Difficult as I found it to ascribe any degree of sensitivity to Adrian, I was prepared to believe that his surface self-assurance disguised an underlying human frailty, or at least to accept that Miriam saw it in this light. Scenting my chance, I waited until she had holed her putt before continuing. 'His job is kind of hush-hush, I gather? He hedged a bit when I asked.'

For a moment or two she made no reply. Thinking she had taken offence on his behalf, I resigned myself to a silent completion of the half-round. But as we crossed the footbridge over a stream to the next tee, she spoke again with more animation.

'He never likes to talk about it. Not even to me. It has to do with communications, I believe: that's the most he's ever let slip. Obviously he's in no position to blab about his work.'

You can say that again, I thought. Judging from what I had seen and heard of Adrian, communications—on his own terms—were what the little fellow was all about. A master of the self-sales pitch, he had Miriam as a captive client: how many had he previously enslaved? Watching her tee up and address the ball with a certain earnest diligence, I felt a small, unexpected stab of sympathy for her. As a rule, besotted middle-aged females aroused a sense of impatience in me. Anybody who could fall victim to the most blatant verbal cajolery deserved, in my view, all that was coming to them, and there was little point in trying to divert them. Miriam at this moment, however, for all her high-flown manner, struck me as a genuine and vulnerable person. If I read the situation correctly, she was going to get hurt, and for some reason the prospect annoyed me. Why, I could not have said. I hardly knew her. Perhaps her obvious basic intelligence, coupled with Adrian's equally apparent shallow slickness, had something to do with it.

On our return to the clubhouse I bought her a drink.

Thanking her for her company, I added politely that I hoped we might repeat the occasion some other time, and rather thankfully made my escape. She was, to be truthful, slightly heavy going as a conversationalist. I doubted whether Adrian found it a handicap.

Possibly it was mere journalistic curiosity which took me, that afternoon, to the suburban residential street in which, according to the club membership list, Mr A. C. Whitechapel resided. My purpose in driving out was to do some shopping at the supermarket: on the way back, finding myself at the mouth of Rowan Chase—as leafy a boulevard as its name implied, stuffed with properties that any estate agent worth his salt would have described as 'highly sought-after'—I made an idle detour as far as No. 48, Tudor Gables. Large, square and detached, the house was considerably more up-to-date than its nominal period. The extensive front garden was part-lawn, part-shrubbery, and residually a paved area of pink and grey flagstones upon which, at various angles, squatted three cars: a huge and glistening white Jaguar, a Renault hatchback, and a high-powered BMW saloon. Halting my Ford Fiesta at the opposite kerb, I sat looking across at the spectacle.

Again, without knowing why, I felt resentment. Envy is foreign, I hope, to my nature. But something about that mass of opulent metal smugly installed upon Mr A. C. Whitechapel's dual-toned forecourt scraped against a nerve. I felt I wanted to get out, walk across the street and dent all the bodywork with a brick.

An irrational impulse. Summoning a self-deprecatory quirk of the lips—it was, after all, no concern of mine how Adrian chose to spend money, albeit the source of it remained a puzzle—I restarted the engine and engaged gear. About to move off, I throttled back as the front door of Tudor Gables opened to release a figure into the porch.

I was still curious. And, since I had taken the precaution of wearing dark glasses and a cap, there was little chance of my being identified by Adrian, even at such relatively close range.

It was not, however, Adrian who stepped out on to the flagstones. It was Captain Stevens.

The surprise was considerable. Asked to compile a list of improbable visitors to Adrian's domain, I should have placed the Captain at or near the very top. From his tone of voice in the clubhouse the previous Sunday, I had inferred that he had little time for people of Adrian's stamp, still less for Adrian in particular: the notion that he would dream of paying him a social call on a Wednesday afternoon would never have occurred to me. But this, maybe, was no social call. A demand for a withheld subscription? As a committee member, the Captain would have been a natural choice for such a mission.

The affability on the face of the Captain, however, seemed to rule out such an explanation. Behind him, framed in the doorway, Adrian was looking correspondingly cheerful as they exchanged parting words. With a final friendly gesture, the Captain marched over to the BMW and swarmed in behind the wheel. Smoothly the car came to life, surged backwards, hesitated, swept clear of the driveway into the street and departed with a toot. From the porch, Adrian watched it out of sight, threw a casual glance in my direction, stepped back into the house and closed the door.

Preoccupied, I drove home.

Several other possibilities offered themselves for inspection. Bizarre as it might seem, Adrian could conceivably have been invited on to the committee. The Captain might have been delegated to sound him out, extend an informal invitation prior to official notification.

Alternatively, it might have been decided to ask Adrian, a golfing rabbit, to act as the next tournament referee. Or look after the bar accounts. Assuming he had book-keeping experience, or had once been in charge of a pub . . .

All plausible solutions, yet somehow unconvincing. On Sunday, everything the Captain had said about the little upstart had tended to condition me to the belief that he rather despised him, would have felt reluctant to address him directly if the very ceiling of the clubhouse had been about to collapse on the spot where he stood. Such a disaster, indeed, would not have caused the Captain undue distress, according to the scenario I had been led to devise.

Now, three days later, here he was fraternizing with the man, seemingly on the most amicable of terms. It made no sense.

Unless, just feasibly, he had succeeded in warning Adrian off his widowed acquaintance, Miriam. Such an achievement might well have accounted for his evident good humour as he drove away. But how did it explain Adrian's answering sunniness?

A pay-off, perhaps. A back-hander . . .

My reflections were getting fanciful. Undoubtedly the explanation was straightforward, and in any case the episode had nothing whatever to do with me. Sheer chance had made me a spectator. My interest in either man, or in Miriam herself, for that matter, was minimal. There was no reason for me to pursue the matter. It wasn't worth the trouble.

Over an early supper I went on pursuing it doggedly, and I came to one conclusion. Between them, Adrian and the Captain were up to no good. The precise nature of what they might be plotting eluded me; beyond question, however, their association was unnatural, faintly sinister.

And this set me wondering about Miriam. Did she have money? To judge from appearances, the Captain stood in no particular need of a fast buck: but appearances could deceive. He might be up to his neck in gambling debts, running his BMW on borrowed cash, hopelessly in hock to the sharks. As for Adrian, he lived ostensibly in impressive style and ran, apparently, at least two cars; but it might all be a façade. There could be an insupportable mortgage around his neck. If Miriam, a widow with a good income of her own, had let slip to either or both of them that she had assets . . .

Lucy dropped in on me that evening and I put the question to her. A columnist herself, Lucy Chalmers had opted to remain with the *Comet*, the local weekly that I had abandoned four years previously for a sterner journalistic climate; but as I still lived in the district we had kept in touch. There was nothing of a heavy-breathing nature between us. We just liked one another. Assaulting the dish of ice-cream I produced for her—Lucy had a rueful weakness for such confections—she gave the matter a full half-second's consideration before offering an opinion.

'She's slap-bang in the target area, I'd say, this Miriam of yours.'

'Not mine. I'm nothing to do with her.'

'Then why are you asking?'

'Out of interest. Well, maybe there's an element of altruism. Wipe that look off your face. I do have my finer side. Let's say I dislike seeing somewhat naive ladies in their middle years offering themselves for possible sacrifice. In her case, it irks me.'

Lucy cast me a lopsided grin. 'What if she *wants* to be taken for a ride?'

'In that case there's nothing anyone can do. If there are spoils to be had, Adrian and the Captain will just have to be allowed to pocket the damn stuff.'

'This Adrian. What's he like?'

I described him. Lucy sucked in her cheeks. 'Any idea where he lives?'

'Rowan Chase. He's got a Tudor-style—'

'Good grief. Adrian Whitechapel? I know him.'

'You do?'

'Sort of. His mother was a friend of my grandmother's, believe it or not. I used to see him occasionally when they met up. He kind of went with the furniture. Bored the pants off me. He could always talk, I'll say that. Which probably explains later events.'

I gazed at her. 'Events?'

'You don't remember? Come to think of it, it was probably a year or so before you joined the *Comet*. Also he was using a different name at the time, rather cannily. So obviously you wouldn't have linked him with the episode. Nor would anyone else, unless they happened to have been involved.'

'Involved in what?' For a punchy writer, Lucy could be maddeningly circumlocutory in conversation.

'It was some shady investment trust that he and a partner

set up.' Taking a spoonful of ice-cream, she dissolved and swallowed it with a reminiscent expression. 'As I recall, they sweet-talked several hundred hopefuls into parting with their life's savings and pouring it all into something called the Peterson Profit Plan which was meant to give a cast-iron return of twenty-three per cent, tax-free. It went bust, of course. Eighteen months later every investor had lost the lot.'

'Ho, hum. Were he and his partner prosecuted?'

'There was talk of bringing charges. Finally, though, it was decided that all they'd done was indulge in outrageous over-optimism, taken on more than they could chew and ruined a few gullible souls in the process. Strictly speaking, they hadn't broken the law. There was some tax loophole they'd tried to exploit. It's been plugged since.'

'A trifle late for the victims.'

'Stable doors and horses department,' she agreed. 'Anyhow, after that Adrian supposedly retired from the scene of high finance. Last I heard, he was some kind of a clerk with British Telecom.' Clearing the ice-cream dish with gusto, Lucy licked each of her fingertips in turn. 'Maybe he's decided the time is now ripe to get back into the skulduggery market, in a small way.'

Meditatively, I passed her a table napkin. 'You don't happen to recall the name of his partner at the time?'

She squeezed her eyes. 'Daniel? Damwell? No, sorry, I don't. Give us a day or two, I could look it up.' Her glance was shrewd. 'He was young, I can tell you that. Self-styled City whizzkid. How does that description match up with your Captain Stevens?'

'Badly,' I admitted. 'He's pushing seventy. But then, if Adrian was scheming a comeback, he'd hardly rejoin forces with his old crony-in-catastrophe, do you think? He'd try somebody new.'

Lucy sat rubbing her hands reflectively with the napkin. 'If you ask me,' she said finally, 'Miriam Parfett might be well advised to have a rethink about her relationship with the little creep. But who's going to offer the advice?'

★

The following day, I did a little research in my newspaper's microfilm records department.

The crash of the Peterson Profit Plan in 1975 had received a fair amount of coverage. It was a dismally familiar story. Alan Whitney, as Adrian was then calling himself, had teamed up with a dynamic young financier to launch an investment trust dealing with precious metals, including gold and platinum. An ingenious-sounding tax arrangement was designed to give investors complete protection on their gains, either on capital or from income. Additionally, those handing over their money were promised the security of a bond which guaranteed the return on demand, in full, of the sum originally invested. The bond, said the promotion material, was underwritten by the resources of the established and respected financial advisory firm of E. P. Dansell, a founder-member of the Small Investors' Warrantee Association.

In fact, as it transpired, the established firm of E. P. Dansell consisted of the dynamic young financier, operating from a telephone number at his private address in Bayswater and sending out prospectuses typed by his wife. For a few months all had gone swimmingly as the cheques rolled in from eager speculators, lured by the predicted returns and reassured by the certainty of getting their money back if necessary. Needless to say, there proved to be no such body as the Small Investors' Warrantee Association—or rather, there was, but it had been set up and registered by E. P. Dansell himself, who was its sole member and had omitted to take the fundamental precaution of allocating funds to its coffers for emergencies. When the Profit Plan overreached itself—foundering on the twin shoals of inept management and a sharp fall in the price of the metals in which it specialized—there was nothing left. E. P. Dansell retired, chastened or otherwise, to the Isle of Man, leaving behind him four hundred and eighty-three highly dissatisfied customers furiously demanding compensation from thin air. Sums of more than £50,000 were among those said to have been lost.

Adrian himself—or Alan Whitney—dropped prudently

out of circulation until the threat of prosecution was lifted. Whether he personally had lost money was never determined. The one indisputable fact was that he continued to dwell in apparently uninhibited comfort at his Rowan Chase address, run a large car and retain his membership of the golf club. A year or so after the crash, in reply to questions from a Sunday newspaper, he declared himself to be 'actively investigating ways of achieving reimbursement of those adversely affected by this unfortunate chain of events'. There was no record of a fruitful outcome to his endeavours.

I came away from the microfilm department musing yet again upon the fallibility of human nature. While there were the Whitneys and the Dansells around to exploit it, the casualties would go on piling up. A cynic might have called them legitimate victims of greed for fat profit. Many of them, on the other hand, might well have been motivated by a wish to provide adequately for their families, and could hardly be condemned for seeking the best returns on their savings, especially in view of the Press advertisements that had seduced them in the first place. Devised by Adrian, who was nothing if not a wizard with words, the promotional blandishments would have tempted a Swiss banker. For those left penniless, it was difficult not to harbour a certain sympathy.

Early on the following Sunday morning I paid another visit to the golf club to try my luck. Again, hardly anybody else had arrived, but the sight of Miriam Parfett in her chair by the window, sipping coffee and gazing out abstractedly at the waiting course, activated switches within me that subconsciously I had known were there, waiting to be thrown. I walked across to her.

'Hi.'

She jumped a little, spilling some coffee. 'Oh—hello.' Her tone of voice lacked a welcome. She looked less than delighted to see me.

Disregarding the frost, I threw myself into a chair facing her. 'Care for a repeat of last weekend? Or are you waiting for somebody?'

'Two people, actually.' She glanced at her watch. 'I've a threesome arranged.'

'That's nice. You managed to find two other ladies, then?'

'It's with Adrian Whitechapel and Captain Stevens.' She turned her head to peer at the door. 'They should be here shortly.'

'I could tag on, make it a foursome,' I suggested jovially.

Ignoring me, she devoted her attention to stirring the coffee. I sat watching her for a moment. 'Sorry if I'm out of line,' I remarked presently, 'but I had the impression that Adrian and the Captain weren't exactly buddies. What's this, a fence-mending operation?'

Her eyebrows rocketed. 'I'm sure I've no idea, Mr Hooper. The Captain suggested it, and Adrian had no objection.' A twist of her body and a resumption of her outward gaze informed me that as far as she was concerned the dialogue was over, but I sat on. After a few moments she felt obliged to accord me another glance.

'Normally,' I added at once, 'the Captain's choosy, isn't he, about playing standards? With the greatest respect, I wouldn't have thought Adrian . . .'

The faintest of smiles disturbed her mouth. 'I'll be doing my best to make up for Adrian's deficiencies. It's more of a social occasion, in fact.'

'Sounds fun. I expect you've plenty in common, the three of you. Lots to discuss.'

This earned me a hard stare. 'We do have something to talk about, as it happens.'

'Not business, I hope,' I said lightly. 'Not on a Sunday.'

She blinked twice. 'Nothing too demanding, if the thought bothers you. There they are now.' Relief showed in her voice as she rose, waving through the window at the two men who had appeared at the first tee with their clubs and were making beckoning gestures towards her. 'I hope you manage to find yourself a partner,' she said by way of farewell, and went off to collect her carrier. A few moments later I saw her join them. After some animated talk they drove off—Adrian achieving his usual fifteen-yard trickle into the rough—and headed down the fairway. Remaining in my chair, I watched them thoughtfully until they were out of sight beyond the crest of the slope.

Could I have said more? I decided that I could, but that no purpose would have been served. Women of Miriam's breed were not to be swayed by words, however blunt. She would have to learn the hard way.

Soon after the trio's disappearance, another member arrived. A general practitioner called Smithers, in his early sixties but still possessed of a mighty swing by club standards, he accepted tolerantly my proposal of a nine-hole saunter before lunch, and we set off immediately. It shortly became evident that Miriam and her companions were a bare two holes ahead of us, and losing ground. The culprit was Adrian, who was hacking his way along a few yards at a time. I glanced uneasily at Dr Smithers. He had a reputation for impatience, and I was in no mood for a fraught morning. I was here to relax.

From the fairway of the fifth, however, I was relieved to see that Adrian—no doubt at the tactful behest of the Captain—had abandoned the struggle. With his own clubs slung over a shoulder, he was now caddying for Miriam, trotting behind her like a rounded puppy, hauling her wheeled bag and clutching an assortment of jackets. Lining up his second shot, Dr Smithers noticed it too.

'That's good,' he grunted. 'Maybe they'll get along faster now. I was afraid we were going to have to play through.'

'Best to avoid that,' I agreed. 'I hate having people on my heels.'

'Don't know about you, but it makes me hurry my shots.' Delaying his stroke, Dr Smithers continued to gaze contemplatively across the intervening distance. 'That fellow Whitechapel,' he said suddenly. 'I wonder what she sees in him.'

'His tongue has a way with it, from all accounts.' I watched Miriam and the two men vanish behind a belt of trees between ourselves and the stream which ran alongside the seventh fairway. From what I could discern at that distance, she and the Captain were having a lively chat as they walked, while Adrian was keeping well within range of them as if poised to throw in a helpful word. On Miriam's behalf, I offered up a short prayer.

Another grunt came from Dr Smithers. 'What you mean is, the little bugger can talk the hind legs off a giraffe. The Captain's no slouch at that, either. I hope the lady's a good listener.'

I said, 'I'm very much afraid she might be.'

He threw me a quick, suspicious stare, saw that I was serious, decided it wasn't worth asking what I meant, and hooked his ball into some gorse. By the time he had found it and chopped it out I was waiting for him on the green, from which the remainder of the course was entirely concealed by encircling slopes. With the threesome out of sight, I resolved to forget about Miriam and concentrate on my game. So far, Dr Smithers had been outplaying me too comprehensively for the good of my pride. Surveying the immense putt he had left himself, he scratched his head testily.

'Beats me why they make this a par four. Always come a cropper on it. By comparison with . . . What was that?'

'I didn't hear anything.'

'Sounded like a squeal. Fox, maybe. Do foxes have shrill voices?'

'The vixens, possibly. Hedgehogs squeal.'

'But only at night, I fancy.' Steadying himself, Dr Smithers made the putt and missed by a yard. He dealt his beefy thigh a slap. 'Two over already, and I've left myself another stinker. You got your par? At this rate we'll be level by the next hole, and serve me right. Lapse of concentration. In this game, I find, the slightest . . . *Now* what?'

Irritably he swung about to glare at the hillside behind us from which, unmistakably this time, a call had reached our ears. Turning, I saw the approaching figure of Miriam. She was heading for us at a stumbling trot, grasping an iron in her left hand and gesticulating with the other. 'She can't have mis-hit this far,' Dr Smithers growled incredulously. 'There's a three-acre wood in between.' He raised his voice to a roar. 'What's the trouble, Mrs Parfett?'

'Please come,' she panted, reaching the green. 'We need help. There's been an accident.'

'Captain Stevens?' Dropping his putter, the doctor came swiftly across. 'Chest pains? He was telling me—'

'No, no.' She grabbed his arm. 'It's Adrian. Please come quickly.'

Accompanying her over the hill, we descended the far side at a run to a spot at the edge of the stream where the kneeling figure of the Captain was performing pumping actions upon Adrian's prostrate rotundity. Both of them were drenched. As Dr Smithers hurled the Captain aside and took over, applying the kiss of life, I said to Miriam, 'What happened? Did he fall in?'

'A ball hit him,' she said distractedly. 'He was near the stream, searching for one I'd lost, when . . .'

Her voice tailed off. With a desperate anxiety in her eyes she stood watching the efforts of the doctor, who was being grimly efficient to no avail: Adrian continued to lie there like a spent balloon tyre on a dump. Presently she added, 'He couldn't have seen it coming. If he hadn't been standing so close—'

'I'm the culprit.' Captain Stevens interposed gruffly. He looked shaken. 'Sliced my drive, I'm afraid. Ball just flew at him and in he went.'

'God, how awful.'

'Worst of it is, he was carried out midstream. Time I got to him, he'd been face-under for quite some time . . .'

Like Miriam's, the sentence remained unfinished as he gazed at the doctor's abortive activity. His fists were clenched hard at his sides.

'It was nobody's fault,' Miriam said faintly.

After ten minutes or so, Dr Smithers abandoned his efforts. Rising slowly from the body, he placed an arm around Miriam's shoulders and led her aside. 'Nothing more I can do. I'm very sorry,' he told her.

Giving a kind of sigh, she began to weep quietly. Still ashen-faced, the Captain watched her briefly before, directing a final numbed glance at the corpse, he turned away, producing from a hip-pocket a small flask which he unstoppered and put to his mouth. He took a gulp or two.

'Needed that,' he said, on a gasp. 'Can't quite . . . take

it in. What a thing. What a thing.' Vacantly he held out the flask. 'Anyone feel like a bracer?'

I took him gently by the elbow. 'Come back with me, Captain, to the clubhouse. We must get you dried off.'

It took most of the rest of the day for the dust to settle. By late afternoon the police had taken statements, the Coroner had been informed, and the body of Adrian had been carted off. Not without misgivings, I had telephoned a story through to my newspaper, which splashed it the following morning under the headline SLICED SHOT KILLS GOLFER. As a result, the club secretary had to endure a minor bombardment of calls from other sections of the media during the next day or two, and I felt it diplomatic as well as expedient to stay out of range until the fuss had expired.

Hence, it was not until the formal opening of the inquest that I resumed contact with Miriam and the Captain. Both of them looked, still, a little haunted, and we exchanged few words. Later, when the adjourned inquest was reopened, all of us including Dr Smithers had to give evidence. The Coroner was sympathetic. Having elicited from the pathologist that Adrian's death was due to asphyxia from drowning, caused by his immersion unconscious in water as a consequence of a blow consistent with the impact of a golf ball travelling at speed, he gave special consideration to Miriam and the Captain, urging the latter not to blame himself for 'this unhappy mischance' and to do his best to put it out of his mind; and wishing the former a speedy recovery from her ordeal. Miriam smiled at him wanly and bowed her head. The Captain puffed his leathery cheeks.

A verdict of Misadventure was recorded.

After the hearing, the Captain invited Miriam and me to lunch at a nearby hotel. Dr Smithers had had to return to his practice. No longer subdued, the Captain ordered for the three of us. 'I've quite an appetite, at last,' he announced. 'How about you, my dear?'

Miriam confessed to feeling less like refusing food than she had for some while. 'It's the relief,' she said, 'of getting the inquest over. Illogical, really.'

'I don't know. It's the same as funerals. Good to have 'em out of the way.'

'And a favourable verdict,' I remarked, 'into the bargain.'

They both looked at me. 'What other verdict could there have been?' demanded the Captain.

'Alternatives do exist,' I said vaguely. I turned to Miriam. 'Feeling better now? Over the hump?'

'A great deal, thank you.' Although she spoke primly, I received an impression of buoyancy underlying the response. The Captain was eyeing her closely, almost proprietorially, like an agent vetting the public utterances of his charge. Dismantling her bread roll and nibbling at a morsel, she added, 'What alternatives?'

'It could have been an open verdict.'

'That would have suggested,' the Captain said heavily, 'that there were some doubts about what occurred.'

'Whereas there are none. As we know.'

'*We* know,' he echoed with emphasis. 'You sound a shade uncertain, Mr Hooper, yourself.'

'Do I?'

The soup arrived. When it had been served, I went on, 'There's no uncertainty, as far as I'm concerned. I know what happened.'

'Of course you do. It's been described umpteen times, in detail.'

'Oh, I don't dispute that Adrian was hit by a golf ball and fell into the stream. What I find harder to credit, Captain—' I gave him a quizzical glance—'is that you managed to perpetrate such an atrocious slice to cause the accident. I'd have said your technique ruled it out.'

He took a bubbling inhalation of soup. 'We all have our lapses,' he said mildly.

'But you're a sporting all-rounder.' Leaning back, I contemplated him. 'Quite a cricketer, weren't you, in your younger days? Demon bowler, I'm told. Middle stump, every time.

'You flatter me,' he murmured. 'But what are you getting at?'

Miriam's gaze was fastened upon me. I said meditatively,

'It's odd, you know, that Adrian should have met his death just now. Or perhaps I should say, fortuitous.'

'In what way?' Miriam's soup-spoon rested on the rim of her plate. She was now making no pretence of eating.

'He was on the point of a comeback into high finance. Or low finance, if you prefer. As I dare say you might.'

The Captain studied the tablecloth. 'I take it,' he observed after a pause, 'you've been investigating. That news media mind of yours.'

'I did a spot of research. The full list of ruined investors in the Peterson Profit Plan wasn't easy to come by, I might tell you: but one has one's contacts. And persistence usually pays, as in this case.' I sat looking at him until he met my eye. 'Twenty-eight thousand quid,' I said quietly. 'You couldn't have enjoyed losing that.'

The head of the Captain shook slightly. 'Nobody could have found it funny, Mr Hooper. Believe me.'

I turned back to Miriam. 'The biggest loser of all, though, was somebody else. A gentleman by the name of Parfett. R. M. Parfett. He crashed to the tune of eighty thousand.' I waited a moment. 'It's not that common a name. A member of your family, perhaps?'

She held my gaze steadily. 'Since you've obviously done your homework, you must know that he was my husband. The exact sum, for your information, was seventy-eight thousand, nine hundred and thirty.'

'Not peanuts, in anyone's language. Took it hard, didn't he?'

The Captain leaned forward across the table. 'Bob Parfett committed suicide five months later. You know that too, I'm sure. Any need to distress Mrs Parfett by dragging it up?'

'It's all right, Adam.' Miriam's eyes were calm. 'I don't mind talking about it. Not now. I'm feeling much better about everything.' She paused, and then repeated, '*Everything*. Besides, I believe Mr Hooper is just trying to tell us something.' The lift of her voice conveyed a challenge.

I sipped at some soup. 'My function,' I said carelessly, 'is to report. I don't make judgments. One or two small things do still intrigue me, I must admit. Such as the panic in both your faces when Dr Smithers set to work on trying to resuscitate Adrian—almost as if you didn't want him to succeed. Which is absurd, of course. And then, the fixing up of a threesome like that in the first place. If I didn't know better, I'd have guessed that Adrian had been tempted previously by talk of a possible business deal of some kind. But, as I say, it's nothing to do with me.'

The Captain's smile was enigmatic. 'I never talk business, Mr Hooper, during a round of golf. Nor over lunch, for that matter.' Lifting his wineglass, he bowed slightly to both of us. 'Drink up, and we'll order another bottle. After all, we're celebrating.'

Paula's People

At five o'clock they all assembled in the dining-room for tea. All except ancient Mrs Blatt, who was rumoured to have suffered 'a turn' and to be bedded down for the night; another rumour said she had been taken off by her young, seventy-year-old nephew for supper at his house and would not be returned until ten. Whatever the truth, her three pills, two yellow and one pink, had been deposited as usual on the rim of her plate. This, her table-companions agreed darkly, was the mistake of Julie, who never knew what was going on, having thoughts only for her young man or the formation of her next hairdo.

It was perhaps imprecise to say that the residents assembled for tea. Since lunch, most of them had never been dispersed. Even the decampment from lounge to dining-room had been undertaken more or less in unison, with just a handful of independent spirits such as Miss Jameson and Mr Cuthbert—both contenders for the coveted post of Matron's Pet—hanging back for the few seconds required to give an impression that they were making their own way through, at their own pace, to arrive at a time that suited their tastes and appetites.

By three minutes after the hour, all the tables (apart from No. 5, where the gap created by the absence of Mrs Blatt stood out like a missing galaxy in the heavens) were heavily occupied, and the first strafing runs had been made by Julie and her colleagues with their combined armoury of hot-plates and metal dish-covers, blitzing each place-setting with its allocation of poached whiting and baked beans. Six minutes later, the laggards were toiling to clear their plates in time to snatch their shares of the buttered sultana scones that were fast vanishing from the central cakestands, and the staff had carried out their third and penultimate low-level swoop with giant teapots. By this time, tongues and brains which had been ossified for most of the afternoon had achieved their greatest flexibility of the day.

'Looks like she's in love again,' rickety Mr Dodds confided jovially to his neighbour, Miss Cranleigh.

'Who?'

'Our Julie, bless her. Got that look in her eye.'

Miss Cranleigh sniffed. 'Been at the sherry again, if you ask me. I've seen her, when she thought nobody was looking. Residents only, those drinks are meant for. Can I trouble you for the preserve?'

Looking vague, Mr Dodds passed her the honey. With a sigh, Miss Cranleigh stretched across him for the pineapple jam and heaped a liberal spoonful on her remaining half-scone. Swallowing the vestiges of his whiting, Mr Dodds arranged his cutlery scrupulously together at the side of his plate, picked up the purple, torpedo-shaped tablet next to his saucer, placed it upon his tongue, added some tea, retracted the whole and gulped strenuously. 'She's in love,' he repeated. 'No mistaking the signs.'

'I wouldn't mind what she is,' Miss Cranleigh said practically, 'if only she'd remember I like my tea in the cup before the milk. If I've told her once, I've told her a thousand times. Still she does it the opposite way round. A scatter-brain, that's what she is. I pity any young fellow *she* gets hold of.'

'He won't need sympathy.' Mr Dodds said it good-humouredly, albeit on a detectable note of envy. For a moment, while the pill travelled down, he eyed Julie with the frankest interest as she refilled the cup of Miss Jameson, whose voice could clearly be heard in all parts of the room from its source at the furthermost corner table, by the bay window with its view over trimmed lawns and the mallard-infested pond that was known as The Lake and boasted, at its narrower end, a rustic wooden bridge from shore to shore. Miss Jameson was telling Julie that she ought to get more sleep.

'Fat chance, with you lot to see to,' retorted the girl, tossing hair back from her eyes.

'If you were better organized, my dear, you could get all

the relaxation you need and still have heaps of time for your duties.' Miss Jameson's arch great-auntliness was gruesome to hear and to behold. Julie, who was accustomed to worse, took it unflinchingly on the chin.

'I relax okay,' she said with a giggle. 'You should see me sometimes. More tea, Mrs Davenport?'

'Of course you do, my dear. At the wrong times.'

Miss Jameson looked around for applause. One or two acolytes tittered. At the next table, old Mr Cuthbert champed stoically away at a few resistant shreds of whiting and seemed to have heard nothing of the exchange. Julie feigned a look of injury.

'That's not very nice. Run off my feet all day, I am, looking after you, making sure you're comfortable. Then you've the cheek to say I'm slacking. I've a good mind to pour your tea back in the pot.'

'You can't,' Miss Jameson said complacently. 'I've nearly drunk it.' She knew to a nicety how far she could go. 'And who might it be this time, young Julie? Anyone we know?'

'Miss Jameson, you're *wicked*.' Wriggling her hips, the girl glanced across the tables at an older colleague, who grinned back. 'I'm not telling. You'll only gossip. Don't forget it's bingo tonight. Six o'clock, on the dot.'

'No use trying to sidetrack me, my girl. I got used to that with my great-nephews and nieces. Quite often they thought they'd got the better of me, but in the end I always showed 'em.'

Until they shoved you away in here, thought the girl, mostly in pity. Aloud, she said, 'It's double-prize evening—got that, everybody? Some lucky person could clean up.'

'You haven't answered my question.'

'I'll write you a letter about it,' teased Julie, moving on with the teapot.

'Takes it very well, doesn't she?' observed the table-companion at Miss Jameson's right hand. 'Not touchy, not a bit.'

'She knows I'm only pulling her leg. All in fun, my dear. What's life without a dab of fun? If you can't—'

'Paula!' An apple-cheeked woman in her forties had appeared at the dining-room door and was gesticulating. Rising majestically, Miss Jameson weaved her way between tables to join her, tracked expressionlessly by Mr Cuthbert from the shelter of a mouthful of scone and honey. 'We've been let down again,' explained the Matron, Mrs Harding, 'by our caller for this evening. Do you think you could fill the breach?'

'You know, my dear, I'm always ready to oblige.' Miss Jameson was indiscriminate in her distribution of endearments.

'What should we do without you, Paula?' Matron squeezed her hand. 'All those who are playing, try to have them in their places quite by six, won't you? We don't want it to drag on. The staff like to get away.'

'Leave it to me.' Miss Jameson laughed musically. 'I'll see they're installed.'

Without bothering to return to her table, she went out into the hall and back to the lounge where the TV set, tuned to a children's programme, was thundering away to nobody. Reducing the sound, she turned to cast an assessing eye over the chairs lined against three of the walls. Clicking a fussy tongue, she pushed one of them back into line and plumped the cushion, lifted a half-filled ashtray from the floor beneath it and carried it across the carpet for emptying into a plant-pot. While she was attending to cushions on other chairs, Mr Cuthbert shuffled into the room. Still chewing, he inspected her briefly. With an air of preoccupation he began altering the seat alignment along the wall facing the screen. Miss Jameson jumped at him.

'No, Harry! It's bingo night, don't you remember?'

'I thought, if these were brought forward a bit . . .'

'Leave everything to me. I know what's wanted.'

'You can do with a spot of help, Paula, now and then.'

'I don't need any help. Go and sit down.'

Vanquished, he retired to his corner armchair and sat contemplating the silently active screen, registering no reaction to its visual messages. He continued to chew. Thumping a cushion, Miss Jameson said severely, 'You should clear your mouth before coming back in here.'

Mr Cuthbert's jaw movements became more furtive. Hissing and shaking her head, Miss Jameson returned across the hall to show herself at the dining-room doorway. 'Bingo starts in twelve minutes,' she announced. 'All those taking part, I want you seated in the lounge by five minutes to six, at the latest. Quick sharp, now.'

'Paula's got the whip out,' Julie remarked in the kitchen.

'Thrashing 'em into shape,' agreed a colleague, a cynical older woman who came in four afternoons a week. 'Pity she can't do the same with her relatives, when they get round to visiting.'

'They seem to get along all right.'

''Course they do. Butter wouldn't melt in her mouth, 'cause she knows they're paying for her to stop here. What'd happen if they didn't? She'd be in a council home—snap!—like that. So it stands to reason, she's on her best behaviour.'

'You mean she *wants* to stay here?'

The older woman eyed the incredulous Julie dispassionately. 'Never said that, did I?' After a moment of baffled silence from the girl, she added, 'Going out with Rod tonight?'

Julie perked up. 'He did say we might be able to. Depends if he's wanted here past seven.'

Miss Jameson was a good caller of numbers. Her voice had retained a resonance—'You don't spend a lifetime in catering,' she was wont to observe, 'without developing strong vocal cords to deal with backsliders'—and her eyesight was as keen as ever. By eight o'clock, bingo prizes had been briskly distributed among three recipients: two pounds for Mrs Davenport, a pound for Mr Dodds, and a fifty-pence booby award for the bottom scorer, venerable Miss Willis, who accepted the coin with a fixed smile of incomprehension, having not the slightest idea what the evening had been about. At eight-thirty the surviving staff came round with warm malted milk and biscuits. By nine, the residents had retired to their bedrooms. Noting the silence, Julie stroked the muscled arms that were pinning her to the bed-coverlet and said drowsily, 'That's them in their cages for the night.'

The human factors responsible for the existence of his job as porter held little interest for Rodney; especially at moments like this. 'Glad you ain't a pensioner yet,' he remarked in her ear, sparking a splutter.

'Supposing I was. What would you do about it?'

'Not a lot, I reckon.' A second splutter rewarded the witticism.

'It's my half-day off, Thursday,' said Julie.

'Yeh?'

'When's yours?'

'Not till the weekend. Can you make Saturday?'

'Might do. What's on?'

'Disco at the Barn Owl. Get the Harding dame on your wavelength.'

'She is already.' Julie undulated her limbs smugly under his weight. 'She's all right, Mrs Harding. I can twist her round me little finger.'

'Okay, then. Do a bit of twisting. Not now! Keep still, you little . . .'

'Tomorrow,' remarked Julie, twenty minutes later, 'we're meant to be getting a couple of new ones in.'

'Two more to thump into shape.'

'You'll be old yourself, Rod, one day. I feel sorry for them. Most of them. One or two, I wouldn't mind seeing the back of. Still, though. How'd you like it, to be shunted off in here?'

'I'd take a cyanide pill first.'

'Half the time,' murmured the girl, frowning at her hair in the mirror screwed to Rodney's bedroom wall, 'I can't make out if they know what's going on but can't join in . . . or whether they'd join in if they had a clue what was going on.'

From the bed, where he was flipping the pages of a hi-fi magazine, the young man eyed her warily. 'Join in what?'

She suspended operations with the hairbrush to consider. 'Life, I suppose.'

'They're okay. Plenty to eat, lots of time to sleep.'

'And they've got Paula.' Julie chortled. 'She looks after 'em. They're her people.'

On cue the following afternoon, the newcomers arrived. One of them, Miss Scarborough, had been sent along from the local geriatrics ward, which was being closed as an economy. In her ninety-third year, she was the shape of a crescent moon but hardly matched up, Matron thought resignedly while greeting her, to the brilliance of such a heavenly body: to be candid, Miss Scarborough's cerebral faculties had seen better days.

The other, Mrs Manners, was something else. Only seventy-four, she was small, bright-eyed, alert and bustling. Had her daughter not already been along to scout out the home and make arrangements for her mother to become a part of it, Matron would seriously have suspected an administrative blunder which had brought the wrong prospective incumbent into her office. Mrs Manners seemed entirely capable not merely of adapting to the place, but running it.

Matron permitted herself a small surge of cautious relief. An intelligent and mobile addition to the strength was never to be deprecated. After showing Miss Scarborough her shared bedroom and then committing her to the care of Miss Jameson in the lounge, where afternoon tea was imminent, Matron returned to the office to find Mrs Manners inspecting the wall-prints with every sign of appreciative authority. Their owner gave her a warm smile.

'Fond of Art, Mrs Manners?'

'Taught it, for many years.' The reply was crisp, person-to-person. Matron blinked a little. Shading her eyes, Mrs Manners intensified her scrutiny of the wall. 'These are good. Are you a collector?'

'In a small way, perhaps. You paint, yourself?'

'Pencil sketches, mostly. The occasional oil.' Returning to her chair, Mrs Manners stood bolt upright beside it, as though scorning to fold her limbs into its embrace twice in one afternoon. 'Do any of the other residents . . .?'

'I'm afraid not.' To cover a vague feeling of shiftlessness, Matron added, 'It sounds like a splendid idea. We might start classes.'

'Excellent therapy,' Mrs Manners said firmly.

'Let me take you along and introduce you to our Miss Jameson. She does a lot for the other residents.'

In the lounge, the tea-trolley had arrived. Young Julie was pouring and Miss Jameson was supervising the allocation of cups, keeping a hawkish eye upon those who were too far slumped in post-prandial catalepsy to know what they were about. At Matron's summons, she hurried over with devoted alacrity.

'We've had a spillage, Mrs Harding, I'm sorry to say. Miss Evershaw—'

'Never mind, Paula. Julie will cope, I'm sure. I just wanted you to meet our—one of our new arrivals, Mrs Manners. Alice, isn't it? Paula Jameson. Is there a cup of tea, Paula, for Alice?'

When the three of them were provisioned, Matron steered the two older ladies to a deserted corner and spoke confidentially. 'Alice has come up with rather a good idea, Paula. Art lessons.'

Miss Jameson smiled and nodded. 'Art lessons. I see.'

'For those who want to take advantage. Alice knows about painting, you see.'

Matron elaborated. Having listened, Miss Jameson inclined herself forward and placed an arthritic hand upon the newcomer's cardigan-clad shoulder. 'My dear! We shall all have to look to our laurels. I've never put brush to canvas in my life.'

'Never too late to start,' Mrs Manners informed her. 'Look at Grandma Moses.'

'Oh, my dear!'

'I see no reason,' declared Matron, 'why we shouldn't get something organized. If I attend to the materials, can the two of you . . .? I'll leave you to talk it over.'

Back in her office, she put a call through to headquarters and obtained clearance for an investment in a dozen sketch pads, pencils, plastic paints and brushes. 'Just a trial run,' she explained. 'If it catches on, we may need more. I'll let you know.' Ringing off, she sat back and mused for a while. If the idea took off, she thought, it could make life easier all round. Good for the residents, a blessing for the staff.

Perhaps Mrs Manners and Paula, between them, could make a go of it.

A week later, the class was thoroughly into its stride. Five took part at the outset. Mr Cuthbert; Miss Cranleigh; antique Miss Willis, to whom the procedure was plainly a mystery but who seemed to enjoy sitting in a different chair; Paula herself; and Mr Dodds, whose interest openly was centred upon the possibility of invoking at some point the aid of Julie as a life model, preferably of the undraped variety, notwithstanding Mrs Manners's forthright denial of any such intention. After a few days Mr Dodds, disheartened, dropped out, but was replaced by two further recruits, Mrs Hammond and Mrs Petworth, both octogenarians who until now had evinced no awareness of anything that occurred in their vicinity. Mrs Manners took them in hand. By sheer force of personality, she got them out of their lounge chairs at ten-thirty each morning and into the solarium, where the art class was held. Furthermore, she kept them there for the full hour and even conjured a pencilled line or two out of each of them, although the results were not readily identifiable. This, she assured everybody, mattered not a jot. What counted was their willingness to soldier on.

'To look at them,' Julie bawled in Rodney's ear above the howl of amplified electronics at the Barn Owl Disco, 'you'd never think they was the same bunch. Three more joined this morning. That's nine altogether. Good, eh?'

'Fantastic.' Rodney looked sardonically at her down his nose. 'When's the exhibition?'

She jabbed him hard with an elbow. 'It's just a load of tripe. You should see it. Point is, though, they're occupied. They've got an interest.'

'Give 'em another month, they'll all crash out.'

'What if they do? At least they'll have tried. And it's given us a breather, I can tell you. Some of the others go into the solarium to look on, so it means we can tidy the lounge a lot easier.' For a few moments Julie jogged ruminatively, solo, rippling her arms to the beat. 'There's only one thing,' she added presently, wiggling back to him.

'Wot?'

'Paula seems a bit down. You know how she was always buzzing around, like, heading the action? Now, she's . . . I dunno. Not much life in her.'

'Maybe it's her arthritis.'

'She's always had that. She still takes the same amount of pills every day, so it can't be any worse. Hope there's nothing else wrong with her. I quite like Paula, even though she can be bossy. At least you can talk to her. Most of the others, you can't.'

Matron, too, had noticed the change in Paula. It bothered her enough to prompt her to speak privately to the old lady's nephew, Mr Frank Jameson, when he made his next duty call. 'Your aunt,' she told him, 'seems a little under the weather. We had the doctor take a look at her and he says she seems all right in herself . . . but she's certainly less bouncy than she was. I thought I should mention it to you.'

'Is she eating?' A simple rule of thumb guided Frank Jameson's attitude to well-being: if food was being ingested, there was little to worry about. Matron looked dubious.

'She's never been a great one for her meals. Small fads . . . Whether she's eating less now than she used to, it's hard to say. Mainly I'm concerned about her demeanour.'

'She seems all right to me. She was telling me about these art classes she runs. Sounds a promising venture.' The nephew, who was with a merchant bank in the City, had eyed speculatively a few of the residents' efforts, having in mind the feasibility of promoting them commercially (an Exhibition of Mature Art, perhaps, at the Waring Gallery?), although what he had seen so far was hardly in line with his ultimate remark.

'Yes, it's taken off rather nicely. Of course,' Matron said tactfully, 'the actual, um, technical instruction is being given by another of our residents, Mrs Manners. But your aunt does invaluable work in getting people along there and . . . and . . . assisting in a general capacity. She produced quite a few sketches herself at first, as you probably saw.'

'Doesn't she now?'

'Well, the supervising takes up so much of her time. At least it did.'

'She's let up on that, too?' Frank Jameson inquired keenly.

'So I gather. Yesterday morning she went along and just sat there, you know, watching the others. Then this morning she never turned up at all. Stayed in the lounge. Didn't seem to want to talk, or read. So unlike her. This is why I thought I should have a word with you.'

'Going through a withdrawn phase,' the nephew said comfortably. 'She's had 'em before.'

'She has?'

'Oh yes. I remember my father—her elder brother—saying once: "The trouble with Paula, when she was younger she was cock of the roost: now if she doesn't get what she wants, she sulks." Which I think probably hits the nail on the head.'

'I shouldn't have described it,' Matron said cautiously, 'as *sulking*, exactly.'

'Whatever. I wouldn't worry about it, Mrs Harding. I'll be along again the week after next. By then she'll be back in the groove, you mark my words.'

That evening had been earmarked for a bingo session. It was to be a somewhat more elaborate affair than usual. Refreshments had been laid on, and some of the outside staff were staying on duty to serve them and also to take part in the games. There was to be a grand top prize of fifteen pounds, plus second and third consolations of five and three respectively. And, to cap it all, Rodney the porter had been prevailed upon to give a demonstration of his home-produced electronic music afterwards. A faint aura of expectancy—it could scarcely be called a buzz—had been discernible throughout the home all day, and during tea it was the prime topic of conversation, easily shouldering aside the quality of the fried sausages.

One or two of the more cognizant inhabitants, like old Mr Cuthbert, noted that Paula Jameson took no part in the discussion. She sat, smiling remotely at the others on her table, volunteering no opinion upon the mooted question of where the prize money was coming from. Towards the end of the meal, Matron loomed at her left shoulder.

'You'll do the honours again for us, Paula, this evening?'

'What's that, my dear?'

'We're relying on you to call the numbers.'

'I'm afraid I've a bit of a sore throat. You'd better ask somebody else.'

'Got a cold coming?'

'Just a spot of October inflammation, I expect.' Paula beamed round at nobody in particular. 'Why not ask Mr Cuthbert? Or Mrs Manners, over there?'

'We'd much rather you did it. You've such a knack.'

Paula laughed on a key of mechanical merriment. 'I'm sure I can't be the only one. No, my dear, you'll have to excuse me. I'd hate to ruin everyone's fun.'

'As if you would!' Matron straightened up, doing her utmost to mask a feeling of slight irritation. 'Shall I invite Mrs Manners to deputize, then?'

'Why not?' Paula smiled myopically across the tables. 'She'll be an absolute whizz.'

After tea, it was Mrs Manners who took the initiative in rearranging the lounge chairs and herding the residents; Mrs Manners who helped Julie and her colleagues to set up the refreshments trolley; Mrs Manners who launched the proceedings with a neat preamble incorporating a quip or two, before bringing to the task of caller the clarity and aplomb of a seasoned college lecturer. Paula, meanwhile, had disappeared. Searching stealthily, Matron finally nosed her out in a corner of the Games Room upstairs. Seated erect in a wicker chair, Paula was gazing at a copy of *Rural Life* which she was clasping in front of her nose as if studying herself in a looking-glass in a poor light. After some hesitation, Matron decided not to intrude. Before quitting the Games Room, however, she had an opportunity to observe that the copy of *Rural Life* was being held upside down.

Throughout breakfast the next morning, Mrs Davenport remained the heroine of the hour, having walked off the previous evening with the fifteen-pound first prize. A close second in popular esteem was Rodney, whose electronic assault was generally agreed to have given things the biggest gingering-up since the invasion of the reggae group from the village last Christmas. Some of the glory reflected upon young Julie. Mr Cuthbert went so far as to clutch her by the wrist as she passed behind him with a tureen of porridge, and advise her to 'tell that young man of yours to get himself on telly if he wants to do any good for himself. You tell him that.'

'Only give him a swelled head,' Julie retorted, releasing herself by means of a diplomatic lateral skip. 'Glad you liked it, though. Bit tough on the eardrums, I thought. Where's Miss Jameson this morning?'

Blank faces greeted the query. It was Mrs Manners who answered from table No. 7. 'She said she might not be down to breakfast. She was feeling a little under the weather.'

'Have you told Matron?'

'Matron was informed,' Mrs Manners said reprovingly, 'at the earliest opportunity. But I doubt if it's anything serious. A touch of the sniffles, I dare say. Miss Jameson was complaining of a sore throat last night.'

'Is she having breakfast in bed?'

'Where,' asked Mrs Manners, 'is Miss Jameson's bedroom?'

The girl looked startled. 'Upstairs, of course.'

'And where are we, at this minute?'

'Down here,' Julie said faintly.

'Then how could I know about Miss Jameson's gastronomical arrangements? You'd better ask Matron.' Mrs Manners looked about her for applause. Julie flushed.

'I'm supposed to know,' she muttered resentfully, 'because of her arthritis tablets. She's meant to take them straight after the meal.'

'That's right,' Mr Cuthbert informed the company at large. 'Them big pink ones. Two, she has.' He cocked an eye at the girl. 'Like us to pop upstairs, love, and find out if she's swallowed 'em?'

'I'll see to it.' Upending a gluey mound of porridge on to his plate, Julie passed on, contriving to make Mrs Manners wait until the very last for her helping. It was a revenge which gained in piquancy from the fact that porridge oats and Mrs Manners had a special and permanent rapport, much publicized. On her return to the kitchen, Julie found Matron herself preparing a tray. She said plaintively, 'Is that for Miss Jameson? Nobody told me she wasn't coming down.'

'It's only just been decided that she won't,' Matron explained, placing a crispy half-slice of toast alongside a butter dish and accepting a steaming teapot from Cook. 'Don't worry, Julie. I'll see she takes her pills. She'll have to try and eat something first.'

'What's wrong with her?'

'Nothing much. She's just a little off song.'

Taking the lift to the first floor, Matron carried the tray to Room 16 which Paula shared with Mrs Davenport. She found Paula out of bed, fully dressed and seated on a hard chair by the window, gazing out at The Lake below. 'I've brought you a little something,' she said brightly, planting her burden on the chest of drawers. 'Glad to see you're up. Feeling better?'

Paula smiled vaguely round. 'Oh, my dear, I'm *quite* all right. Mustn't get in the way. The staff all have their jobs to do, don't they? How sweet of you. Toast and marmalade. Very nice . . . very tasteful.' She peered attentively at the tray's contents, making no move to extend a hand towards any item. Matron eyed her uneasily.

'Shall I pour you a cup of tea?'

'Just leave it there, my dear. I'll get around to it.' Paula laughed briefly, a two-note chime. 'I'm perfectly capable, you know.'

'I've reason to.' Matron grinned at her. 'Which reminds me. We've two extra people joining the art class this morning. Will you be there to lend a hand? Mrs Manners would so appreciate your help.'

'Mrs Manners can get on *far* better without me.' The vague smile directed itself out at the garden.

'Not true, actually. She misses your touch with the likes of Miss Willis. She hasn't—'

'Miss Willis doesn't need *me*.' The tone was almost waggish.

'She may think she doesn't.' Matron thought deeply about her next observation. 'Quite often, people don't appreciate what's being done for them . . . just as others may not realize how indispensable they are.' Allowing a moment's pause, she added casually, 'I'll leave you to take your tablets, Paula, after you've eaten your toast. See you downstairs, later.'

At eleven o'clock, Matron peeped hopefully into the solarium. The art class muster was busily at work under the admonishing eye of Mrs Manners. Of Paula there was no sign. Matron beckoned.

'Has Miss Jameson been along, at all?'

The lips of Mrs Manners snapped together, like two elastic bands. 'If she has,' she replied, separating them again, 'it wasn't to favour me with her cooperation. I and Mr Cuthbert had to put out all the chairs, besides handing out the materials.'

'She wasn't feeling too chirpy, earlier,' Matron apologized. 'I thought she seemed on the mend, but I wonder if . . . I'd better scout round for her. She may have gone back to bed.'

Paula was not in bed. Nor was there any sign of the breakfast tray. Upon inquiry, Matron learned that it had been collected at nine-thirty by one of the room cleaners and returned to the kitchen, where somebody else recalled that no toast had remained on the plate and that inroads had been made upon the butter. 'She must have got that down, then,' Matron said, a little relieved. 'Was there a bottle on the tray with a couple of pink tablets inside? I left them for her to take.'

Nobody could remember a bottle. Trying not to get agitated, Matron hurried back upstairs and searched the bedroom, checking in particular through Paula's wardrobe. The only garment obviously missing was the heavy camel coat presented to her by her nephew the previous Christmas . . . a cast-off, Matron had surmised, from his own wife's plentiful reserves. This apart, everything seemed tidily in place. Accelerating downstairs, Matron sought out Rodney the porter, who was sweeping out the storeroom.

'I can't find Miss Jameson,' she told him. 'You've not seen her, Rodney, on your travels?'

Rodney hadn't. 'Maybe she took off for a stroll,' he suggested, resting thankfully on his broomhead.

'In this weather?' Matron peered through the storeroom window at the heavy drizzle. 'She's not wild about the damp, at the best of times. And I've never known her to venture out before lunch.'

'Library?' The Library was four shelves in a corner of the Games Room.

Matron shook an impatient head. 'I've hunted everywhere indoors. All the toilets. She's nowhere inside the building.'

'So,' Rodney concluded reasonably, 'she went out.'

'Not from choice, I'm certain. I mean,' Matron enlarged, 'it could only be that she felt in urgent need of fresh air or something. And since she hasn't come back . . .'

'Want us to take a look?'

'Could you, Rodney? Just in the grounds.'

'How about dragging The Lake?' he asked flippantly, relinquishing the broom. The Lake, as they both knew, was a uniform six inches in depth: nobody could have vanished beneath it.

'Try anywhere that seems possible,' Matron said neutrally. 'Oh, and Rodney—take Julie with you, I should. In case Miss Jameson needs any . . . attention. Off you go.'

The grounds attached to the home covered two acres and a half. The bridge that spanned The Lake led on to a shrub-bordered path which took a devious course to the perimeter fence before lurching to starboard and tacking through a rose-garden, a midget pinetum and a copse of silver birches before heading back for the rear terrace.

In waterproofs, Julie and Rodney carried out a more or less conscientious sighting mission, at intervals calling Paula by name, at other intervals pausing behind convenient clumps of evergreen for moist embraces. On the third such occasion, Julie said, 'Proper fusspot, isn't she—Matron? I know what Paula's gone and done.'

'Wot?' Rodney thought Julie was looking a particular

turn-on in her circular rain-hat. The droplets glistening on her nose gave her a gamine appeal.

'She's gone into town to buy something. She did it before, once, without telling anybody.'

'Two miles?' Rodney said sceptically.

'Not walking, stupid. She could hitch a lift.'

'So what are we scraping round out here for?'

'Because Matron's a fusspot.' Julie eyed the rain-speckled surface of The Lake with all the teenage assurance of one who had seen, heard, experienced everything that institutional employment could hurl at her. 'She's dead scared of copping any blame.'

'So would I be, in her shoes.'

'Well, you can see her point, I s'ppose. We'd better go right round, case she's watching.'

Completing the circuit without result, they reported back to Matron. Reluctantly she lifted the telephone receiver and dialled the police station. 'I don't want to make a thing about it, too soon,' she told the duty sergeant, an old friend of the home, 'but I'd be grateful, Chris, if you could have your people watch out for her. We think she may possibly have gone into town. I'm going to drive out there, see if I can spot her. If you hear anything, you can get in touch with my deputy here, Miss Dewhurst. She'll be standing by.'

Passing as it did through cultivated fields, the road into town lacked footpaths. Even the grass verges were spasmodic, which meant that anyone foolhardy enough to undertake the pedestrian's role had to walk mostly on the carriageway and trust to the charity of drivers to avoid spinning them over the nearest wire fence. Although there was no overt compulsion, residents at the home were strongly urged not to tempt fate but to await the twice-weekly minibus if they craved a shopping expedition. Problems were rare. The biggest scare to date had been created by Mr Cuthbert when he walked out with his visiting niece's pet Labrador and was narrowly missed by a passing juggernaut. Until now, Paula's inclination for a tramp along the tarmac had seemed to be nil. As a rule, she disliked walking in open space. At present, however, she was unquestionably in a strange humour. Matron felt nervous about her.

Along the entire two-mile stretch there was no glimpse of Paula's stooped figure or of anyone else. In the town centre, Matron made some faintly despairing inquiries, called fruitlessly at a few shops, then visited the police station and spoke again to Chris the sergeant. He was disposed to take a relaxed view.

'Probably took a meander through Chard's Farm,' he suggested, 'and went further than she'd reckoned on.'

'Could you send someone over there, Chris, to take a look?'

'Sure, okay. Don't want her registered as missing yet, do you?'

'It's too soon.' Matron twisted her fingers. 'Be an angel, will you, and ring Miss Dewhurst at the home? Find out if Paula's arrived back?'

Paula hadn't. Without waiting to be urged, Chris the sergeant had a call put out to Patrolman Swift, instructing him to reconnoitre in the region of Chard's Farm. Matron said distractedly, 'What I'm half afraid of, you see, is that she may have done something silly about her tablets.'

'Tablets?'

'For her arthritis. Either forgotten to take them, or somehow got hold of a few more and taken too many. That could be so dangerous. They're aspirin-based. An overdose can cause internal bleeding . . . lethal.'

The sergeant looked grave. 'Does she have access to 'em?'

'Not in theory. We keep them and dole them out. But she might somehow have been at the cupboard. You never know.'

'If I were you,' he counselled, 'I'd get straight back and take a look.'

Driving like the wind, Matron took his advice and, on her return, made a dive for the medicine cabinet in the sickroom. It was locked, and when she opened it she found, to her relief, that Paula's supply of pink tablets had not been tampered with. There remained, however, the bleak fact that there was still no sign of Paula herself. The other residents were at lunch. After discussion with Miss Dewhurst, Matron took the opportunity to conduct yet another exhaustive search of the building, all bedrooms included. Nothing resulted.

By the time lunch was over, a decision could no longer be ducked. She rang the police station and asked that Paula should be listed officially as missing. After that she dialled the City office of Frank Jameson, to be told by his secretary that he was out for a couple of hours. Cravenly glad of the respite, Matron left a message for him to call her back. Meanwhile the search for Paula continued.

It was established that she had taken no money with her. The small hoard of pound coins and silver, known only to Matron and Miss Dewhurst, that she kept at the foot of her wardrobe was in its place, manifestly untouched. Her pension book was held by the home. Apart from her nephew, she had no one to go to. And she had not gone to him. This, Frank Jameson made emphatically clear when he telephoned in the late afternoon.

'Of course not, Mrs Harding. Why would she? And how? If she'd travelled to my house for some reason, my wife would have let me know. Anyhow, my aunt would do no such thing. We're not on those sort of terms. Frankly I don't understand it. How could she just walk off, without being seen?'

'We're puzzled, too,' Matron assured him nervously. 'We've hunted everywhere. The police are scouring the district now.'

'It's highly disturbing,' Frank Jameson said bluntly. 'My aunt was in your care.'

'We do realize that.' After a taxing few hours, Matron felt close to tears. 'We take our responsibilities here very seriously and we're doing all we can.' She hesitated. 'If you remember, Mr Jameson, I did mention to you that I've been disturbed lately about your aunt's . . . mental attitude. She—'

'If it was that noticeable, perhaps she ought to have seen a specialist.'

Matron took in a breath. 'You yourself,' she reminded him, 'spotted no particular change in her. It was nothing that obvious.'

'I'm not trained to detect these things.'

There was silence while the implied rebuke hung on the line between them. At last, restrainedly, Matron said, 'I'll be keeping closely in touch with you, Mr Jameson. The moment we hear anything, I'll let you know.'

'I shall be obliged.' The setting down of the distant receiver was not noisy, but it was firm. After staring wretchedly across her office for a while, Matron heaved a sigh, squared her shoulders and walked over to the dining-room where the residents were at tea.

'As you all know by now,' she announced, 'Miss Jameson has gone missing. Now I want each of you to think back very carefully, try to remember anything she might have said, any little action of an unusual . . .'

Miss Cranleigh thought she might have snatched a glimpse of someone who could conceivably have been Paula, descending by the main staircase at about a quarter to eleven that morning. She couldn't be positive. The view of the stairs from the solarium, where Miss Cranleigh had been intent upon a still-life study, was only a partial one, and she had glanced up only briefly. Even if the figure had been that of Paula, she demanded, how did that help?

Only, responded Matron, by indicating a time when the missing woman had still been around. For all they knew, she could have left the building an hour earlier. Old Mr Cuthbert thought this unlikely.

'Slow to get going of a morning, she is,' he observed sagely. 'Likes her cup of coffee at ten. Gives her some pep.'

'Normally, perhaps,' agreed Matron. 'But this morning she was below par. Perhaps she didn't fancy coffee.'

Inquiries about the coffee service that morning drew a blank. None of the staff could remember whether or not Paula had been around to partake of any. The general blankness was frustrating. Matron felt let down. She had always nursed the impression that among the residents there was an almost minute-by-minute observational exchange, backed up by staff members who provided a vigilante patrol. To discover that Paula had been allowed to evaporate under the noses of the lot of them was disillusioning, to put it mildly. A brief reading of the Riot Act seemed called for. At present, however, Matron felt too dispirited to pursue the matter. Finding Paula was the priority.

Sergeant Chris at the police station had done sterling work. Mindful of the circumstances, he had prevailed upon his superiors to deploy considerable manpower resources in the search: by nightfall, he was able to report that no trace of Paula had been found within a mile's radius of the home, which suggested that she must be further afield, which in turn appeared to indicate . . .

'A vehicle,' breathed Matron, taut-faced with worry.

'Would she have accepted a lift?'

'She might. I'm not sure. I don't like to think of it.'

'Easy to imagine the worst,' said the Sergeant's soothing baritone down the wire. 'If she was set on making off, for reasons of her own, she could have flagged down some kindly motorist who took her into town. Then she could have got a bus. We'll make inquiries. For the moment, Mrs Harding, there's no more you can do.'

Except telephone the nephew. The conversation which resulted confirmed Matron's fears. Mr Frank Jameson wanted his aunt located and he wanted it done fast. If, by morning, nothing had been heard . . . Four minutes later, as she hung up, Matron felt shaken and drained, a shell of a woman. She drank a stiffy brandy and then called in her deputy.

A quietly-spoken woman in her late thirties, Miss Dewhurst had opinions of her own. In her view, Matron was taking the matter too personally.

'They're not prisoners,' she pointed out. 'We're just here to see to their needs. We don't keep them under lock and key.'

'We're responsible for their wellbeing.'

'Up to a point. It's a question of what's reasonable.'

'I wish her nephew saw it that way. But in any case, I'm

quite fond of Paula. I can't bear to think of her lying ill or injured somewhere. Can you think of any place,' beseeched Matron, 'where we haven't looked? Do you think we should make one more effort inside these walls?'

Looking dubious, Miss Dewhurst proffered a suggestion or two. Matron summoned Rodney. 'I realize you're off-duty,' she told him, 'but I wonder if you'd mind working a little overtime, just for this evening?'

'Okay by me, Mrs Harding. Where jew want us to start?'

'You might try all the outhouses again. You've been through them once, I know, but I'd like them double-checked. Every nook and cranny. And after that . . .'

Duly programmed, Rodney set out. Privately he regarded the furore as premature: the old girl had gone off for a day or two, that was all. She'd be back. He knew, because Julie had told him, about the mild agoraphobia that Paula was supposed to suffer from in addition to her arthritis: as a practical bloke, however, with countryside roots, Rodney was inclined to scoff at such diagnoses. People had been known to use such 'illnesses' as an excuse for the cushy life. Still, if Matron wanted to get steamed up and pay him overtime to pull open cupboard doors, who was he to object? The company of Julie would have been nice, but this evening she was tied up in the kitchen, helping to prepare tomorrow's menu. Sighing at the thought of her, Rodney stepped into the drizzly night and headed for the main barn.

In the kitchen, Julie finished removing meat and vegetables from the freezer and turned her attention to the cutlery. 'I'll lay this lot,' she informed her colleague at the sink. Bearing the tray through to the dining-room, she began scattering knives and spoons over the tables; tomorrow was a cereals-only morning. As she reached table No. 9, a movement tweaked at the corner of her left eye. She glanced round.

A door of the oak dresser against the wall behind her had drifted open. Moving across to secure it, she hopped back with a startled cry as a small, wrinkled hand appeared, lowered itself over the base edge, commenced to paw the carpet. Eyes bulging, the girl watched it speechlessly. The hand was followed by an arm, swathed in purple wool. A second hand joined the first. A face appeared.

'Miss Jameson! Whatever are you doing in there?'

'Shhh!' The old lady started to crawl out, disturbing glassware in her progress. Reaching the floor, she hoisted herself from a crawl to an upright kneeling posture and placed a finger warningly to her lips. 'Keep your voice down, my dear. We don't want anybody to hear us.'

'How long've you been inside?' Unconsciously Julie did as she was urged, speaking in an astonished whisper. 'We've been looking—'

'Since this morning.' Reaching back, Paula hauled from the interior her glossy beige handbag and set it down conspiratorially on the carpet between them. 'I've got this,' she announced, looking up with shining eyes. 'Kept it by me all day.'

'Got your money inside, have you?' The girl thought it best to humour her. 'You're right to look after it. Aren't you cramped? You must be hungry. Why don't we—'

'I've eaten some toast. Money, did you say?' Paula laughed gently. 'What would I do with money? Nothing to spend it on, around here. I'll show you what I've got, if you can keep a secret. Can you?'

'Zip-lips, they call me.' Since Paula was displaying no wish to rise, Julie sank to her knees to confront her on her own level. 'Show us, then. What've you got?'

Unclasping the bag, the old lady produced a small Polythene bag containing a number of pink capsules. With an air of quiet triumph she held it up. The girl looked at it blankly.

'Your tablets. Where'd you get all them? Matron—'

'Aha! You thought I was taking two a morning, didn't you? That's just where you're wrong. I pretended to, but I've only been taking one.'

'Why?'

'Well, I had to build up a stock, didn't I?' Paula spoke on a good-naturedly reasonable note. 'There was no other way. Matron would never have given me any extra.'

'How about your arthritis?'

'Oh, one a day keeps it fairly well under control. These are very strong, you know.'

'But what did you want a pile like that for?'

'Her, of course.' Paula nodded towards a table. The girl turned to look, before twisting back to stare.

'Mrs Manners?'

'I'm only telling you this because I know you're to be trusted. I need your help, my dear. You will help me, won't you?'

'How?' The query emerged huskily. Julie felt distinctly sick, more than slightly disorientated. The nap of the carpet was rough against her kneecaps.

'I'd have thought that was obvious.' Rotating the plastic bag in her fingers, Paula eyed its contents with some complacency. 'These,' she explained, 'have got to be crushed.'

'Crushed?'

'Otherwise she'll spot them, my dear. She's got very sharp eyes. Artist's eyes. But she's greedy. Oh yes. Have you noticed how she wallops through her porridge? She'll never taste it in that.'

The girl said carefully, 'Mrs Manners has her own tablets, Miss Jameson. She doesn't need any more.'

'It's only for tomorrow,' Paula admonished her. 'One helping should be quite enough.'

Julie put out her right palm. 'So you want me to crush them up and add them to her porridge in the morning?'

'I knew you'd help.' Paula beamed at her. Then she looked anxious. 'Do you think I need go back and spend the night in there? I *am* getting rather stiff.'

'I shouldn't think so.' Taking the bag of pills, Julie stuffed it into her overalls pocket before helping the old lady arduously to her feet. Paula stood puffing for a moment, flexing her limbs. The girl put an arm around her. 'Why not come up to your room and lie down? I'll fetch you a nice cup of tea. How about that?'

'And I can leave the rest to you?'

'Leave everything to me.' Swivelling her, Julie steered

her for the door. En route, she said, 'I'm glad you trust me, Miss Jameson. You could've made a right hash of things, by yourself.'

Paula gave her a beatific smile. 'I kept out of sight, though, didn't I? The whole day.'

'Yes, you did that. You're a smart one.'

As they were crossing the hall, Mrs Manners emerged from the lounge. Pausing, she shielded her eyes from the glare of a nearby lamp. 'Paula—you're back! What a fright you gave us. Are you all right?'

'Yes, my dear, thank you. I'm fine. See you at breakfast in the morning.' Slipping Julie a broad wink, Paula preceded the girl into the lift.

From another door, Matron and Miss Dewhurst entered the hall. '. . . could try the Games Room once more,' Matron was saying, 'although how we could have overlooked . . . What is it, Mrs Manners?'

'Paula's turned up.'

'She *has*? Oh, what a relief. Thank heaven. Where has she been?'

'I've no idea. Julie found her, I think. They've just gone upstairs.'

'I'll go straight up and see her.' Whey-faced from emotional reaction, Matron turned to her deputy. 'Would you do something for me, Glynis? Give Mr Jameson a call, tell him his aunt's back with us. You'll find his home number on my desk. Tell him I'll ring him myself later, after I've seen how Paula is.'

The returned prodigal was seated on the edge of her bed, being helped off with her cardigan by young Julie, who glanced round as Matron entered and gave her a deeply significant look. 'Miss Jameson,' she explained on a casual note, 'is going to have an early night. She's a bit tired.'

'Not tired, my dear. Still a little cramped, perhaps.'

'We've all been frantic, Paula,' Matron told her reproachfully. 'Where ever did you get to?'

'I'll tell you about it, Mrs Harding,' the girl interposed. She had removed the bag of pills from her pocket and placed it behind a photograph on Mrs Davenport's locker near the door. 'It's a long story. You'll find something over there on the—'

'All right, Julie.' Matron could read smoke-signals when they were puffed at her. 'Help Paula into bed first, and then bring her a glass of warm milk, will you? Oh, and while you're downstairs . . . Would you mind trotting over to the barn? You'll find Rodney there, or in one of the other outhouses. Tell him he can call off the search, there's a love.'

'Okay. But there's something—'

'When you come back, Julie. We'll talk in my office. Now, Paula. Let me help you with this other sleeve . . .'

After putting her head into the kitchen and placing an order for heated milk, Julie took an umbrella from the hallstand and paddled across to the barn. Behind cracks in the door, light was visible. Rodney was still inside, using a flashlight. Half an hour earlier, the notion of Paula skulking in a concealed recess of an outbuilding would have seemed outlandish to Julie: now, she would have taken it in her stride. Thrusting at the door, the girl was propelled backwards as it rebounded. Something was impeding it. Pushing again, more measuredly, she eased herself through the gap and promptly tripped over an obstruction. 'Damn!' She regained her balance. 'Rod? You there, Rod?'

The light was blinding her. Half-averting her eyes, she made out the reason: the flashlamp was glaring up from floor-level, having evidently been left there by Rodney to illuminate his search. But why was it aimed at the door? Stepping past the torch, Julie got behind the beam and blinked several times to adjust her pupils. A larger shape, close to the foot of the door, slowly came into focus. She frowned. Surely he hadn't gone off to sleep on the job? Picking up the flashlamp, she directed it floorwards.

'Rod?'

He didn't stir. The crimson mass that was the top of his head glinted stickily in the glare. Close alongside stood an object, a metallic one with projections. A mechanical cultivator. Parts of its surface were smeared red. Directly above it, fifteen feet up, was the hayloft. Everything was perfectly, obscenely plain. Julie had an instant in which to work it out before her knees buckled and with a tiny sigh she collapsed in a heap.

After the police had done their work, taken statements and supervised the removal of the body, the doctor gave Julie a powerful sedative and ordered her consignment to bed. 'She seems,' he commented, 'to have taken it extra hard, even allowing for the shock. Was she . . .?'

'Yes,' Matron confirmed in anguish. 'They were close. Poor child. If only I hadn't sent Rodney out again . . .'

'No fault of yours,' the doctor said tersely, 'that he chose to trip out of the hayloft. Sheer accident.'

'I can't look at it that way.'

'Hasn't been the best of days for you, has it? One bright spot. I've had a look at Miss Jameson, and you'll be glad to know she's in fair physical shape. Mentally alert, too. Nothing wrong with her, that I can see.'

'That's something, at any rate.' Matron gazed unhappily at Julie's bedroom door, outside which they were standing. 'The girl was going to tell me where she found her, but we never got around to it.'

'Tomorrow,' grunted the doctor, 'will be more than soon enough.'

'Is she likely to sleep till then?'

He smiled thinly. 'If that young lady wakes before mid-afternoon, I'll be surprised.'

Having seen the doctor off the premises, Matron sat limply in a hall chair and looked at her watch. Eleven-thirty. Everyone else had retired to bed. Forcing herself to rise again, she walked wearily across to the lift.

Conscious of a simmering resentment towards Paula as the unwitting cause of the tragedy, Matron had to work hard to be solicitous at the bedside of the old lady, who was lying peacefully gazing at the ceiling while Mrs Davenport snored. Taking the empty milk-tumbler, she said heroically, 'Delighted you're back with us, Paula, and looking so rosy. Had all you want?'

'Yes, my dear, thank you. Where's Julie?'

'She's . . . had a bit of bad news. She'll be on leave of absence for a little while.'

'Oh. I am sorry.' Paula looked more disconcerted than grieved. 'Does that mean she won't be on duty at breakfast?'

'Tomorrow? I'm afraid not. We're going to be short-handed.' A thought struck Matron. Laconically she added, 'I suppose, Paula, you couldn't be prevailed upon to help us out? We could do with somebody competent, who knows the ropes.'

After the briefest of pauses, Paula said brightly, 'My dear, I'd be only too pleased.'

Beneath the bedclothing, her fingers tightened upon the plastic bag, producing a faint scrunching sound which Matron failed to hear. 'Perhaps,' the old lady suggested, turning over comfortably, 'you'd like me to lend a hand in serving the porridge?'

The Loss Adjuster

'We're over here,' called Lorraine.

Celia altered course to join them. She did so with caution, because the rocks on which they were walking amounted, she had discovered in secret horror, to no more than a latticework of solidified lava eighty or a hundred feet above the breakers pounding in from the ocean. All about her, holes yawned underfoot. It was like being strung high in a mesh which might at any moment come apart. Apart from her dread of heights, uncontrolled descents into churning salt water figured largely on Celia's personal Richter Scale of undesirable pursuits.

'Wait a second.' Instead of the light-hearted cry she had intended, the phrase emerged as a quaver. Paul wouldn't care for that.

She was not enjoying the day. The realization came at her yet again as she scrambled warily through a gully that seemed—unless the topography was deluding her—to lead in the direction the others had taken. The entire morning had been spent on heights. First, there had been the castle. A mundane affair, though supposedly historic . . . two hours later, she couldn't even recall its name. Nothing but battlements, reached by spiral stone steps of dizzying rake and altitude. At the top, battered flagstones with jutting edges. One false step . . .

Next had come the cliffside restaurant. Undoubtedly a Sight, and Celia had welcomed the coffee which they drank while looking out across sparkling water and the lesser island facing them; but then afterwards it had been deemed necessary (who actually had made the suggestion?) to venture out on to the pencil-slim pathway at the cliff's very brink and peer over a balustrade at the sheer drop beneath. All of six hundred feet, Mark had knowledgeably observed. Celia had believed him. Six hundred, six million . . . what difference did a few noughts achieve?

In the event, she had been the last to return to the security of the restaurant. It was a kind of defiance. When she finally came inside, Paul had greeted her quizzically. 'What happened to the cowardess I married?' As he spoke, his eyes had flickered towards Lorraine.

Celia had responded with a smile. A show of teeth, testifying to limitless reserves of good nature, pliancy, a readiness to please. Ever since their arrival it had been swelling in size, that smile. By now, it seemed to be occupying her whole face, bursting it at the seams.

From the restaurant, they had driven straight down to the coastline and the lava rock. Unquestionably the area was another phenomenon, in line with the rest of the island: every mile covered produced a fresh surprise. Even the weather had chimed in. The Canaries sunshine guaranteed so glibly by the travel agent had, for the time being at least, petered out. Cloud patterns obscured the sky, and a buffeting wind made it difficult to keep one's balance on ordinary footpaths, never mind jagged corridors between twisted outcrops suspended above a restless shore. Having assessed the nature of the terrain, Celia had hung back, feigning an interest in the rock-formation. But it was no good. They were still calling.

'Take the track to your right.' Mark's voice, vibrant with holiday good spirits. 'It's less precarious. But mind how you go.'

'Don't worry. I'm minding.'

Apart from the odd fissure sneering to her left, the recommended route was, she supposed, marginally safer than the alternative. As she embarked, a sudden gust spun her round, fetching a gasp out of her as she clutched at a projection. For a second or two she hung on. To be allowed not to proceed, to make her own way back—what bliss! Hopeless. The others were watching her, vetting every shaky movement as she advanced, gritting the teeth that she maintained on display. When she had five yards to go, Mark added encouragingly, 'It's worth the effort, you'll find. Come and take a look.'

'If it's another bottomless chasm, you can keep it.'

'Everyone,' Lorraine said languidly, 'has to take the ritual peep.'

Standing alongside Paul, she seemed unaffected by the wind. Was his left palm supporting the back of her waist? From where she stood, Celia couldn't be certain. She came on again. Reaching the spot, she braced herself against a lava column and gazed appalled at the circular vacancy to her right. The greenish water below seemed to beckon spumescently at her. Rigid with terror, she forced liveliness into her voice.

'Not exactly Westgate-on-Sea, huh?'

'I wouldn't know.' Lorraine switched weight to the other hip. 'I've never been to Thanet.'

'Take my word for it.' Relinquishing her grasp on the lava, Celia edged closer to Paul, who extended his right hand to her in a gesture that implied a grudging sense of duty rather than spontaneity. She reached out to take it.

The sensation was dreamlike. The hand was there, hovering, waiting to be clasped: her aim, Celia felt convinced, was true, and yet somehow contact was missed. Cheated of arrest, she tottered on down the slope. Ahead of her, directly ahead, a second natural manhole waited in ambush. Impetus carried her on. The dream had become nightmare.

At the last instant she was jerked back. Mark's grinning face loomed above hers. 'Steady on! You're meant to be looking down at the surf, not taking a header.'

Breathless, shaken, she couldn't answer. Higher along the slope, Paul and Lorraine were regarding her with a sort of half-frowning curiosity, as if she had purposely launched herself towards catastrophe. What exactly had occurred? Her mind refused the analysis. She knew only that she had to get back to the road, fifty yards distant, where they had left the car. Clinging to Mark's arm, she toiled upwards to rejoin the other pair. On an amused note, Paul said, 'If you're that keen for a swim, maybe we should have come here earlier when the sun was out.'

By some miracle, Celia found fragments of her voice. 'A swim? Don't know about that. What I need is a nice, safe public highway infested by homicidal motorists. If it's all the same to you, I'm going back.'

'We want to see what's over there,' Lorraine objected, pointing.

'You and Paul go,' suggested Mark. 'I'll go back with Celia.'

She could have hugged him. At the same time, perversely, she felt a despairing vexation rise within her; she itched to slap his beaming face. Committed, she said lightly, 'Okay, we'll keep the car warm while you explore—but for goodness sake watch your step. You don't want to do what I nearly did.'

'No,' Lorraine agreed coolly. 'We'd hate to do that.'

With Mark's biceps to keep hold of, the return journey was less hair-raising, but the wind was now against them and she felt chilly. Pausing, she fastened the top button of her sweater. 'I should have worn two of these,' she remarked, summoning a laugh. 'What happened to the climate?'

'Here.' Removing his windcheater, Mark slipped it across her shoulders. When she started to protest, he brandished her words aside. 'I don't need it. Keep it on till we're back in the car.'

'It's very kind of you.'

A guffaw burst from him. 'Why not send me a formal note of thanks? Loosen up, old thing. We're here to relax.'

She gazed at him in silent despair. 'Speaking of gratitude,' she said presently, zipping up the windcheater, 'I think I owe you more than the others seemed to realize. I was darn nearly a goner, you know.'

'Oh, you'd have hopped over it.'

'A hole five feet across? Not the way I was stumbling. For heaven's sake, Mark,' she added testily, 'but for you, I could have been down there impaled on a rock by now. You'd think they'd have handrails.'

An earnest glaze formed over his eyes. 'Yes, you would. You're right. Or at least they should have warning signs. If I were arranging personal accident cover for a typical family of four, including one child of eight and another of, say . . .'

All the way back to the road, Mark continued to apply

his professional zest to the hypothetical matter of insurance cover for the incautious. Happiness exuded from him. Following at the shortest distance she could decently contrive, Celia was able to take stock of his tall but stringy frame, the sloping shoulders, the bony elbows loosely encased in the sleeves of the blue Dralon pullover which sagged almost, though not quite, to the waistbelt of his badly pressed fawn cotton trousers. His straw-tinted hair flew in the breeze. Although he was taller than she by half a foot, the windcheater he had lent her was a passable fit. She had more flesh on her arms. And its colouring suited her. With her dark hair and complexion, she had always been able to wear scarlet, the more vivid the better: it enhanced her personality. In this department, at least, she could claim one over Lorraine, whose Saxon blondeness was apt to quail at the mere sight of primary hues. Not that this seemed to cause Paul the slightest concern. Whatever Lorraine appeared in, he mutely applauded with his pupils. To be fair, of course—Celia was the fairest-minded of young women—she did have irreproachable taste. Which, considering her vocational background, was hardly surprising.

Paul, too, wore his clothes well. Even now, Celia could gain a secret kick from just looking at him. Whether in T-shirt and slacks for a lava-strewn coastline or dark grey suit and white collar for the office, Paul exuded the same air of having been fitted by specialists who had run every measurement of his torso through a computer scan. In this, as in practically everything else Celia could call to mind, the contrast between himself and Mark could scarcely have been starker. Making every allowance for their shared activities in the insurance business, Celia occasionally wondered how the two men could possibly have remained close acquaintances over the years.

They did, it was true, occupy the same building in the centre of Manchester. Each had purchased a house on the same executive estate at about the same time. And there was, of course, the existing relationship, dating from schooldays, between their respective wives. All this had established powerful fetters.

Just the same . . .

Back inside the car, a rewarding warmth had somehow built up. With a flourish, Mark held a rear door for her. Slamming it punctiliously, he then went round and admitted himself to the front passenger seat. 'Snug,' he said on a chuckle, over his shoulder.

For want of somewhere to look, Celia peered out at the sky. 'Hope it hots up a bit tomorrow.'

'Sure to. That stuffed penguin in Reception—'

'They always make hopeful noises.'

'Still, you know, he might be right.' Mark slid her the kindly smile of a maths teacher applauding the plucky efforts of an innumerate student. 'Technically it's their winter here, at the moment.'

He sat humming to himself, admiring the shoreline. The sound he was making drove Celia to the borders of desperation. Opening her bag, she hunted through compartments. 'Like a boiled sweet?'

He looked faintly startled. 'Thanks, but I—Well, perhaps I will. Three or four hours till dinner, isn't it? Must keep the old tissues together.'

As they sucked, the car rocked a little in the gusts. Unable to remain silent, Celia said casually, 'They must have hit upon some other geological freak.'

Mark looked round blankly. 'Sorry?'

'The intrepid pioneers,' Celia explained, holding on grimly to the shreds of her patience.

'Those two, you mean?' Mark squinted at the rocks. 'I'd be surprised if they hadn't. This entire island, you know, is packed with phenomena. I was mugging it up. That booklet, back at the hotel . . .'

Not for the first time, Celia speculated upon possible reasons for Lorraine having consented to marry Mark.

During and after their schooldays, Celia had envisaged a far more dramatic husband for her blonde and willowy friend. A career diplomat, at the very least. A thrusting politician, with Cabinet prospects. An industrialist, with vast estates in Mayfair and Shropshire. Given a comprehensive list, Celia would have applied a dubious tick to a

Lancashire-based insurance man, devoid of dress sense, only when all other possibilities had been eliminated. What could Lorraine have been thinking of?

Half-listening to Mark now, taking detached note of the guileless good nature that shone from every feature of his lean, sallow face, the plonking tones of his professional delivery, she began to have an inkling of what had led up to so ill-assorted a match. While she could earn money from her modelling, Lorraine had been content to keep her independence. But she had never become a top name, and at thirty, casting around for security, she had homed in upon Mark's unlikely attractions for the very reason that they gave her the best of both worlds: support and freedom. Nothing incompatible about that. It was, on reflection, a natural consequence of Lorraine's stated aim in life, which was to get all she could out of it while putting the minimum in.

Their failure, after seven years of marriage, to start a family could no doubt be traced to the same cause. Children would have spoilt everything. Lorraine would have vetoed the idea and Mark, in his amiable, blinkered way, would have gone along with her wishes because no other course of action would have occurred to him. Yes, Lorraine had chosen prudently. She always had.

'. . . no time at all, in geophysical terms,' Mark was intoning from the front seat. 'I mean, if the last major eruption was in 1824, who's to say there mightn't be another one tomorrow? Those Fire Mountains are simply alive with subterranean activity. The volcanic potential—'

'Is that them?'

Jerked to a halt by her interruption, he shaded his eyes to peer across the road. 'Lorraine and Paul, you mean? I believe so. Yes—no mistaking Paul's sun-hat. A bit surplus to requirements today. Wonder how far they got?'

Celia had been wondering, too. She had a feeling that the object of her speculation was not quite on the same level as Mark's. Disliking herself for harbouring such thoughts, she delved for a change of topic. 'How are we for petrol?' she asked.

Obediently, Mark leaned across to switch on the ignition and examine the fuel-gauge. 'Enough,' he pronounced, 'to get us back. But we'll need a fill-up in the morning. Hi, you two. Seen all you want?'

'We managed to complete our scientific research.' Joining Celia on the rear seat, Lorraine removed her thick-knit sweater and stowed it on the shelf behind. 'Saw all the sights.'

'Anything outstanding?' prompted Celia, alert and interested.

Lorraine transmitted a faint smile to Paul, who had installed himself in the driver's seat and was lighting a cigarette. Inhaling, he breathed smoke into the car. 'If it's configuration you're talking about, we saw plenty of that.'

'Pretty antique, too,' Mark informed them in his uncomprehending way. 'That rock formation goes back a bit, I can tell you. The primary upheavals . . .'

Lorraine had produced a handkerchief and was holding it delicately to her nostrils, hiding the lower part of her face. Waiting until Mark had finished, Celia said, 'I still think it's risky to let people roam across at will. It's a miracle there haven't been accidents.'

Her voice emerged shriller than she had intended. Paul's gaze flicked towards her in the rear-view mirror. 'Maybe there have.'

'Yes,' agreed Mark, beaming round at them past the neck-restraint of his seat. 'It's quite feasible we wouldn't have heard of them, if there had been. Not likely to publicize such things, are they?'

'No, dear.' Lorraine's tone was that of an aunt absent-mindedly indulging the verbal fantasies of a nephew with whom she has been saddled for the day. At the wheel, Paul spouted more smoke into the roof-trim and fired the engine suddenly.

'Who's for a snifter?' he demanded.

'I wouldn't say no to a cup of tea.'

'Celia, for God's sake. Tea!'

'You three can have what you like,' she said firmly. 'Tea for me.'

Casting his eyes heavenwards, Paul let in the clutch. 'Let's see what we can find.'

A few miles inland, they came across a small bar with outside tables on a gravelled terrace. Paul had a beer; Lorraine a glass of the local wine. Celia and Mark shared a pot of something described by the Spanish bartender as tea, diluted with what tasted like goat's milk heated nearly to boiling point. The sun had ventured out and, away from the coast, the wind was less troublesome. The hills facing them in the middle distance reminded Celia a little of a Scottish landscape on a warmish day. Pouring second cups with fussy attention to sequence, Mark said optimistically, 'Fire Mountains tomorrow, you guys? I believe they're worth a visit.'

Lorraine raised languid eyebrows. 'In that case, who's arguing?'

'Someone might have other ideas.' He gave her a self-deprecating grin as he passed Celia her refilled cup.

'You're the ideas man,' Paul said with gravity. 'What do you think we pay you for? A trip to the Fire Mountains, by all means.'

From where she sat, Celia had a view of Lorraine's profile. The tip-tilted nose gave it a piquancy that was countered by a resolute chin: a child/woman image. It could be an expressive face: at this instant it registered nothing beyond a bland acceptance of events. Celia recognized the look. She had seen it across the school classroom, and later. It had always disturbed her.

By the time they returned to the hotel, the sun had been out of retirement for a couple of hours and body-toasting was in full spate around the pool and the private beach. Paul announced his intention of taking a dip. 'In that case,' said Celia, 'I'll sit on the balcony and catch up with yesterday's *Guardian*. I presume we're meeting later, in the bar?'

'Seven o'clock,' suggested Mark. 'Okay, darling?'

'If that's the consensus.' Lorraine seemed about to pat him on the head, as if he had been a Labrador. Turning to Paul, she said, 'Don't swim to the bottom and stay there, will you? We wouldn't want to lose you.'

'No fear of that.' An inscrutable look passed between them. Placing a palm against the small of Celia's back, Paul added, 'Come on then, love—let's get you fixed up in the ultra-violet. See you at nineteen-hundred hours, you two. Last one there buys the first round.'

As though steering a trolley around a supermarket, he impelled Celia towards the lift. Unlike Lorraine and Mark, whose room was on the first floor, they had to ascend to the seventh. On the way up, Paul stood whistling softly to himself, his hand maintaining light contact with Celia's spine. When they emerged from the lift, she hurried on ahead to open the door to their room. The screen dividing it from the balcony had been left open, so that the atmosphere was warm but airy. While Paul was changing, Celia had a quick wash.

On her emergence from the bathroom, she found that Paul had left for his swim. Bare-legged, in blouse and skirt, she arranged one of the sling-back chairs in the sunniest corner of the balcony and settled herself with the arts page of the *Guardian*. She didn't read for long. The warmth and the drama reviews conspired to bring heaviness to her eyelids: before long she was dreaming.

Lorraine was in the dream. An identifiable Lorraine, albeit subtly different, faintly alien, as if she had been taken apart and reassembled without strict reference to the diagram. She and Celia were together in some kind of boulder-strewn wilderness and were being quite exceptionally chummy until another figure appeared on the scene: a tall, commanding silhouette holding a length of chain. The newcomer could not be mistaken. It was Miss Merrick, their old headmistress, and she was wrathful. 'Come here, both of you,' she instructed curtly. Lorraine gave a snigger. 'You can,' she told Celia, 'if you like. She's not catching me.' When Celia glanced round, Lorraine had vanished. In her place stood Miss Merrick, swinging the chain—no, it was a cane with a metal tip—in a pensive, deliberate fashion. 'I've seen this coming for some while,' she declared, gazing away from Celia towards the horizon. 'You wouldn't listen.

Now you're reaping the harvest.' Celia felt indignant, but beneath this superficial reaction lurked terror . . .

'You'll burn, if you're not careful.'

Paul was looking down at her from the edge of the screen. He was clad in a beach-wrap and his hair glistened wetly. Feeling a little dizzy, she said, 'Have a good splash? How's the water?'

'Moist. Bracing.' Removing the wrap, he revealed himself in a pair of trunks that did justice to his fairly impressive build. Celia retrieved the *Guardian* from the floor, to which it had slipped, as he stepped past her to take up position at the edge of the balcony, gazing over the handrail at the pool below. 'Quite a few paddling about,' he remarked, pulling a towel idly to and fro across his shoulderblades. 'You should try it, love. It's nothing like as hideous as you make out.'

'I never said it was hideous,' she protested.

Climbing out of the chair, she joined him at the rail. The chlorinated water of the pool was being thrashed by a dozen bodies; more reclined at the edge. It looked a long way down. Fighting the urge to step back, Celia added, 'I might take the plunge tomorrow, if it's hot. I get chesty so easily. The air has to be calm.'

'Sheltered down there,' he said abstractedly.

He was leaning over, studying the scene. As if to show that he was still aware of her, he repeated what he had done in the lift: placed his palm against her lower back and held it there, just in contact. Celia's muscles became tensed. Say something, she thought frantically. Keep the dialogue going. 'I'll take your word for it. Still quite a breeze up here.'

'Mind you don't get blown over.'

Afterwards, she was uncertain as to just what happened next. Her body seemed to perform a twisting movement. Her left knee scraped the rough concrete facing of the balustrade, and pain seared her left arm. Her neck whip-lashed, as in a car smash.

Paul's bulging eyes were close to hers, almost up against them. Beyond them, she could see a section of the pool previously hidden from her view, the tiled expanse immediately beneath the balcony, dotted with striped reclining chairs. This, she knew, was terribly wrong. Paul, grasping her elbow, released a kind of puff.

'Celia, for Christ's sake . . .'

Again the concrete abraded her knee. Miraculously, she was back fully on the safe side of the balustrade, clutching the rail as if it had been the edge of a life-raft on a gale-tossed sea. Paul was in an odd position. Half-slumped across the barrier, he was bracing himself with one hand against a steel stanchion that helped to support the rail, and yet she had the impression that its support would have sent him the wrong way unless he gripped it with his fingers, which in fact were hanging slack. As she looked at them, they moved upwards and closed around the metal. He thrust her clear of the danger zone, then stepped away himself. Their eyes met for an instant.

'That was a close call.'

'Too close for comfort.' Her own voice was astoundingly level, conversational almost. 'Shall we give it more of a berth in future? I don't fancy stunt diving at my time of life.'

From putty-colour, his face was covering the spectrum back to crimson-brown. He gave a laugh which sounded more than forced: it seemed to have been synthesized in a laboratory. 'You nearly got your first ducking sooner than intended.'

'When I do immerse, it'll be step by step at the shallow end.' On shaky knees, she followed him back into the room. 'Well, after that I think I'll return to ground level. I thought I might stroll round to that shop in the village, in case today's newspapers have arrived.'

'Sound scheme.' Paul stood regarding himself irresolutely in a wall-mirror, rubbing his neck with the towel. 'See what you can get hold of.'

Descending in the lift, Celia leaned into a corner and took deep, calming breaths. When she arrived in the lobby she made for one of the low leather chairs amid potted palms and sat quietly for several minutes. Her left knee was severely grazed, she could tell. Luckily the marks were covered by her skirt. The flesh needed bathing. Members of a sizeable English family she had noticed before trooped by and smiled across. One of them, an elderly woman of muscular build who invariably wore bright green cotton trousers coupled with a range of short-sleeved blouses—regardless of temperature, Celia had so far seen her in nothing else—gave her a cheery wave.

'Hullo! Enjoying yourself?'

Patently she was the keen, rallying-point grandmother of the party, which included two mute teenage girls. Celia waved back. 'Very much, thanks.'

'Nice to relax, now and then.'

'Certainly is.' When they were through the automatic swing doors she waited a few moments before taking the same route, more slowly. To her consternation they were standing, the five of them, in a huddle on the asphalt outside. 'White as pastry,' the grandmother was asserting. 'If she hadn't just had some kind of upsetting . . .'

At Celia's appearance she broke off, gave her another brilliant smile. 'Just the afternoon for a walk. Work up an appetite.'

'I'm hoping so.' With a parting display of teeth, Celia walked past them and headed for the nearby arcade, alive again after the siesta. A shock-headed, intense young man tried to interest her in his leather goods laid out on the paving. Barely conscious of his endeavours, she made for the newspaper and gifts shop and captured a disfigured copy of the *Daily Telegraph*, the last in the rack. Then realized she had come out without her bag. About to replace the newsprint, she remembered the 500-peseta note she had folded away the previous afternoon into the breast pocket of her sweater, part of her change for the coffee which the four of them had drunk in a dockside restaurant outside Arrecife. It was still there, behind a handkerchief. Using it to pay for the *Telegraph*, she returned outside and spotted the English family again, three shopfronts along. Wheeling to her right, she walked briskly towards the unkempt fringes of the village, gazing like a diligent tourist at the faintly Moorish architecture of the villas, seeing nothing. Somewhere at the top of her mind, she was aware of feeling overdressed. Most of the people she passed wore shorts and a top, and little else.

Lorraine would have mocked. 'Always the last girl out of winter knickers—that was you, Celia. I remember, Miss Merrick . . .'

Lorraine had always known just what to wear. And when, and how. Small wonder she had become a model.

Appearances mattered to Paul. Knowing this from the start, Celia had done her best, but she lacked the flair. For this reason, his eventual selection of her as a bride had perplexed her even more than Lorraine's choice of Mark. For a while, she had nursed the delusion that he saw in her qualities that he missed in other women: it was only recently—within the past few hours, in fact—that an alternative explanation had begun to dawn on her.

It had everything to do with her new theory concerning Lorraine. If a go-getting female could marry a humanoid, from ulterior motives, the same could apply in reverse. The difference was, some semi-automatons had feelings.

Celia had always hoped she would be able to cope. But she had reckoned without a holiday in the Canaries, the four of them together.

Whose inspiration had it been?

Celia rather thought the idea had simply evolved. She herself had chanced to mention Lanzarote. A day or so later, Paul had come home with brochures: somehow, Lorraine had got wise to the project and turned her guns upon Mark, who within a week had suggested to Paul that it might be fun to do a package as a quartet and share the cost of hiring a car for the fortnight, to see the Sights.

Soon afterwards, it became a reality. Celia had been a little dazed by it all. As a foursome, hitherto they had not been especially close. They lived within a mile of each other, Paul and Mark had the office connection, and Celia and Lorraine had maintained contact of a fairly loose nature through the years. Each couple had attended the other's wedding. That was all. Up until now, they had never even dined together. What in heaven's name were they doing, sharing a package holiday and a hired Renault?

Finding she had reached scrubby, charred fields populated by the occasional goat, Celia turned back. Her knee smarted and her head throbbed. She wanted to get back to the hotel room and yet at the same time she was anxious to keep away. She felt bemused. Near the foot of the slope leading down into the village, an approaching figure reminded her of Paul, and her heart skipped a beat. She paused to study souvenirs in a shop window. When she turned to look again, she found she had been right: it was Paul. They waved to each other. She stood waiting for him to come up.

'How did you know I came this way?'

'Simple.' There was a certain wariness in his manner. Or was she imagining things, as he was fond of telling her she did? 'I met that crowd from Leicester—the hearty family with the bustling gran. They said they'd seen you come out of the shop and head inland.'

'I might have guessed.'

'Actually I was grateful. I was a bit concerned about you. Our balcony scene—'

'I soon got over that,' she said easily. 'Thanks for checking, though. Look, I got the last, tatty *Telegraph*.'

Paul eyed it. 'Caught in the starboard engine, I'd say, coming over. Still, bits of it may be decipherable. Smart girl. Sure you're not shaken up?'

'I'm fine.' Celia smiled brightly up at him as they turned to walk back. 'So, is it fixed for tomorrow? The Fire Mountains safari?'

'If that's what you want to do.'

'You mustn't go by me. This is meant to be a joint venture.'

'Yes, but you might prefer some other activity,' he said with an air of solicitude that sat on him like an ill-fitting jacket. 'If it's sunny, we could sit by the pool. I'm sure the others won't mind. They're quite flexible.'

'I think I'd sooner be doing things. There's a lot to see. And I've never got on close terms with a volcano.'

'Worth a visit, Mark tells me. He's been swotting up his

pamphlets. Apparently you can feel the heat coming up through the cracks, and if you chuck straw down into the . . . Talking of cracks, love, mind where you're treading.'

The footway they were using was still under construction, and just ahead of them a square pothole had been left to give access to a drain-cover. As he stepped over it, Paul pressured Celia to the left. She took a step on to the road. As she did so, something rushed past her, appallingly close, brushing her elbow and creating a draught against her cheek. With a gasp, she jumped back. Paul exclaimed.

'Damn traffic! I keep forgetting they drive on the right. Sorry about that. Still intact?'

'Yes. He missed me.'

'No further damage to the nervous system?'

She dredged up something shaped like a laugh. 'It's case-hardened, by now. Proof against all shocks.'

For the remainder of the return journey she hung back a little so that when obstructions loomed they could revert to single file. Paul went on talking, over his shoulder, about volcanic ash, and at intervals she said 'Really?' or 'Fancy that!' to show that she was listening. She had some difficulty in getting along, because a skilled surgeon with a knife seemed to have been at her legs, systematically removing the nerve and bone, leaving only a jellied mass of flesh and skin that had never been designed for the automotive function. Back at last in the stifling sanctuary of their room, she retreated into the bath and stayed there for nearly an hour, attending to her abrasions and regaining a degree of sinew. By the time she had dressed, they were overdue in the bar and Paul had reverted to petulance.

'I can't think what takes you so long. It's not as if the result was all that special.'

Swallowing the several retorts that trembled on her tongue, Celia accompanied him down to join the others. Mark, formal in a lightweight suit which did its utmost to accentuate his jagged knees and elbows, had set up the drinks—sweet martini for Celia, whisky-sour for Paul—and was reading extracts from the hotel pamphlet to Lorraine, who looked a vision in a brief emerald dress and a double string of pearls. At their arrival he leapt up. 'Thought you'd decided to give us the cold shoulder. I've been adding to Lorraine's education while we were waiting. Lot of interesting stuff in this guidebook.'

'Lorraine doesn't need educating,' said Paul, seating himself directly opposite her.

She gazed dreamily back at him, her mascara'd eyes unblinking. Planting herself behind the martini, Celia took a determined sip and regarded the pair of them with the outward detachment she had once employed upon a feared and detested form-mistress when under verbal assault. 'Lorraine might have a few things to tell *you*, Mark. She used to surprise us at school, now and then.'

'I'll bet she did!' Mark slapped his knee. 'Come on then, darling—petrify us with your education. We're all agog.'

'I'm tired,' she said languidly.

'She's tired!' Mark sent a comical glance across the table. 'Four days of festing and feasting, and she's worn out. Hard graft, these holidays, you've got to admit.' He sat with an elbow on the table, admiring her. 'Wake up, gorgeous. Mustn't ignore the guests.'

'We don't feel left out,' Paul assured him with a smile, man to man.

'That's a relief. Here, Paul, this'll fascinate you. Apparently at the time of the third eruption, the island inhabitants . . .'

Half-listening in a state of tortured disbelief, Celia watched Lorraine's expression. It was one that she knew well. At school, she had worn it to demonstrate her special immunity from censure: few of the teachers, in Celia's experience, had ever shown the smallest disposition to take Lorraine down the peg or two that other students had been lowered regularly as a matter of course. Celia had wondered why, then, and she had gone on wondering since.

After dinner there was a fashion display in the terrace lounge. Leather garb was the motif. The models, dark-eyed and smiling, were studies in magnetic sensuality as they marched in rhythmically to music. Celia found them more arresting in themselves than the garments they were showing, and experienced an extra spasm of self-doubt: could most of the trouble lie within herself? But Lorraine too, she could see, was entranced. Hers was the eye of the professional. Although her own modelling career had come to little, she still regarded this as her world. Paul, seated next to Celia but out of reach, divided his observation between Lorraine and the proceedings, viewed the outfits with brooding intensity and kept his own counsel.

Mark enjoyed the whole thing. He tapped his left foot to the music, commented knowledgeably on the styles, and exchanged greetings in Spanish with the models as they bustled past. When it was over, he was the first to start clapping and the last to stop. To Lorraine, he said teasingly, 'What did you think of that lot?'

She smiled slightly and shrugged. Celia said, 'Awfully pretty girls, weren't they? I'm not so sure about the rig-outs.'

Cigar in hand, Mark considered the matter. 'I'm not really sure why they bother to stage these displays, to be quite honest. I mean—it's just leather wear, isn't it? Been around a fair time, now. Why flog it?'

Lorraine said tiredly, 'You shouldn't pontificate on things you know nothing about.'

With a fingertip, Mark administered a playful flick to the frontal wave of her hair. Frowning, she leaned away. Paul watched impassively. Mark appealed to him across the table. 'What do you think, fellah? Is it just an excuse for a cabaret?'

'Racing cars,' Paul said slowly, 'have been around for quite a while, too. They go on staging grand prix events. It's entertainment, but it's also the best way to develop a breed.'

'That's true.' Mark looked impressed. 'Damn good analogy, that.' He looked at Lorraine with a pleased air. 'This the way you see it?'

She turned to gaze directly back at him. 'Your cigar smoke's getting in my eyes.'

'Whoops—sorry, darling.' He ground the butt into an ashtray, giving Celia a sidelong grin. 'Let's bring Celia into the discussion. From the woman's point of view, would you say there's a case to be made out for—'

Lorraine rose. 'I need some fresh air.'

'Ah—why not? Paul will escort you on to the terrace, if you ask him nicely. I'll stay here with Celia and we'll examine the—'

In her turn, Celia came to her feet. 'I think I must be off to bed, Mark, if you don't mind. I'm so sleepy.'

'Must have been the sherry trifle,' he said slyly, 'on top of the T-bone steak. Actually I'm ready to nod off myself. Think I'll go and hit the hay. If you're having a meander outside, Lorraine, I'd slip a wrap on if I were you. There's still quite a breeze.'

Celia went up alone in the lift. She took time over her preparations for bed, draping her evening clothes carefully on hangers and putting out fresh informal garments for the morning. She had another wash, cleaned her teeth with the aid of bottled water, and changed the dressing on her knee. Having finally got into bed, she stared at the home news and women's feature pages of the *Telegraph* for twenty minutes before switching off the overhead light and lying down on her right side, facing away from the door. When Paul came in, half an hour later, she pretended to be asleep.

The sounds he made while undressing resembled those of darting rodents in an attic. Their cessation signalled his retirement to the bathroom: he remained there some time. On his return, he moved around for a while longer, more stealthily, then doused the light. The bed bucked under Celia as he joined her on the mattress, contorting himself this way and that in his habitual quest for a posture that he could tolerate. Finally the bedsprings quietened. Celia opened her eyes.

It was, she had read somewhere, an infallible way to induce sleep. The Law of Reverse. Lying motionless, she stared through the near-darkness at curtains palely lit by floodlights in the date-palms outside. The faint beat of music was audible. It persisted for a time, augmented at one point by a Spanish male voice pitched remorselessly, it seemed, on high C and a couple of semitones above and below. Beside her, Paul stirred briefly. She made her body rigid. The movement evaporated. She allowed her eyes to close.

There was weight upon her arms, a choking sensation in her throat. Something was smothering her, something soft and yet immovable. She wanted to struggle, to scream. Somebody was calling to her.

'Celia! *Celia*!'

Abruptly, the weight upon her upper half was lifted. Her mouth was unclogged. She could breathe. She lay panting, restocking her lungs. A light clicked on. Paul, towering above her, glared down: he was grasping her wrists. She tried to free them. He held on.

'What the hell do you think you're up to, Celia? Trying to throttle yourself, or something?'

She hoisted herself to a sitting position. The upper of the two pillows on her side of the bed was between her arms, against her chest. As she sat up, it flopped away. She stared at it blankly. Releasing one of her wrists, Paul thrust some loose hair clear of his eyes.

'For Christ's sake. If you're going to start having nightmares . . .'

'It wasn't a nightmare. I was being suffocated.'

'I'm not surprised. You had the pillow tight over your face.'

'*I* had?'

The stress she placed on the personal pronoun was a challenge. Paul looked angry, flustered. 'There's no one else, Celia, here in the room with us. You must have been dreaming, grabbed hold of the pillow . . . Lucky I heard you spluttering. You might have done serious harm to yourself.'

Celia got shakily out of bed. Barefoot on the cool tiled floor, she stared down at her watch on the bedside cabinet. 'Two-fifteen? It can't be.'

'Why the hell not?' Hurling back the bedclothes irritably, Paul strode across to the bottled water they kept on the table, poured some into a tumbler, took a gulp or two, returned to offer her the glass. With a shake of the head she sat on the mattress edge, folding her arms to control the shivering.

Finishing off the water, he dumped the tumbler. 'If we're to get any more sleep,' he said curtly, climbing back into bed, 'I suggest in future you keep the pillow *under* your head, where it belongs.'

Presently, his regular breathing told her he was asleep, or on the brink. Regaining her original position on her right side, Celia refocused her eyes and mind upon the curtains. Sleep was far over the horizon, and this time she wanted it to remain there.

Against the patterned fabric she fired a series of mental images. Her girlhood. School and college incidents. Trivial landmarks in an eight-year stint at Lovejoy's.

How had she first drifted into a broker's office? Security. That had been the cornerstone of her family's collective mind. Don't chop and change about, Ceelie. Take my advice. Stick with something. People had always been free with their advice. Possibly this had something to do with her almost invariable willingness to take it. Malleability possessed a scent, to which others were attracted as hounds were drawn to a trail. Celia knew better, now, than to accept the first counsel that came along, but in any case the point was academic; there was no longer anyone around to make the offer.

Advice, persuasion, or the muzzle of a gun . . . nothing would have swayed her when she first met Paul. Or rather, the second time she met him. On the initial occasion, he had merely breezed through the office on his way to the Chairman's sanctum: from the shelter of her desk, Celia had recorded a swift impression of dynamism harnessed to screen-star looks, and had forgotten him in moments. When their paths crossed again, a week later, it was because she had gone to him on loan from the Chairman to help him in computing some figures relating to a commercial insurance package that was being assembled as a joint venture. This time, she was floored.

Paul, for his part, seemed oddly taken with her computer software abilities. What turned him on, he told her on their first dinner date, was a woman who could handle a keyboard. It occurred to her, even then, that he saw her perhaps as some kind of secretarial appendage, a human visual display unit, worth a small speculative investment which, in the event of its failing to produce a yield, could be written off.

Awakening from an ultimate feverish doze, Celia found half-light seeping through the curtains and a vacant space alongside her where Paul had been lying. To her surprise, she felt hungry. Getting dressed, she went down to the dining-room for an early breakfast. Midway through her second croissant she was joined by Paul, who explained that he had gone for a daybreak jog along the sand.

'Were you able to fight your way through the mob?'

'Just me and the gulls.' Pouring coffee, he studied her intently over the spout. 'You look fairly chipper. No more fantasy-horrors last night?'

'Unless you count the gurgles in the plumbing.' The conversation was tilting dangerously on its runners. As a steadying touch, she added, 'What's it like out? Nice day for the hills?'

'I doubt if we'll have to face blizzards.'

As arranged, Lorraine and Mark were waiting for them at nine-thirty in the lobby. Mark was clasping under one arm a bag of necessities for the day, and under the other a bundle of leaflets, guidebooks and maps. 'Background gen,' he explained earnestly to Celia. 'When you're seeing something in the flesh, so to speak, it helps to be able to look up the odd detail. I'm looking forward to this trip, are you?'

'Rather,' she replied, managing a smile at his enthusiasm. 'Are you the chauffeur for today?'

'Yes, my turn to scare the daylights out of you. Good night's sleep?'

'So-so. How about you?'

'Lorraine was a bit restless, weren't you, darling? Excitement of the floor show, I expect. Made her itch to get back to the catwalk herself. She's a bit headachey this morning, aren't you, love? Not much to say for herself yet. Needs a coffee fix. Outside, then, folks. Let's head for the uplands. Last one to spot molten lava's a cissy.'

Having trundled them cautiously out of the village, Mark set a northerly course between fields of black ash and pursued it at a constant thirty-five, declaiming upon features of the landscape to which he had already called attention half a dozen times on previous excursions. Seated at the back with Lorraine, Celia awaited an outburst from Paul. Mark's driving, she knew, sent him to the outer limits. This morning, however, he seemed prepared to sit back and take it. Lorraine, wearing a fixed half-smile and an aura of dreaminess, sat silently observing the scenery. Nearing the Fire Mountains, they passed a lethargic file of dromedaries ferrying trippers up a barren hillside.

'We ought to give that a try,' Mark exclaimed, twisting perilously in his seat-harness to peer back at them. 'I can just see old Lorraine hanging for dear life on to that front creature's neck. Not your favourite domestic pet, eh darling? Camels.'

The half-smile stayed in place. Celia said, 'I don't suppose Lorraine's had much chance to get acquainted with the species.'

'Oh, I don't know,' Paul said innocently.

Mark dealt him a nudge. 'Less of your lip, my old son. Remember who's piloting this thing.' Leaning forward over the wheel, he peered anxiously ahead. 'Pretty soon, we should be coming to the pay kiosk. They charge for entry, did you know? It's a sort of national park. According to the handbook . . .'

Once inside the boundary, they headed straight for the elevated restaurant overlooking the moonscape that constituted this part of the island. Celia did her diligent best to absorb the bleak fascination of the scene. Clearly it was unique. The absence of vegetation hinted at the seethings below ground, although it was faintly disappointing not to see steam rising from the rocks, or bubbling lava in spate. She had half-expected red-hot fissures to be in evidence on all sides. But as soon as the four of them emerged from the car they were waylaid by a tall young Spaniard who with shouts of 'Hey!' steered them to a pit in the hillside from which heat emanated, waited until he had their attention and then threw down bundles of straw, which obliged by bursting into flame. While they marvelled, he picked up a chunk of rock, hot to the touch, and passed it round. Lorraine, to the Spaniard's amusement, dropped it.

Mark joined in the guide's hilarity. 'Now if that had been hot money, my wife would have clung on till her fingers were raw. Sorry, darling. Only my joke. Headache still bothersome? We'll have coffee soon. Tell you what, Paul—we could use some of this stuff back home, right? Ideal for chucking at awkward clients.'

Turning, he led them in pursuit of the guide, who was striding uphill to an open space where a number of metal cylinders protruded from the ground. When they were gathered in an expectant circle, the Spaniard seized a pail of water and poured its contents into one of the funnel tops. Almost instantly a jet of steam exploded twenty feet into the air. Lorraine jumped back with a shriek. Celia said 'Gosh.'

Pleased with the reaction, the guide said 'Hey!' and brandished them towards the restaurant building.

During the demonstration, a familiar station wagon had arrived in the car park below and was disgorging its occupants. 'God Almighty,' groaned Paul, turning to gaze. 'They've tailed us here, too. Is there no peace?'

Celia saw that it was the family from Leicester, once again. The energetic grandmother, swathed in anorak and headscarf against the chill mountain breeze, was supervising the locking of doors while, at the rim of the car park, a second Spanish guide lay in ambush for them. 'Well, after all,' Celia remarked as she followed Paul into the restaurant, 'this is one of the major sights. We can't expect to have everything to ourselves.'

'Personally, I expect just that.'

Paul's tone was casual, and yet downright. He means it, she thought; every syllable. Suddenly, a new perspective opened up to her. With a racing mind she hung back for a moment, carrying out a reassessment that in the space of an eye-blink seemed to encompass the entire span of her existence. Momentarily she lost touch with the surroundings. Then the mental fog rolled aside and she saw with a new, acute clarity all that had hitherto been out of focus, tricky to define. She gave a soft gasp, took a breath or two, before hurrying through the entrance to link up again with the rest of the group.

They were inspecting gravely a sizeable joint of pork which was roasting slowly on a spit suspended in the centre of a railed-off circular hole in the floor of the ante-room that led to the restaurant. Mark was putting learned questions to the guide, who smiled uncomprehendingly back. Lorraine was leaning on the rail with her eyes partly closed. Celia moved to her side.

'Better than having to light the cooker, every time.' She glanced at her friend. 'Head-thump getting worse?'

'Heights and cold winds don't help.' Removing a blonde tress from her sightline, Lorraine puffed her cheeks and gave the pork joint a jaundiced glance.

'Coffee might do the trick. Shall we leave the men to be scientific, and steal a march on them?'

'Best idea I've heard all morning.'

On the far side of the rail, Paul had joined Mark in his quest for information, using a phrase or two of Spanish which he had picked up from a language course on tape. Leaving them to tie the hapless guide in knots, Celia ushered Lorraine through to the cafeteria, secured two coffees and carried them, with Lorraine in tow, across to the window-table that she had earmarked from outside. Lorraine flopped down. Seating herself alongside, Celia said, 'Like a couple of painkillers?'

'Have you got some?'

'I usually go equipped.' A search of her bag revealed a phial from which she shook a pair of capsules. 'These should dull it down in twenty minutes. You've probably got a touch of holiday liver.'

Lorraine washed the capsules down with coffee, and pulled a face. 'They taste bitter. How long have you had them?'

'I'm not sure. It's all right, though. They last.' Celia returned the phial to her bag and sipped at her coffee, gazing out through the window. The Leicester family were midway through their tour of local phenomena. As she watched, the second Spaniard produced a geyser, earning applause. The headscarfed grandmother pointed to her camera; obligingly he led the way across to another funnel and waited, pail in hand, while she made fussy adjustments to range and angle. She was still marshalling her daughter and two granddaughters into position near the spout when Paul came into Celia's view, trudging past them on his way back downhill, evidently on his way to re-examine the pit that ignited straw. Restless by nature, he had never been one for idle coffee-breaks. From the ante-room, the voice of Mark could be heard galloping on in his interrogation of the guide. Celia saucered her cup. 'The boys are happy.'

'What?' Lorraine sounded faraway.

'They're too engrossed in physics to worry about refreshment. How do you feel now?'

'Rotten. It's this pain in my stomach . . . You're sure those tablets were okay?'

'Absolutely. You won't feel a thing in half an hour, I promise.' Celia gave her friend a rallying smile, patted her shoulder. 'Sit quietly for a while.'

'There's not a damn thing else I can do.'

Outside, the Leicester family were regrouping for an advance upon the final objective, the roasting pork. Keeping them under his wing, the second guide was waiting anxiously for a party of newcomers from a minibus to reach them from the car park: evidently he preferred a crowd. The grandmother was looking restive. Having secured her snapshots, she was keen to get on. She reminded Celia, with her incessant gesticulations, her interest in all and sundry, of a relative she had known as a child. Great-Aunt Bessie. The family Spark, was how Celia's mother had dubbed her. Interfering busybody, was her father's darker description. However one viewed her, in Celia's recollection there had been no doubt that Great-Aunt Bessie had enlivened every scene of which she was a part. The Leicester grandmother seemed built on similar lines. Clearly, the present lull in proceedings was not to her liking. Already she was showing signs of breaking away from the party, drifting back, like

Paul, in the direction of the straw-burning pit. The first Spaniard, who had reappeared outside with Mark in train, still apparently asking questions, put out a cry of 'Hey!' to her retreating figure, but was ignored. With a shrug, he exchanged looks with his colleague and picked up a bucket.

Producing some coins, Mark pressed them into his free hand and wandered off, stooping at intervals to pick up and investigate rock samples. Having watched him out of sight, Celia turned back to the semi-recumbent figure of Lorraine. 'Still suffering?'

'It's like hot needles.' With eyes closed, Lorraine rubbed feebly at her abdomen.

'What did you eat for breakfast?'

'Half a croissant.'

'Maybe they're hunger pangs.'

'It's more than I normally have.' Clutching herself, Lorraine rocked in her seat, moaning softly. The man at the serving counter, possibly out of earshot, took no notice. Apart from him, they had the cafeteria to themselves. Presently Lorraine said with a gulp, 'I need the Ladies.'

Celia helped her outside to the annexe. 'Want me to come inside with you?'

'No. I'll be okay.'

'Take your time. No rush.'

Having watched the crumpled figure of her friend vanish into the toilet, Celia walked across to the mini-plateau where the minibus group had now joined forces with the Leicester family, minus grandmother. The geyser scene, to the clicking of cameras, was once more being enacted. As she arrived the combined party was swept on into the building by the two guides, leaving her solitary on the escarpment with the wind knifing her hair. Staring out over the shattered hillsides, she strove to pull her thoughts into a semblance of shape. Like darting pets, they refused to come to heel. There was an insistent buzzing in her ears.

Suddenly she spotted Mark. Approaching at a trot from the slope below the escarpment, he was waving both arms. She plastered a smile on her breeze-whipped cheeks. 'What is it?' she called cheerfully. 'An eruption?'

Breasting the rise, he pulled up directly in front of her. His expression was unfathomable. It put her dimly in mind of yet another incident at school: the day when Miss Merrick called her out of class to break the news that her mother was in hospital after a stroke. A similar blankness had occupied her features, as though everything inside had been switched off. Mark's hand made a tentative dab at her left arm.

'I'm sorry, Celia. Something's happened, I'm afraid.'

She looked at him inquiringly.

Half-turning, he stabbed with a thumb. 'Paul was over there, but he slipped.'

'Slipped?'

'That hole . . . where they burn the straw. Don't go near. I'm off to fetch help.'

She gaped at him stupidly. 'What's happened, Mark?'

'Wait here. Don't try to . . .'

With an aimless gesture he hurried off towards the restaurant. Celia stood vacantly watching him. No action on her part seemed to suggest itself. The moment he disappeared inside, it was as though the incident had not occurred. Had he been there, talking to her? Perhaps she should follow him, and ask.

Below the escarpment, a little way to the left, another movement caught her eye. The headscarf was unmistakable. It was coming her way. Celia waited passively for its owner to get within range and call to her. 'There's been an accident. Can you raise the alarm?'

'Is it my husband?' she called back.

'Oh my God.' The Leicester grandmother halted, dithered. 'I never realized . . .'

An upsurge of activity near the restaurant distracted her. She began to wave furiously. 'Over here! Quickly!'

The two Spanish guides loped across. 'Down there.' She pointed. 'The hole—comprendi? I doubt if there's anything you can . . .' Again her voice trailed off. The two men took off down the slope. Huntedly she looked round at Celia. 'Best come back inside with me, dear. You'll want to sit down.' She shielded her eyes. 'Is this a friend of yours?'

Lorraine was approaching at a limp pace, coughing a little. She seemed unaware of anything but her own discomfort. Reaching the spot, she ignored the older woman and addressed Celia. 'I threw up,' she announced. 'Good grief, that was some experience. The trifle last night, and then the coffee . . . Boy, was I sick. Those pills you gave me . . .'

Pausing, she glanced around. 'Something happened? What's going on?'

Mark re-emerged from the restaurant. Walking methodically, setting his feet down with fastidious care between the impeding rocks, he came over to join them. Lorraine turned on him. 'What's all the commotion?' she demanded. 'Where's Paul?'

He nodded at the slope. 'Paul's down there.'

His wife stared at him, frowning in perplexity. 'What's he up to?'

'Nothing. He tripped and fell in the pit.'

Lorraine regarded him doubtfully. She was trying, Celia thought, to decide whether or not she was expected to laugh. While she was making up her mind, the Leicester grandmother took a step forward. She aimed an accusing finger.

'You were responsible,' she declared. 'I saw what happened. He was just standing there when you crept up behind and threw that lump of rock. That's why he fell in. I saw it all.'

'Don't be absurd,' Mark replied with dignity. 'Paul was a friend of mine. As though I'd think of doing such a thing.' Without warning his face puckered, fell apart. Dropping to a crouch, he stared vacantly at the ground, sifting the warm cinders with his fingertips.

Bye-bye, Shimmy

'Her name's Shimmy,' said Mike. 'She's eight months old. Getting on for nine.'

'She's beautiful.' The schoolgirl extended slim fingers to be licked. 'Why do you call her Shimmy?'

'If you watch her from behind, trotting along,' Mike explained, 'you'll see why.'

The girl laughed, rumpling with her other hand the glossy nape fur of the spaniel. 'Can't help the way you walk, can you, Shimmy?'

Her laughter was low, amused but moderate, an expression of pure appreciation without excess. Her knees as she crouched were rounded below her plain, dark skirt. Gazing upwards into her face, Shimmy administered a solemn tongue-flick to the tip of her nose. The child's laugh became a giggle.

'Shimmy!' reproved Mike. 'You're not to.'

'I don't mind.'

'Have you got a dog?'

'No,' the girl said sadly. 'We've got a cat. We had two, but one went missing.'

'That's a shame. No idea what became of it?'

She shook her head. 'They say there are gangs going about, snatching pets for . . . you know. Experiments.'

'Oh Lord. I hope not.'

'I don't think about it. I can't. Do you let Shimmy off the leash?'

'Up to now,' Mike admitted, 'I haven't dared.'

The girl rose and they both stood looking down at the spaniel, whose attention had been seized by some movement, real or imagined, in a distant corner of the park; it stood with forelegs planted firmly apart, raptly at gaze. 'She's very skittish,' he elaborated. 'I'm afraid she might bolt.'

'Not worth risking,' the girl agreed. She looked thoughtful. 'You could try one of those extending leads—like a fishing line. I've seen people using them.'

'It's an idea. I might give it a whirl.'

Side by side, they began moving slowly towards the park exit. After initial resistance, Shimmy came along with fast-mounting gusto, snorting against the collar, hind legs pounding sturdily into the turf like a rabbit's. Mike held on diligently. The girl, whose head of brunette hair came up to his shoulder, regarded the dog with a kind of detached fondness: she reminded him of a besotted mother trying hard, in the company of others, to be realistic and non-tedious about the entire subject of parenthood. He liked the style of her hair. Hatless, she wore it in a series of controlled festoons around a face that seemed to have arrived at maturity well before its time. But for this, he would have described her features as elfin. If he had ever had a daughter, this was the model he might have selected from some celestial brochure. She walked neatly, unhurried, responsible. He glanced at his watch. 'What time do you have to be at school?'

'Nine-fifteen.' The air of maturity dissolved in a solution of childish rebellion.

'Sounds as if you don't care for it much.'

'I like school,' she averred. 'Only it's English, first period.'

'And you're not hooked on English?'

'It's Miss Barkworth. She hates me.'

'I'm sure she can't do.'

'She's always making fun of me. Whatever I do isn't right. We've got her again this afternoon,' the girl said despondently. 'She takes history, too.'

'What subjects do you prefer?' Mike inquired. They were almost at the park gates. A middle-aged man in City suit and bowler, using a furled umbrella as a walking-stick, stood pondering an ornamental flowerbed laid out by a beneficent local authority at the ratepayers' expense. Mike had seen him several times before. They had reached the nodding stage, and in a few weeks' time might well be exchanging stiff ''Mornings'. Turning from his contemplation of the salvias, the man gave the schoolgirl a brief though searching glance before awarding Mike his nod, then went on his way through the park towards the railway station beyond the far side. For London commuters, the route provided a daily taste of urban countryside. Alongside the path were steep grassy slopes, topped by trees and shrub thickets; downland in miniature. Neighbourhood folk were jealous of the park's character. A local councillor had once suggested levelling it to accommodate soccer pitches: he had been pitched out at the next election.

'I like science,' announced the child, after some thought.

'Any particular kind?'

'We only do chemistry.'

'I was never any good at that,' Mike confessed. 'How about maths?'

'I like it, but I'm no good at it.'

He rubbed his neck. 'Sounds contradictory.'

She looked up at him with a beguiling grin. 'Mr Bradshaw takes us for maths. He's great.'

Mike threw back his head in a guffaw that was a shade louder than it might have been, masking a sudden ripple of jealousy in respect of the unknown but great Mr Bradshaw. 'That explains it. Any maths periods today?'

Her face fell. 'No. Not till tomorrow.' She cheered up. 'But then it's a double period, straight after lunch.'

'Something to look forward to.' They had reached the main road. Hauling Shimmy away from the kerbside, Mike shortened the leash and established the dog in roughly the right direction for home. 'Have a nice day,' he advised, not displeased with the transatlantic flavour of the remark. 'Don't let Miss Barkworth get you down.'

'I won't,' the child said cheerfully. 'Bye, Shimmy. Be a good girl.'

Lurching homewards behind a spaniel with the scent of arrival in her nostrils, Mike held the image of the girl's face in his mind while dwelling with pleasure and relief upon the thought that not everything one read about today's younger generation was necessarily accurate. To his sister, clearing away breakfast dishes in the kitchen, he recounted the events of the walk, as was his custom, leaving until last the episode of the schoolgirl in the park. 'Intelligent little thing,' he remarked, struggling to remove Shimmy's collar. 'Quite restored one's faith in modern childhood. Shimmy captivated her.'

'She does most people,' his sister retorted. A small, sharp-featured woman of nearly sixty, seven years his senior, she had a brain and a tongue to match her appearance. In her presence, Mike trod softly. She threw him an acute look over the frying-pan she was wiping. 'How old was she, this girl?'

'I suppose . . . around twelve.' Releasing Shimmy into the hall, Mike hung the collar and leash on their hook before helping himself to the remaining coffee in the pot that had been put aside for him. 'Older than her years, though, in some ways. Cute kid. I thought they'd stopped making 'em like that.'

'What would a bachelor know about it?' His sister returned the pan briskly to its rack. 'Underneath the charm, she's probably a knowing little hussy.'

'No need to wreck my illusions, Beth,' he protested mildly. 'I like to think there's still some innocence around.'

Taking his cup and the newspaper into the living-room, he browsed for twenty minutes before leaving by the patio door and treading the flagstone path to his garage workshop. He had a pinewood dresser to finish for Mrs Swift along the street. After that there was a requirement for a cocktail cabinet from the Mathesons at Stable Cottage, in The Crescent. Mike liked a full order book. Besides giving life a purpose, it kept him from under Beth's feet. They lived together quite amicably as long as they were apart most of the time.

Several days elapsed before he again met the schoolgirl in the park.

The fine spell had broken. She had covered her festooned hair with a rain-hat and was wearing a short, translucent waterproof jacket over her striped blazer. When he first spotted her she looked abstracted, as though preoccupied with school concerns—the idolized Mr Bradshaw, perhaps?

—but at the sight of Shimmy she returned delightedly to her surroundings and, regardless of the wet grass, sank to her knees to enable the spaniel to give her a greeting proper to its instincts. 'Shimmy . . . Shimmy . . .' she murmured into its shaggy left ear. 'You're getting a podge, did you know that? You must watch your diet.'

'She has the scraps out of dishes,' Mike said apologetically. 'I tell my sister she shouldn't, but you know how it is.'

'Shimmy, you're a greedy-guts.'

'She is, that's true. I think I'll take her around the Thorne Estate this morning, work some of it off. How's school?'

The girl wrinkled her nose. 'English twice today,' she said dejectedly.

'Oh dear. The dreaded Miss Barker.'

'Barkworth. Barky, we call her. She gave me an extra poem to learn.'

'How rotten. Why?'

'For slamming the desk lid when she was reading from *David Copperfield*. I didn't mean to. It slipped.'

'That seems unfair.'

'She's always doing it,' the child said philosophically.

'I thought you seemed a bit worried this morning.'

'Not about her.' Straightening up, the girl glanced across the park to focus upon the children's play area. Mike, whose long-distance eyesight was poor, gained a blurred impression of a figure on one of the swings, pendulating languidly. 'I don't like the look of *him*,' said the girl, resuming course for the gate.

'Have you noticed him before?'

'He's often around. Just sits there and stares. Gives me the shudders.'

'Is he young? I can't see very well.'

'Oh no. He must be over twenty. I wish he'd go away. Do you live far?' asked the girl, patting Shimmy as the dog wriggled into the space between them.

'Half a mile. Oaks Avenue.' Mike spoke a little absently. He was giving some thought to the aging twenty-year-old on the swing. Perfectly harmless, in all probability. An idler or one of the unemployed, with time on his hands, poor wretch. The girl, though, was right to be cautious. The hazard was there, although it was not great as long as she kept to the main path. At the times she came through, somebody else was generally likely to be about. The bowler-hatted City commuter, for example, who on the previous occasion had made rather a point of demonstrating that he had not failed to notice the pair of them together, Mike and the child. Life could be awkward. The complications were endless.

'I've got an auntie,' volunteered the girl, 'in Oaks Avenue.'

'You have?'

'Well, she's not really my auntie. She's a friend of my mum's. I call on her sometimes. She's fabulous.'

'Gives you tea, does she?'

The wide smile travelled up to him. 'Iced buns,' the child said reverently.

'My. They're favourites of mine. I'll have to get acquainted with your auntie myself. Do you have a tuckshop at school?'

She shook her head. 'We can buy rolls from a kiosk at morning break, but there's no proper shop. We're organizing a petition for one.'

'Hope you have some luck. You turn right here, don't you? See you again. Take care.'

'Bye-bye, Shimmy. Don't you go eating too much.' The child gave the spaniel a pat on the rump before turning away. 'You'll ruin your figure,' she warned, over her shoulder. With a little skip, she started uphill towards the school.

Before setting off for home, Mike went into the newsagent's for a copy of *DIY Monthly*. He liked to keep track of trends. The shop's owner cast him an indulgent look. 'Getting off with the schoolgirls, Mr Owen? Better watch it. You know what they say about juvenile crushes on older men.'

'Believe it or not,' Mike informed him, pocketing his change, 'we were chatting about food.'

'Nice to be young again,' the shop owner said lugubriously. 'Eat what you please. No weight problems.'

Indeed, Mike reflected as he plodded home, the girl was lath-slim. Sticky buns evidently did her no harm . . . yet. Would it be indiscreet to . . .? Yes, it would. Accepting confectionery from strangers was undoubtedly top of any schoolchild's proscribed list, these days more than ever in the past. Mike sighed. He found himself worrying about the young man in the park. Suppose he carried a bag of sweets? A quiet word, perhaps, with someone at the local police station . . . Not trouble-making: just a precaution. He decided to give serious thought to the idea.

When Beth asked him about the walk, he delayed any mention of the girl until the end, sliding it in as an apparent afterthought. Beth gave him one of her harder looks. 'You mean the one you met the other morning? The innocent little charmer?'

'She always goes through the park at the same time,' Mike explained. 'If I take Shimmy that way, naturally we meet.'

'Naturally.'

For the next few mornings, Mike avoided the park. He would have found it hard to explain, even to himself, why he should do such a thing. It was depriving Shimmy of a much-needed scamper; and it was denying himself a small pleasure of such harmlessness that it was laughable, absurd, to imagine that anyone might ascribe a questionable motivation to his actions. And yet, somehow, there it was. For the time being, he couldn't bring himself to enter the park again.

Shimmy, for her part, took all that failed to come her way with supreme good nature. If she missed the grassed expanses, she made no detectable protest. She could find interest in a garden gatepost or a road bollard. An accommodating dog. However, she was getting noticeably plumper.

Mike didn't go to the police station. The risk, he had decided, was minimal: it was summer, the daylight was abundant, and there were always responsible people walking through the park. Besides which, schoolgirls these days knew what was what. They could look after themselves. The particular young lady he had in mind had shown, by her speech and actions, that she was fully alert to danger. Who was he to interefere? The police had enough to do, without being urged to hound people who were doing no manifest harm to anyone.

On a Thursday afternoon at the beginning of July, Beth found that she needed a postal order and some stamps.

'I must write to Aunt Marjorie,' she declared. 'It's her birthday on Saturday and she'll expect to hear. She looks forward to her five pounds. Unless it's posted tonight or tomorrow morning . . .'

'I'll nip down to the shop,' Mike offered.

'All right. And take Shimmy.'

'No. I can't handle cash with her tugging at me. I'll manage better by myself.'

The newsagent's by the park entrance was also the sub-post office. Reaching it via the main road, Mike obtained the things that Beth needed and a copy of the evening paper for himself. On impulse, he also bought his sister a slab of her favourite fruit-and-nut milk chocolate. The shop owner, who was filling in as sub-postmaster for the afternoon, leaned forward to peer through the glass panel. 'No four-legged friend today, Mr Owen? Not off-song, I hope?'

'She's fine. I was in a bit of a hurry so I left her behind.'

'That'll be seven pounds thirty altogether. Don't eat the whole slab at once, will you?'

Mike gave him a wink. 'It's not for me.'

Outside the shop, he hesitated briefly before heading for the park gate. It was a quicker way home, and at three in the afternoon he would be just ahead of the school exodus. And he hadn't admired the salvias for a week. They were, he discovered, as refulgent as ever, pert from the showery weather that had followed the heatwave. He stood for a minute or so, surveying the bed. The park was cocooned in mid-afternoon peacefulness. He was glad he hadn't brought Shimmy. She would have dragged him off to explore a hilltop shrubbery, robbed him of his moments of reflective renewal.

Suddenly he felt hungry. Having worked through to complete an order, he had missed lunch and was starting to feel the lack of it. Feeling for the chocolate bar, he broke off a third and ate it, square by square, with a half-guilty but sensual enjoyment while circumnavigating the flowerbed as a prelude to heading for the opposite side of the park and the way out. It was while he was so engaged that his gaze drifted across to the corner playground and settled hazily upon the shape occupying one of the swings. Indistinct though it was, he felt sure that it was not the figure of a child.

Slightly altering course, he followed a path that took him closer to the play area before bending away in the direction he wanted. At the nearest point, he was able to get a clearer picture of the figure on the swung. An unshaven man in his early twenties, clad in jeans and bomber jacket over a checked shirt, he was sitting with an air of indolence, staring across the park at the main-road gate. Mike gave him an intent look, which the man ignored.

Pursuing the path as it veered back, Mike tried to commit to memory details of the young man's appearance. Copious brown hair, swept untidily back. A saturnine, brooding face. There was little else to grasp. Before leaving the park he looked back, in time to see the figure detach itself from the swing and begin to saunter towards a clump of conifers at the foot of a steep bank which flanked the park on that side. Aimless. The word should have summarized the man's demeanour, and yet somehow it fell short. There had been something else: an extra dimension that he couldn't identify.

Reaching the mouth of his own street, Mike hesitated again.

The police station was half a mile further on. There and back, the diversion would cost him another half-hour at least, and Beth was waiting for her postal order. He turned into Oaks Avenue and walked smartly home.

When he got inside, he didn't tell his sister about the partly-consumed chocolate bar. Now that it was started, he might as well finish it off. He would buy her a replacement next morning.

But he did tell her about the man in the park. 'I'm wondering,' he said, 'if I ought to tip the wink to the police.'

'What were you doing in the park?' demanded Beth.

'I just thought I'd come back that way. It's pleasanter.'

'Except for the prowlers.' She gave her brother a penetrative survey. 'What were you thinking of saying to the police, exactly?'

Mike shrugged. 'Suggest they check up on him, in a quiet way. He may be quite harmless. But he does seem to hang around the kids' section a fair bit. I wouldn't want to feel I'd been remiss if anything . . .'

'If anything what?'

'You read of all kinds of things happening, these days,' Mike said uncomfortably.

'Not just these days.' Beth paused for her words to sink in. 'I wouldn't bother about it now,' she continued briskly. 'I might call myself tomorrow, on my way into town. Just mention it to them. If that would settle your mind.'

'Better than nothing,' Mike said quietly.

That night he slept badly. He never passed a completely restful night, but about once a month his internal wiring, as he phrased it to himself, seemed to go berserk. During these phases he awoke regularly every fifteen minutes from a series of weird kaleidoscopical images that could barely be described as dreams, and he sweated a lot. This time it was really bad. It began the moment his head touched the pillow, which instantly became filled with jagged rocks instead of duck feathers and in no time succeeded in creating a burning sensation inside his right ear. He perspired and tossed. His mouth felt sulphurous. Tiny, unidentifiable sounds tormented him. He had no dreams, for the sufficient reason that sleep eluded him completely. At midnight he made coffee, and again at three in the morning. He also nibbled a few more squares of the chocolate. If the night was a lost cause, he reasoned, he might as well put the failure to some advantage. He read *DIY Monthly* from cover to cover. As he stared at the print, obscure thoughts and images trotted across the horizon of his consciousness, defying definition. At six o'clock he could no longer endure the confinement of his room. Creeping downstairs, he informed a suprised Shimmy that he was taking her for a walk to clear his head. The early streets greeted them like unexpected guests, granting a reserved welcome overlaid with touches of resentment. Rain splinters drifted in the breeze. Allowing the dog to set the pace, Mike followed in the wake of her pistoning hindquarters, relishing escape.

He returned with an appetite for bacon. He told Beth he had slept quite well.

'Thought I heard you moving about.' She had to raise her voice to compete with the Radio Four announcer.

'I did take Shimmy for an early hike.'

'Whatever for?'

'Just felt like it.' He glanced up from his plate. 'No harm, is there? She enjoyed it.'

'Can't see the sense, myself.' His sister was a woman of routine. 'You're not taking her again, afterwards?'

'A quickie, perhaps. I want to get on with that table for the . . .'

Mike paused. Something that the announcer was saying had tugged at the fringe of his attention. 'Listen a moment.'

The announcer was alluding to a police search. 'Having covered the route taken by Susan to school, they're now switching their attention to other neighbourhoods which are known to have been visited by the girl on recent occasions. In particular . . .'

'Another missing child,' sniffed Beth. 'What were you saying about a table?'

'Listen, listen.'

'. . . the street of a relative with whom she sometimes has tea. Emphasizing that Susan had been missing for only one night, a police spokesman said that nevertheless, the fact that she was a level-headed child who was not in the habit of—'

Beth flicked off the radio. 'Just what they always say.'

Mike gazed at her in anguish. 'I wanted to hear the rest.'

'Why? There's nothing we can do.'

'How do you know?'

His sister eyed him. 'You sound quite upset. Do you

think you might be acquainted with this Susan who's gone missing?'

'I'd simply like to have heard, that's all.'

'Too soon in the morning to be morbid.' Beth engineered another sniff. 'You'd do better getting on with some work. Pass me that plate, if you're finished.'

Although he worked assiduously all morning upon the pinewood table for the Pitt-Joneses, Mike found less than his usual satisfaction in the task. To an extent, he felt that he was under auto-pilotage. He might have put it down to the sleepless night, but insomnia had never had this effect on him before. At midday he knocked off. He returned to the house, hoping to find that Beth was out shopping; she was, however, in full cry around the kitchen units, and there was no chance of his getting to the radio without her intervention. The morning newspaper had said nothing about a missing girl. There was, he believed, a twelve-thirty news bulletin on TV, but if he tried switching on the set in the living-room Beth could be relied upon to erupt from the kitchen at precisely the moment to catch him at it. Viewing of any kind prior to five-thirty in the afternoon was, to her, anathema.

After lunch he trudged back to the garage. For a couple of hours, until four, he forced himself to plane and saw and mitre. By that time, it was reasonable for him to take Shimmy for her afternoon walk and to buy the evening paper. As a special treat for the spaniel, he took the park route. That was all it was, a bonus for Shimmy. She had put up with hard pavements stoically for too long.

When they got there, it was to find—to Shimmy's delight—a rival occupation force of assorted juveniles which sent Mike, in some dismay, to the perimeter fence in a bid to avoid balloon-tyred cycles and rocket-propelled footballs. The park at this time of day was a different kettle of fish from the park at eight in the morning. Diverting, with some difficulty, Shimmy's attention from the rival attractions, he hugged the fence as it mounted a hillock and pursued an erratic course between thickets and bramble-patches. Thirty per cent of the park's forty acres, he discovered, was barely navigable. Such footpaths as existed tended to expire in the midst of clumps of tangled foliage; he had to keep doubling back.

Shimmy was in ecstasy. Plunging into and out of undergrowth, she subjected to a stern test the extending lead that Mike had finally acquired for her. It gave her a degree of controllable freedom, justifying the outlay. Experimentally he played her in and out, like an angler subduing a fish. After a few minutes the inevitable happened. Vanishing into a clump of particularly dense foliage on a slope leading down to the perimeter ditch, Shimmy took the line off to the right and jammed it solid.

Mike called sharply, 'Shimmy! Come back here.'

He could hear excited snufflings, rustles, a growl or two. 'Stay where you are,' he told her. 'I'll have to come and get you disentangled.'

Leaves and twigs stung his face. Crouched almost double, he battled into the core of the clump, following the snagged line from point to point. Shimmy's vibrating rear became visible. His calls fell upon deaf ears. 'What is it?' he demanded. 'A hedgehog? They're full of fleas. Stay clear of—'

The words stagnated in his throat, choking him. By now he had reached the spot where the spaniel had exhausted the extent of her liberty, and could see what she had seen.

At the police station, they seemed to consider that he needed strong tea. A cup was planted at his elbow and somebody kept hovering, as though avid to replenish the contents. Tea, as it happened, was low on Mike's present list of priorities. He didn't feel ill, shocked, stupefied. He felt nothing. The questions they asked, he answered mechanically, clearing his throat repeatedly because it seemed to have become congested by dust from the undergrowth. He had a vague notion that he was dishevelled. Shimmy, after an initial frenzy of exploration, lay resignedly on the tiled floor at his feet, jowls and ears spread, awaiting the resumption of the walk.

The man putting the questions was a Chief Inspector Adams. That much Mike had taken in, quite clearly. The questions themselves were cloudier, but he did his best.

'How come, Mr Owen, that you chanced to investigate that particular patch of undergrowth, this particular afternoon?'

'It was her.' He indicated Shimmy. 'She dived in.'

'You always take her that way?'

'Which way?'

'Over the hilly part, near the fence.'

'Not normally. It was quieter. There were a good few kids about.'

'Annoy you, do they? Kids?'

'How do you mean?'

Patiently the Chief Inspector rephrased the query. 'You're apt to steer clear of children, as a rule?'

'When I'm with her.' Again he nodded down at the red-gold fur. 'She's a shade temperamental.'

'Why go through the park at all, then?'

'It gives her a gallop.'

'You always have her with you, when you walk through the park?'

'Generally speaking.' He guided the cup of stewing tea cautiously aside with his elbow. 'Would she have felt much, do you suppose?'

Adams studied him with some care. 'Who are you referring to?'

'The little girl. Would she have suffered?'

'I'm not sure. Maybe you can tell us, Mr Owen?'

Mike closed his eyes. He felt as if he were plunging uncontrollably forward, head over heels through deep space, beyond the pull of gravity. He reopened them. 'You think I did it?'

'I'm asking you.'

'You're not. You're making an accusation.'

The Chief Inspector strolled away to the end of the room, did a turn, came back. 'We've been talking,' he confided, 'to your sister.'

'Beth? What did she have to say?'

'She just filled us in a little. You've been living with her some while, I understand.'

'Eighteen years, five months.'

'You've forgotten the weeks,' the other reminded him, half-humorously.

'No, I haven't. It was exactly—'

'Did you move in with her from choice?'

'I wasn't given a choice.'

'How come?'

Mike glanced up. 'If Beth's filled you in, you ought to know.'

'I'd have liked to hear it from you.' With a delicate cough, Adams looked sidelong at his assistant who was taking notes. 'As I understand it, the vital factor was a court appearance . . . am I right? Remember that, Mr Owen?'

The wavy fur on the back of Shimmy's neck gave a twitch. Mike sat examining it. The Chief Inspector waited.

Presently he resumed. 'Not exactly a pleasant case, was it? Nobody cares much for child molestation. In your case there were thought to be certain mitigating circumstances—the behaviour of the girl involved, for a start—which explains why you were given probation, on stated conditions. The main condition being that you went to live with your sister, who undertook to—'

'Since you know all this, why make a song about it?'

'You don't feel it might possibly have some relevance to . . . current events?'

Painfully, Mike rehashed his thoughts into a modified shape. He tried to keep his phrases concise. 'I did talk to the kid. Susan, I mean. Twice. She took an interest in the dog. Bright youngster, she was. You think I'd have done that to her?'

'I'm not paid to conjecture, Mr Owen.'

'Perhaps you're paid to jump to conclusions? I'm not sure where that leaves me. All I can do is . . . is . . . tell God's truth. I never saw her yesterday. I've never touched her.'

'Nor given her anything?'

'Like what?'

Reaching out to the desk behind him, Adam produced and displayed something on the palm of his hand. 'Found,' he said, 'next to the body. It was—'

'*Her* body.'

'What?'

'*Her* body. It didn't belong to anyone else.'

'Her body. Half a slab of chocolate.' Adams reached behind him again. 'This was found in your jacket pocket. Four remaining squares, in a torn wrapper. Fruit-and-nut. Same chocolate, same brand. Mean anything to you, Mr Owen?'

'Susan wouldn't have accepted anything like that. Not from anyone.'

'Oh? How do you know?'

'A kid of twelve? She knew the score. She was wary of people. There was this character on the—'

'It's you, we're talking about. According to—' The Chief Inspector consulted a slip of paper—'Mr Mark Summers, who runs the sub-post office by the park entrance, you bought a slab of chocolate just like this, yesterday afternoon.'

'So I did. I was going to—'

'And then went off with it in the direction of the park. Without your dog.'

'Does that prove anything?'

'It suggests a thing or two. From the state of the body—Susan's body—it appears she was killed some time yesterday afternoon. You were there in the afternoon. You've said so.'

'I never said I clapped eyes on her.'

The Chief Inspector mused. Suddenly he said, 'Why did you take your dog for a walk this morning?'

'I always do.'

'At six o'clock?'

'I'd had a dodgy night. Wanted to clear my head.'

'What gave you a dodgy night?'

'Indigestion, maybe. The chocolate.'

'You're saying you ate it yourself?'

'I'm telling you what happened. I can't do more.'

'I think you can, Mr Owen. I believe you can give us a full account of events.'

'Look. Why don't you trace this bloke I saw, loitering in the kids' playground? Susan saw him, too. She pointed him out. He scared her.'

Adam surveyed him. 'When was it you spotted this man?'

'Yesterday afternoon. I was coming in here to report it.'

'What stopped you?'

'My sister said she'd do it today.'

'So you were happy to leave it to her?'

'She said she might call in.' Mike rumpled the furry dome of the spaniel, who looked up at him hopefully, scenting departure.

'Why didn't you do it yourself, on your walk this morning?'

'It didn't occur to me.'

'Other things on your mind, maybe. Like revisiting the park?'

'I never went near the park.'

'You did this afternoon.'

'Is there some law against it?'

Chief Inspector Adams sat on the desk-edge to observe him. A thin-faced, worried-looking man, he sounded angry. Subterranean volcanic mutterings were impeding the surface equability of his approach.

He spoke slowly and distinctly. 'You hadn't taken your dog to the park for some days. Why choose this afternoon to get back into the habit?'

Mike sat silently for a while.

'I'd heard something,' he said finally, 'on the radio. Something about a missing girl.'

'What difference would that have made?'

'Perhaps I . . .' Mikc stumbled, stuttered. 'P-perhaps she'd have been there. Susan, I mean. Coming home from school, through the park. I might have spotted her. Then I'd have known it wasn't her that was missing.'

'What made you think it might have been?'

'I wanted to be certain.' Mike hiccuped. 'Pardon me.' Belatedly he put a hand to his mouth. Adams watched it stonily.

'You've already said you took the perimeter path for the express purpose of avoiding the children who were in the park. If Susan—'

'I might still have managed to spot her, from a distance.' Mike shook his head, intending to stop it again almost immediately, but for some reason he couldn't. Without voluntary effort on his part, his head went on shaking: there seemed little he could do to bring it to rest. 'I had Shimmy to think of,' he added, with difficulty.

'You did, indeed. Why did you let her explore that clump of undergrowth?'

'She just went.'

'And made the discovery. The discovery you wanted her to make. So that then, Mr Owen, you could come along here, report finding the body, act out the part of the concerned citizen doing his public-spirited—'

'I *was* concerned,' Mike said simply. 'I *am*. Why don't you want to believe me, Inspector?'

The assistant glanced up from his note-taking. For a few moments they both stared at him. Adams seemed nonplussed, and no less angry. Presently he levered himself convulsively away from the desk and signalled to his subordinate.

'Is the dog all right?' he asked Mike abruptly.

'What do you mean?'

'It's been here a good while. And it may be a long time yet before we—'

A telephone rang. Snatching it up, Adams listened impassively, said, 'Right, I'll be along,' and put it down. As if there had been no interruption, he went on, 'If you like, we can ask your sister to step round here and take the animal . . .'

'If it's all the same to you, I'd sooner she stayed.' Mike fondled Shimmy behind an ear. The dog rubbed her jowl against the back of his hand, pleaded with burnt-amber eyes. 'Getting peckish, are you?' he inquired softly. 'Past your dinner-time. We'll make it up to you later.'

'I might be able to rustle up a dog-biscuit,' Adams said stolidly. He and the other man left the room.

It was quiet inside the building. The clash of a door was a rarity. A multiple tread of feet along the corridor, which occurred once, seemed to have been condoned by accident:

an unaccountable shudder within lubricated parts. Mike had known noisier hospitals. He glanced around the room. Brightly decorated, it possessed a solitary four-paned window set so near the ceiling that, from where he sat, a mere segment of greyish sky could be seen. The time by the digital wall-clock was eight-twenty-three. Another half-hour or so of daylight remaining.

The Chief Inspector's desk bore nothing except the telephone and what looked like a computer terminal. Nowhere was there anything to read. The atmosphere was on the stuffy side.

At his feet, Shimmy began to pant a little. He caressed her again and she rolled upon her back, hind legs elevated to present a pink-fleshed stomach for attention. 'Sorry, old girl,' he murmured, tickling her. 'Not the normal end to the walk, is it? Afraid we've landed ourselves. Keep your paws crossed.'

An hour later, it was almost dark inside the room. Shimmy's tongue lolled; she looked forlorn. Mike went timidly to the door, opened it, glanced along the corridor to meet the eye of a uniformed constable stationed against the wall.

'It's my dog,' he explained. 'She's getting rather thirsty. Would it be possible . . .?'

'I'll see what I can do, sir.'

The constable made no move. Shutting the door, Mike reclaimed his seat by the desk. A slight feeling of sickness was invading his abdomen. He hoped it would pass. If he had to make a bolt for the washroom, Shimmy would get fussed. Was there a washroom?

Twenty minutes later the constable entered with a yellow plastic bowl of water. Shimmy lapped endlessly. Mike said, 'Thank you very much. I'm so grateful. Perhaps you can tell me . . .'

'Chief'll be with you shortly, sir.'

The constable withdrew, closing the door firmly and soundlessly. Her thirst slaked, the spaniel took a restive turn or two about the room, sniffed at a waste bin, returned to Mike and jumped up to place her forelegs on his lap, nuzzling his nose with her own. Presently she cocked her head and said, 'Woof?'

'Don't ask me,' he told her.

Half an hour limped by.

Again Mike went to the door. The constable was no longer there. Rubbing his jaw, Mike walked Shimmy to the swing doors at the end of the corridor and peered through the glazed section. All he could see was a landing and the head of some stairs. The dog scratched impatiently at the varnished woodwork.

For the thirtieth time, Mike said, 'I know, old girl. I'm sorry. Nothing I can do about it. Try to stick it out.'

Disconsolately she accompanied him back to the room. The dent he had made in the chair accepted him once more. The place now was indisputably hot and airless, making it hard to think clearly. A sudden vision of Beth flashed across his mind. He supposed he could have telephoned her. Would they have allowed that?

The door opened with a rattle, startling him. Shimmy let out a yip of suspicion. Glancing down at her, Chief Inspector Adams said brusquely, 'I forgot about the dog-biscuit. Better get along with her, Mr Owen. Give her a bite to eat.'

He came uncertainly to his feet. 'Where shall I take her?'

'What's wrong with home?'

'Home?'

'That's right.' The tone was casual, though brisk. 'We've been in touch with your sister. She's expecting you.'

'You'll want to . . .' Mike's voice quavered, vanished. Clearing his throat, he tried again. 'You'll be needing to see me again?'

'Let's hope not, shall we?' The Chief Inspector's near-smile seemed as genuine as it was capable of being. 'I'm sure you won't be wanting to repeat an experience like this.'

'What's the position, then?' The tremor persisted, but he had to know.

Adams scowled across the room. Mike thought he had taken offence, until he saw that the detective was in fact thinking deeply about his reply. At last it came. 'There's been a development.'

'Yes?'

'The young man you spoke of. The one in the playground . . .'

'Did you find him?'

'No.' The Chief Inspector examined his fingernails before glancing up. 'He found us.'

Mike waited dumbly. On a reflective key, Adams continued, 'You were quite right. He's been knocking around there for some while, staying clear of people. His parents think he's on a building site the other side of town, but actually he's out of a job. He doesn't want them to know. Touchy type.'

'And he'd seen Susan?'

'Oh yes. Noticed her with you, a couple of times. You and the dog.' With a touch of benevolence Adams bent his gaze briefly upon Shimmy, seated in hunch-backed apathy on the floor at their feet. 'That king-sized lead of yours rather took his fancy.'

'So?' prompted Mike, as the Chief Inspector paused.

'Yesterday afternoon he saw you come through the park—unaccompanied. Not long after that, he spotted Susan.'

Mike's hands clenched. 'What happened?'

'So far as he was concerned, nothing.'

Adams surveyed him blandly. Mike said in bewilderment, 'But he came forward, you said. Wasn't it to confess . . .?'

'The reason he approached us was to supply details of the person Susan was with.'

'Who?'

'A highly respectable-looking gentleman. Bowler hat, City suit: the works. He and the girl were strolling along together, chatting.'

The Chief Inspector leaned tiredly against the desk. 'It wasn't the first time the young man had noticed the pair of them. They'd come through the park together the previous morning, too.'

Mike stared blindly at the digital clock. 'I know the man you're talking about. I've seen him.'

'Yes, and he'd seen you.'

'The first time I ran into Susan—'

'In fact, he did his best to chuck the blame on to you.'
'Blame?'
'He's been interviewed. That's what took us so long.'
The room spun around Mike. To steady things up, he crouched and placed a hand upon the supportive back of Shimmy, who blinked soulfully. In a low voice he asked, 'How did you know where to find him?'
Unexpectedly, Adams chuckled. 'Investigative brilliance. That's what I'd like to be able to say. Truth is, though, the young man knew where he lived. He comes from the street next to his. So . . .' He flipped a hand. 'We sent somebody round, and there he was.'
'And he admitted . . .?'
'As I say, for a while he tried to cast you as the culprit. But luckily we had a shred or two of evidence. We found half a slab of fruit-and-nut chocolate inside his briefcase: it matched exactly the piece found near the . . . Susan's body. Also there were bloodstains on a pair of his trousers stuffed into a wardrobe. A spot of verbal encouragement on our part did the rest. We've a full confession.'
Mike slid his palm to the base of Shimmy's spine, patted the sturdy softness once or twice. He could think of nothing constructive to say. He was out of ideas. The Chief Inspector looked a little dashed. 'It seems,' he went on presently, 'that a handy piece of dead branch was used to . . . subdue the child. As frequently happens, once he'd started he lost his head. When he saw what—'
'I don't want to hear any more,' Mike said hoarsely. 'I'd prefer not.'
'Can't say I blame you.' A flash of kindness lent warmth to the remark. 'The thing that concerns you, Mr Owen, is that you're in the clear. Sorry we had to keep you so many hours, but that's the way it is. Now why don't you get off home?'
All the way back, Shimmy pulled strenuously, panting and wheezing in her eagerness to recapture routine. Mike handled her mechanically. He was barely aware of his surroundings. The evening had turned fine and warm, bringing out scents from the damp greenery. In the dusk, some-

body passed him and said, 'Hi, Mr Owen. Hauled you out for a nightcap, has she?' He contrived some gibberish in reply. A car went past, driven raucously: some youngster on urban safari. From an open window spilled a sequence of familiar introductory chords. *News at Ten* was about to commence.

Beth was ironing in the kitchen. Intent on a garment, she said, 'I kept something hot for you. It's in the top oven. There wasn't—'

'I can't eat, just at the moment. Sorry if it's spoiled.'

'I had to improvise. Didn't know what was happening, when you might be back.' She turned and looked at him, meeting his eyes for a third of a second, chewing her lower lip in the way that Mike recalled from their childhood. Glancing away, she restored her attention to the blouse she was pressing. 'You can have it later.'

'Shimmy's ravenous.'

'She doesn't need anything, this time of night.' Turning to the refrigerator, Beth took out the dog's bowl containing a few scraps and set it down under the table. Shimmy threw herself upon the mixture. For a moment Mike watched her, smiling faintly. He had lowered himself on to the stool that stood near the door. Holding up the blouse for critical inspection, Beth added, 'If anybody wants my opinion, it's high time they brought back hanging.'

Mike studied the cooker. He said nothing.

'If I were the wife of that man,' Beth proceeded, biffing the blouse into neat folds, 'which God forbid, I'd do the job myself. Put an end to him. That's if he hadn't had the guts or decency to save anyone else the trouble.'

The blouse went on to the completed heap. 'In my estimation, anybody who could do that to a defenceless child . . . or even consider the possibility of doing it, which is every bit as evil . . . should be expected to take his own life as a matter of course. He's forfeited his right to existence.'

Seizing a skirt, she draped it across the ironing-board, traced the wreckage of a pleat with her fingers. 'It's the only way to atone.'

Mike rose from the stool. 'I think,' he said, 'I'll be getting along to bed. It's been a hectic sort of day.' In the doorway he paused, looked back at the dog who was licking the bowl to a shine. ''Night, Shimmy,' he said.

Beth ironed for another twenty minutes until she had finished. Then she heated a little milk for her bedtime drink. While she stood waiting for bubbles to appear, Shimmy sat up sharply in her basket and uttered a short, shrill bark, ending in a howl. Beth's fingers tightened on the saucepan handle. After some hesitation she switched off the burner, removed her apron, went out to the hall. The house was silent. Mounting the stairs slowly, she rapped on her brother's door.

'Michael? Did you call out?'

When she tried to open the door, she met resistance. A resolute woman, she persevered until she had created a space wide enough to show her the figure sprawled across the floor, the blood still seeping from the wrists into the drenched carpet. Nearby lay the razor-blade. Having taken stock, she reclosed the door carefully, returned downstairs and lifted the telephone receiver. Before dialling, she checked that she had the right number for the police station. She had never liked doing things in a rush.

Kill Before Publication

In the ordinary way, thought Miles, her features would have been striking. But something had happened to distort them a little. Trouble emanated from her, like polluted steam.

'The Editor?' he repeated cautiously. 'He's busy, right now. Can I do anything?'

The woman glanced along the counter. Four yards away, the small-ads girl was attending to a female customer. She spoke again on the same hushed note. 'Is there someone else I can see?'

Miles quelled his irritation. The implication that he himself amounted to less than 'someone else' was one that eleven months in the Beechway office of the *Gleaner* had taught him to be able to ignore. University, he now realized, had given him ideas above his station. A sensible fellow, he was willing to accept that it was up to him to make a fresh start in the real world, and cash in later. He knew he looked young for his age. This woman, whom he judged to be in the region of forty-five, could hardly be blamed for wanting somebody more blatantly mature.

'I'm from Editorial,' he said patiently. 'Maybe I can help.'

'I was rather hoping to speak to . . . someone in authority.'

Her figure was still trim. The merest hints of silver were beginning to touch her dark hair, softly waved about a face that, in Miles's estimation, had only recently commenced to sag just a little, to lose the confident elasticity of the first half of a lifetime. In her youth, she might well have been a knockout. He gave her a cheerful smile.

'If you could just outline to me what it's about, Mrs . . .?'

'Stanhope.' The name burst out as if under pressure. She hesitated, eyeing him. Her voice dropped lower. 'It's concerning a . . . a police matter.'

She glanced again at the customer, who was querying a

word-count. The only other person in the front office, an elderly man with facial blotches, was examining a rack of photographic prints and humming to himself.

'Criminal offence?' Miles inquired briskly. 'Road traffic problem? Neighbourhood dispute?'

'A court appearance.'

'Involving whom?'

'Actually, I was wondering . . .'

Miles waited. He was the kind of young fellow who always summoned a laugh at other people's jokes, especially when they weren't funny. Somebody had once told him he was too soft a touch to be a successful journalist. This was partly why he had taken up the challenge. There was, he knew, a vulnerable side to his nature. On the other hand, he did possess the sort of tenacity, the hatred of letting go of the rope, that distinguished the hack from the newshawk. In tandem, the traits had potential, although in a place like Beechway the scope for development of an investigative technique could hardly be said to be limitless.

A touch of defiance seeped into Mrs Stanhope's attitude. 'I really came in,' she said, raising her chin at him, 'to find out what the position is regarding . . . It was a shoplifting case, in fact.'

'I see. When was it dealt with?'

'This morning. A fine was imposed.'

'On yourself?'

Her eyes closed for an instant. 'That's right.'

'So now it's all over.' He smiled at her.

Neither her eyes nor her lips responded. She reminded him of some dead creature being jerked around by electrical impulses deficient in voltage. 'The court hearing is over. But you'd have had a reporter in court, wouldn't you?'

'We would, and so would the *Mercury*. Then there's the free-sheet, the *Advertiser*. They sometimes—'

'Yes, well. This is why it's so important that I should speak to the Editor.'

Miles studied her with some compassion. 'You'd like our report killed before publication?'

Hope sent the current surging into her. 'Is that possible? It's terribly important to me. There needn't—'

'I'm sorry, Mrs Stanhope. We report all cases. There can't be exceptions. That's the way it is.'

She gazed past him at the mail pigeonholes behind the counter. Her lower lip, like a child's, was quivering. Unlike a child, she awaited the return of self-control before venturing on further utterance.

'Surely there must be flexibility? You can't possibly override every mitigating—'

'If we did it for one person,' he explained, 'what excuse would we have for refusing someone else? It's not for us to judge. The courts are held in public. Either the Press covers them or it doesn't.'

She said hoarsely, 'It seems a rather insensitive system.'

'What's the alternative?'

Her fingernails, polished deep pink, tapped the counter-surface. Although she was watching them she seemed unconscious of their activity, as if it were being powered by a remote sub-station of her nervous system while the main generator roared desperately to open gates elsewhere. Presently she looked up. 'If I were to speak personally to the Editor . . .'

'You'd get the same answer from him, I'm afraid. It would just be a waste of your time, Mrs Stanhope. I'm sorry.'

'How about a doctor's certificate?'

'A medical certificate,' Miles said guardedly. 'To what effect?'

'It's my mother, you see. She's living with us, and she's elderly and not in good health, and if she were to get to hear about this . . .'

'I don't honestly see how you can keep it from her. Whether it's published or not, she's bound to find out, isn't she?'

'Not if I don't tell her.'

Miles rubbed his jaw. 'I think, Mrs Stanhope, you're being a little over-optimistic. I could be wrong, but it seems highly unlikely to me that she wouldn't get to hear of it, sooner or later. And though initially it might come as a shock . . .'

To his alarm, Mrs Stanhope slumped in tears across the counter. She did it quite silently. The sole giveaway was the slight heaving of her suede-clad shoulders. Barbara, the small-ads girl, however, had sharp eyes. Abandoning her customer, she came over. 'Is the lady feeling ill?'

Miles made discreet signals. 'She's a little upset. I'll take her into the interview room for a moment. Come along, Mrs Stanhope.'

The twin upright chairs inside the interview cubicle were of light, tubular-steel construction, enabling Miles to introduce one of them adroitly beneath the buckling form of his client while manipulating the other closely alongside so that he could bring physical as well as vocal succour to bear. The cubicle walls were mere chipboard partitions. Acutely aware of the pointed ears outside, he spoke quietly.

'If it would help at all, Mrs Stanhope, I'll see if the Editor would be willing to talk to you for a moment. But you really musn't expect anything from him. He'll tell you the same as I have. Like me to try?'

She nodded into her sleeve. Her voice was muffled. 'You're very kind.'

Raising his eyebrows in response to Barbara's inquisitive glance as he walked back through the front office, Miles went upstairs. The Editor, Bob Hartley, was on the telephone. Establishing himself in the doorway to his room, Miles waited without qualms. Despite an eight-year age gap and the gulf between their respective positions, he and Hartley were on terms of easy familiarity: to Miles, his nominal chief seemed no more than a likeable older brother, although Hartley's appointment to the top job at the age of thirty was said to have aroused a degree of resentment in certain of his more elderly subordinates in the newsroom. Even they could scarcely deny that he was smart, destined for greater things.

At the moment, however, Hartley looked anything but dynamic. His face had a bleached appearance and he was sagging sideways in his chair. Mumbling a few final words into the receiver, he dropped it with a clatter, picked up a galley-proof and began marking it with limp strokes of a ballpen. Eyes blearily upon the task, he said, 'Yes, Milesy? Trouble?'

'Nothing wild.' Miles advanced to the desk. 'We've a shoplifter downstairs. Wants it kept out of the paper.'

'You know the routine.' Scoring through a line, Hartley scrawled a weary replacement in the margin.

'She's in a bit of a state. Weeping in the interview room. I said I'd see if you felt like talking to her.'

'I don't feel like talking to her.'

'I warned her you wouldn't.' Miles made no move to leave. Immobilizing his pen, Hartley scowled at the facing wall.

'Menopausal syndrome?'

'Well, she's in her mid-forties, I'd say.'

Hartley waggled the pen feebly. 'Got to you, hasn't she, my son? Those tear-streaked jowls . . .'

'I'm only doing this,' Miles said tolerantly, 'in case she has hysterics all over Barbara's domain. I never promised her anything.'

A sigh rose from the depths of the Editor. 'What's her name?'

'Stanhope. Mrs.'

From a wire basket on the desk, Hartley extracted a pile of folded copy paper, covered with neat handwriting, and sifted through the sheets. 'Here we are,' he announced presently. ' "Mrs Sylvia Stanhope (46), housewife, of Lennard Gardens, South Beechway . . . fined £40 with £17.50 costs for stealing from Jepson's Supermarket three tins of red salmon, a tin of pork luncheon meat, five packets of soup, four boxes of processed cheese and a can of creamed rice, total value £7.36 . . ." '

'Didn't do things by halves, did she?'

'I expect she told the Bench they slipped into her pocket by mistake: ". . . an unaccountable lapse, she told the magistrates, which she now bitterly regretted . . . only explanation her mental state arising from domestic stress . . .

dependent mother in poor health . . . worries about the children . . . estranged from husband, now living at another address with a former woman friend of the defendant . . ." '

Hartley peered up. 'In her shoes, I wouldn't be sobbing my guts out in the front office of the *Gleaner*. I'd be clawing the other dame's eyes out in her front parlour. Maybe she's tried that. Well, Milesy, I'm sorry. Seems to me, Joe's turned in a factual report that need do her no harm at all, if somebody in a position to help sits up and takes notice. Which is obviously what she was after.'

'I don't think she sees it that way, Bob.'

'Go back down and explain it to her.'

'I doubt if she'll take it from me. It's the top brass she's after.'

Hartley's second sigh was of dinosaur proportions. 'What do we pay you for? I'm up to my eyeballs, for God's sake. If I felt good, which I bloody don't, I'd still have no time to spare for neurotic females. What can I say to her, that you can't?'

'It's not what's said. It's who says it.'

Clambering out of his chair, Hartley grabbed his jacket. 'Interview room? Give me a call there in two minutes, on the button. Say I'm wanted at the Town Hall. Leave it a second longer and you get the quarterly meeting of the Ratepayers' Federation tonight, and that's no threat: it's a pledge.' Wobbling outside to the landing, he began clumping down the uncarpeted stairs. The building was old and it echoed. With a faint smile at his lips, Miles returned to the newsroom.

'What happened to you?' demanded Polly Chubb, who was Features. 'You're supposed to be looking out that pictures file for me.'

'Sorry, Poll. Got involved with a female in flux.'

'Try concentrating on one cookie at a time. Who was she?'

'Some housewife, up on a supermarket rap. Wants the story killed.'

'Wow, you don't say? Young, I take it? Good-looking?'

Miles pretended to cogitate. 'A dish.'

'I knew it. The only—'

'Twenty-five years ago, that is. Now slightly threadbare. Which isn't to say—'

'No, it's not, and don't. Get me that file.'

When he re-emerged from the file-room, Miles observed through the glazed upper section of the Editor's office door that Bob Hartley had company. It was Mrs Stanhope. Installed in the deep-seated leather chair that Hartley found useful for placing his visitors at a disadvantage, she was gazing up at him from the humiliating half-sprawl that its antique springs engendered, appearing to listen intently to what he was saying. He was gesturing emphatically, although beneath the surface activity there remained a lifeless manner untypical of him. Miles consulted his watch. Forty minutes had elapsed since he had first gone downstairs to attend to the woman. Handing Polly the file, he remarked, 'She's certainly turning the screw. Bob's looking a little crushed.'

'What are you on about?'

'That woman. The supermarket felon. She's been closeted with him for half an hour, and they're still at it.'

'Give him a buzz on the intercom.'

'I've done that. When they were downstairs.'

'No result?'

'He just said "Yep, okay," and hung up.'

'We can't do more.'

Miles returned to a couple of stories that were toasting on his machine. Twenty minutes later he again had occasion to pass the Editor's door. This time he noticed that Mrs Stanhope had left. Hartley was back on proof-correcting, hunched over the narrow sheets as if analysing the paper's very texture for flaws. Idly, Miles wondered about the outcome of their confrontation. He hoped, in a way, that her objective had been gained. The idea of an elderly parent suffering from reflected odium troubled the pappier side of his nature.

He was unable to ask Hartley about it, because an hour later the Editor went home, complaining of stomach pains and a sensation that six-inch nails were being forced through his scalp. Into his place leapt the chief reporter, Geoff Craddock, who deputized in emergencies. Craddock held traditional views upon editorship. Policy issues, in his philosophy, were not up for discussion with staff juniors. Apart from this, his departure from the newsroom threw an extra load upon the others, and for the rest of the day Miles had no time to dwell upon peripheral matters.

The following morning, it became known that Bob Hartley was down with gastric 'flu and would be absent for a week. Entrenched in the Editor's chair, Craddock became still less approachable. Miles forgot about the incident until Friday.

It was while he was scanning the new-minted columns of the Court Page that memory stirred. Having given more careful attention to the headlines, he wandered across to Polly Chubb's littered desk. 'Bob must be more jelly-centred than we thought.'

The Features Reporter peered up perspiringly. 'Why?'

'He spiked that case. The shoplifter.'

'The woman who came in?' Polly shrugged. 'She must have produced a medical certificate.'

Miles eyed her. 'Ever known it succeed before?'

'No, but there has to be a first time. Now leave me alone, before I go bananas.'

Miles mentioned the matter to a couple of the senior reporters. They showed scant interest. Yielding to a feeling of obstinacy, he went downstairs for a copy of the opposition. Although officially it hit the streets half a day later, the *Mercury* generally contrived to get itself on sale simultaneously with its main rival, and a bundle had already turned up. Careful inspection indicated that Mrs Stanhope had been persuasive in more than one office. There was no mention of her conviction.

Returning upstairs, Miles poked his head around the Editor's door, to find the room empty. With the week's issue triumphantly behind him, Craddock had taken publication day off. Miles went back to his own desk, pondered briefly, lifted the phone.

'Hi, Sue. How's the prettiest girl on the town's second-best newspaper?'

'How's the ugliest guy on the town's third?' Although younger than he, by a year, Sue Baxter had joined the *Mercury* direct from school; her practical experience thus outweighed his by a formidable margin, a fact which she rarely allowed him to forget. 'I see your stuff went through the slaughterhouse again.'

'My work isn't appreciated,' he lamented. 'Yet. Hey, Sue. On a serious note—'

'Who's joking?'

'Something I wanted to ask. There was a court case back in the week—a Mrs Stanhope, shoplifting, fined. You don't seem to have carried it. Any idea why not?'

'Sid must have missed it.' Sid Sullivan was the *Mercury*'s resident court man. 'Want me to ask him?'

'Is he there?'

After a pause, a male voice came to the phone. ''Morning, youthful Miles. What's this about a shopfitter?'

'Lifter.' Miles explained.

'I could have missed it,' Sid opined slowly, 'but I believe not.'

Miles was puzzled. 'You mean, you don't recall writing the story?'

'On the contrary, I recall perfectly well that I didn't. It's news to me.'

'You've no knowledge, then, of Mrs Stanhope calling on you to ask for it to be kept out?'

'If I had,' Sid replied logically, 'I'd have known what you were babbling about. What's your interest?'

'Nothing special.' Miles hesitated. 'Thanks, Sid. If I could have another quick word with Sue . . .'

Having fixed a date with her for that evening, he put a call through to the *Advertiser*. Although a giveaway, it carried a substantial percentage of hard news and was particularly strong on court coverage. By chance, its court man, Ray Woods, was available and communicative.

'Sylvia Stanhope? Doesn't clang a bell. This week, you say?'

'Tuesday morning, she came up. Called on us in the

afternoon. It occurred to me she might have gone on to you that same day, or Wednesday.'

'Hold on, I'll check.'

When Woods came back, he sounded mystified. 'You're positive it was Tuesday?'

'That's what she told me. She should know.'

'Well, I've no record of the case in my notes. What's more, the guvnor tells me he's had nobody of that name pestering him with an exclusion plea.' After an interval, Woods added, 'Why are you asking?'

'I wish I knew.' Miles stared hard across the newsroom, seeing nothing that was in view. Presently, with a start, he said, 'Sorry, Ray. Didn't mean to fade out on you. I think I must have my lines crossed. Forget I mentioned it.'

'I shall, old boy, the moment you hang up. Did I miss a good yarn, by the way?'

'Hardly the scoop of the decade. Thanks for your trouble.'

Ringing off, Miles reverted to his contemplation of space. Becoming aware of his vacant expression, Polly Chubb glanced over and said playfully, 'When you make it on to a daily, you'll get this reaction six times a week. Think you can stand it?'

Giving her an absent look, Miles rose. 'I'll be out for ten minutes,' he announced to the room at large, and left.

The courtroom building was an easy canter from the *Gleaner*'s premises. Miles had covered hearings only a few times, but he knew his way to the admin section and had been prudent enough to strike up a working acquaintanceship with one of the clerks, a spinster in her thirties with more than a soft spot for presentable Press trainees in their early twenties, especially those who came equipped with sympathetic eyes and a full complement of white teeth. Since the Bench never sat on Fridays, the building was relatively deserted and the clerk had time to spare. After a few moments of mandatory banter, Miles switched directly to the topic in hand. She wrinkled her somewhat oversized nose at him.

'*Gleaner* losing its grip? If the case was heard, your man Joe Wilkinson—'

'I know, Kathy, but I can't ask him. He's gone off for the weekend, as usual. Be an angel and look it up for me, huh?'

'You newshounds. You're all the same.' She opened her ledger. 'Incessantly on the cadge for priority treatment. Mrs Sylvia Stanhope, Tuesday . . . Sorry. No record of it here. You did say shoplifting?'

'No, but she did. Try Monday.'

'At once, my lord.' Presently she shook her head. 'No one of that name. How about the previous week?'

'Go back to last Thursday,' he suggested.

They drew a blank. The clerk eyed him quizzically. 'Sure you didn't dream it? You didn't *imagine* she came into your office?'

Too preoccupied to deliver a comeback, Miles stood drumming the ledger with the blunt end of his ballpen. 'This is the full court record?' he asked finally. 'There's no subsidiary file for minor cases?'

Her headshake was conclusive. 'It's all here. If your Mrs Stanhope came up and was dealt with, she'd be down there in black and white. Black, anyway.'

'So why isn't she?'

'Because she's a phantasm, that's why. Stick to flesh and blood, my lad, if you want to know what's good for you. Shall I go back any further?'

'No, Kathy. Thanks. I've wasted enough of your time. See you around.'

'Only if you come looking,' she retorted, smiling at the back of his head as he left.

Polly Chubb was once more alone in the newsroom, tapping drearily at her feature. Planting himself on her desk, Miles arrested the typewriter carriage. She scowled up.

'If you're that stuck for an occupation, how about fetching me some coffee?'

'You reckon Bob would object, Poll, if I phoned him at home?'

'Now? Unless he's made a miracle recovery, I'm certain he'd mind like hell. Is it urgent?'

Miles gazed past her left ear. 'Tell me something. Would you take me for a fanciful sort of guy?'

'I wouldn't take you on any terms.'

'I'm serious, Poll.'

'You're about as earthbound as an earwig. Satisfied? Now get off my machine.'

'I'm still baffled about that—'

The telephone bleeped. Polly snatched it up. 'Miles Repton? Hold on.' She passed the receiver across. 'One of your harem,' she said crossly, and blitzed a sentence out of the keyboard.

'Who?' asked Miles. 'Oh—Kathy. Hi. Did I leave something behind?'

'Yes. A feeling that I hadn't been as helpful as I might.' The court clerk sounded contrite. 'So I ploughed back another week or two, but there wasn't anything.'

'Thanks,' he said blankly. 'Very good of you.'

'Then I had a look at last month's ledger. Guess what I found?'

Miles waited. On a deflated note she went on, 'April the ninth—that's five weeks back—there was an entry about a shoplifting case. Mrs Sylvia Stanhope of Lennard Gardens. Is that the one?'

'Bullseye. Five *weeks*? That's incredible. She gave me to understand . . . Never mind. Kathy, you're a sleuth. What kind of chocolates do you like? Oh, I see. Buy you a Campari, then, some time. Thanks again. 'Bye now.'

Cradling the receiver, he sat staring at the paper in Polly's machine as it rattled to and fro. She suspended operations to glare back. 'Now what?'

'That shoplifting case, Poll. It was over a month ago.'

She puffed her cheeks. 'You're getting obsessed. If it's back in the past, what does it matter now?'

'But it was only this week that she called in, asking for the report to be kept out.'

'Maybe she's been in an extended trance. The shock and shame of it all. She finally came to her senses on Tuesday, and thought it had only just happened.'

Miles's forehead went into a dozen puckers. Without answering, he quitted the desk and wandered over to the rack where back-numbers were kept for three months, pending their transference to microfilm. Withdrawing the issue of April 12, he spread it out on the working-top.

His search took moments. On the extreme right of the Court Page, centre-column, an item was headed *Woman Stole*. It related to Mrs Sylvia Stanhope, of 29, Lennard Gardens, fined for stealing groceries worth a total of . . . Miles read it three times. Then he carried the newsprint over to Polly's deak. Resignedly she stopped typing and leaned back, thrusting fingers wildly through her gingery hair.

'You've traced it. You still can't make it out. You want the benefit of my objective opinion. Shoot.'

'If we carried this last month, Poll . . . how come we had a report of the identical case scheduled for this week?'

'Is it the identical case?'

'Down to the last detail.'

Polly meditated. 'It's what I figured,' she said at last. 'Mrs Stanhope suffered a time-warp. She was five weeks late getting to us.'

'You're missing the point. There was a four-slip report of the case from Joe Wilkinson in Bob's tray on Tuesday, waiting to be subbed. I saw it myself.'

Polly sat in silence. Miles added, 'If it were just the Stanhope woman's account, I'd feel you were right—she'd lost touch with events. But Joe's dependable, isn't he? He wouldn't be likely to re-submit something, more than a month after it took place.'

'Unless,' she said slowly, 'that was an alternative version he wrote at the time. It could have got mislaid. Then somehow mixed in with a batch of this week's copy . . .'

'It's a feasible explanation, I suppose.' Miles studied the news item a fourth time. 'The only one that makes any kind of sense. But it still leaves questions.' He scratched his neck. 'You mean to tell me, Poll, the mislaid report turned up again on precisely the same day as Mrs Stanhope happened to call in here, asking for it to be killed? That's more than coincidence. It's uncanny.'

With a shrug, Polly impelled her chair clear of the desk and spun it a couple of times. Coming to rest, she said tentatively, 'Maybe it wasn't Joe who mislaid it.'

'What do you mean?'

'Bob found it, you say, in his in-tray. Perhaps it had been there all the time.'

'Then how did this paragraph—' Miles thumped the newspaper '—get itself published five weeks ago?'

Polly took a breath. 'Joe wrote two versions—right? The shorter one was subbed and published. The longer one went to the foot of the pile, for some reason, and got overlooked.'

Bobbing out of the chair, she marched over to the coffee machine and inserted ten pence. As a plastic beaker appeared obediently, she turned to him again with a long-suffering air. 'Is any of this relevant any more? It's obvious what must have occurred. Bob checked on Tuesday with Joe, discovered the duplication, and sent Mrs Stanhope off to get herself together. That's why nothing appeared this week.'

Miles said nothing.

Claiming her tenpennyworth of foam, Polly returned to her chair and took a few sips, watching him closely. 'Since it bothers you so much,' she said presently, 'why not take a flyer and call Bob at home, after all? He can only chew off your left ear.'

'I just don't like being made to look a monkey,' Miles murmured. He lifted the phone.

The voice that answered informed him that it belonged to Bob Hartley's mother-in-law. 'He's very poorly, so I'm helping out with the children while my daughter looks after him. I'm afraid he's simply not up to talking to anyone. The 'flu's at its height.'

'You couldn't ask him just a couple of simple . . . No, forget it. There's no urgency. I can have a word with him when he gets back. Hope he's soon on the mend.'

'So do we, rather,' the mother-in-law said devoutly. 'The children are being quite a handful. You'll have to excuse me, I can hear breakages . . .'

'Thanks for your help,' Miles said to the abandoned line. For several minutes, while Polly typed and sipped, he sat staring through the window. Suddenly she ripped out the sheet she was working on, crushed it into a ball and hurled it across the room.

'You're making me fidgety,' she announced. 'For heaven's sake. Can't you either do some work or go home?'

Smiling abstractedly in her direction, he sauntered to the door. 'I'll be out for the next hour, you'll be relieved to know.'

'It's Friday,' she called after him. 'Don't bother to come back.'

South Beechway was the lower-middle-class end of the town, a region of dispiriting avenues and crescents, asphalted pavement verges, elderly terraced housing with half-tiled front elevations, and ragged garden hedges stuffed with discarded takeaway containers. Lennard Gardens, a not untypical specimen, was a cul-de-sac with more than its share of motionless metal parked at the kerbside. Leaving his Fiat Uno near the mouth of the junction, Miles proceeded on foot to the splayed gate of No. 29, a mid-terrace habitation whose window-frames had at some remote date received an application of dark-blue paint which was now taking a piecemeal departure. Someone had made a start on paving the front plot. Half a dozen irregular slabs had been bedded in concrete: the remainder of the fifteen square yards was occupied by more slabs in a drunken pile, a mound of ballast sprouting a range of succulent weed, and a platoon of garden gnomes on sentry-go in a corner, awaiting postings. Eyeing the shambles, Miles clanked along the splintered quarry-tile path to the front door and applied a thumb to the bell-push. No sound resulted. While he was searching for a knocker, the door opened suddenly. The clamour of a radio, tuned to heavy rock, became audible. It seemed to come from upstairs.

'Saw yer through the glass. Thought you was the meter man.' The woman who had appeared spoke with a certain good-humoured disregard, as if resigned to making the best of what she had got in his place. Emerging on to the step, she gave him a narrower look. 'Not, are you?'

Miles explained his identity. 'I'm looking for Mrs Stanhope. She lives here, I believe. Is it possible to see her?'

Glancing past him at the street, she focused briefly upon a parked motorcycle before inspecting him again, appraisingly this time. 'I'm Mrs Stanhope,' she said.

'It's Mrs *Sylvia* Stanhope I want.'

'That's me.' Folding her arms, she leaned back against the rotting doorpost. 'You did say the *Gleaner*?' A wary note had edged into her voice. 'What's it about? We take the *Mercury*.'

'Obviously there's some mistake. The Mrs Stanhope I want to speak to . . .' He paused. 'You've a relative, perhaps, living with you? Or did have?'

'I'm the Mrs Stanhope,' she said forthrightly, 'at this address. There's just me, my old man and his dad. Then there's Beattie, our Jack Russell, and the cats. We ain't got no other relations. No room for 'em. What was it you was meaning to ask?' A look of faint intelligence dawned. 'Survey, is it? One of them polls?'

Mile hesitated. With a sense of acute embarrassment he said, 'This is going to sound peculiar, but . . . I wonder if you'd mind telling me something? Did you by any chance appear recently at the magistrates' court?'

Her features tightened. 'They said as I wouldn't hear no more about it. Paid me fine, I did. We've the receipt to prove it. We never—'

'Hold on a minute.' To his amazement she stopped obediently. Irked by the abrupt transition to an officer/recruit relationship, he tried to moderate his approach, to address her informally. 'Sorry, Mrs Stanhope, if I'm confusing you, but there's something odd here. Was it, um, an offence involving goods in a store?'

'I did forget to pay, if that's what you mean. Never did it on purpose, but they wouldn't take *my* word for it. Oh dear me no. All the papers . . . Half a bit.' Heaving herself clear of the doorpost, she inclined forward to examine him in a new way. 'Seeing as you're from the *Gleaner*, why d'you want to hear about it? You printed something at the time.'

'I know that, Mrs Stanhope. But the point is, you're not the same . . . Would you mind if I came in and tried to explain?'

'I'd mind if you didn't.' Almost with eagerness she bundled him into the house. The narrow hall was uncarpeted and smelt of damp wallpaper. From upstairs, the hammering beat of the radio music sent shock-waves through the ceiling. Slamming the front door shut at the third attempt, the woman stood with her back to it while Miles, at the top of his voice, did his best to acquaint her with the situation. Before he had finished, she interrupted.

'You'd best step into the back room. I'll fetch me father-in-law—I want him to hear this. He's just upstairs,' she added informatively. 'Go straight through. Mind Pluto, he's apt to get under your feet and if you tread on him, he'll spit. You'll find Beattie in there. If she barks, take no notice. She's all noise. Dad! You there, Dad? Can you come down a minute? It's somebody from the paper. He wants to know . . .'

Beattie the Jack Russell launched a series of shrill, ear-piercing yaps at Miles's appearance, and maintained the onslaught, despite verbal blandishments and outstretched fingers, until its mistress reappeared, pursued by a small, purple, semi-inflated man of indeterminate years, garbed in a dirty beige woollen waistcoat, cords and leather slippers. 'Pipe down, Beattie,' she ordered. Backing reluctantly into its rag-strewn corner, the dog lay smouldering, showing the whites of its eyes. Upstairs, the music thundered on. 'Take a seat, Dad,' advised the substitute Mrs Stanhope, clearing a winged chair of magazines. 'I'd like you to listen to what this gentleman has to say. It's about the Case. My little dust-up with Jepson's . . . you remember? Just you lend an ear. You're never going to believe this.'

Miles went through it again. Fatigue was starting to steal up on him. Pluto, or some other cat, had gained entrance to the room and was clawing stealthily at his trouser-ankles, now and then penetrating to the flesh; with difficulty, Miles refrained from retaliatory violence. When the story had been retold, Mrs Stanhope and her father-in-law sat in mute communion with one another while Miles waited hopefully. As time passed, and neither of them seemed disposed to carry matters forward, he said promptingly, 'You've some idea, have you, what it's all about?'

The mouth of Mrs Stanhope smacked shut like a steel grille. Reopening it, she said grimly, 'I've more'n a suspicion *who* it's about. What say, Dad?'

The old man indulged in a loud, prolonged sniff. 'Got all the makings.'

Abandoning the niceties, Miles demanded, 'The makings of what?'

Mrs Stanhope began jabbing a thumb. She did it in the direction of the rear garden, portions of which were visible to Miles through a battered french window with small, grime-encrusted panes featuring a crack or two. From what he could see, the fifty square yards at the back were in even worse shape than the fifteen at the front. Grass, shrubs, bushes and trees had become indistinguishable from each other, entangled in a single unbridled mass from fence to fence, throttling the few rambler roses that had made feeble attempts to crawl clear of the wreckage. The fences themselves looked in dire need of replacement. Altogether, the outlook was one that seemed to demand the attentions of a mechanical earth-shifter and site-leveller, prior to total rehabilitation. Mrs Stanhope, however, betrayed no diffidence at calling a visitor's attention to the scene. Manifestly, her own mind was fixed upon the immediate topic.

'Her ladyship,' she intoned significantly, perpetuating her digital pulsations.

'A neighbour?' Miles speculated.

A short bark erupted from Mrs Stanhope. 'Not much neighbourly about *her*,' she observed. 'Eh, Dad? Suffered our ups and downs with *that* party, wouldn't you say?'

A repeat of the sniff indicated assent. 'Downs, mostly.'

'Downs, mostly.' His daughter-in-law came in like an echo. 'Nothink physical, mark you. We've not been chucking things. Not that I'm saying it mightn't come to that.'

Miles craned his neck. 'That house there, facing this one? You've had problems with the occupant?'

'You could say that.'

'So you feel she may have had a hand in this?'

Mrs Stanhope shrugged. 'Can't think of nobody else. For

one thing, she about fits your description. For another thing, it's got her trademark about it—right, Dad? Wouldn't put anything past our Viv, I wouldn't.'

'Do you know her surname?'

'Kemp. Miss Vivien Eleanor Kemp. Told us that, didn't she, Dad, when we first come? Quite proud of her full title, she is. Thinks she's royalty, I reckon.'

'But what would she hope to gain?' asked Miles. 'The whole exercise seems pointless. If Miss Kemp wanted to get at you, surely she'd start a false rumour or something, not try to squash a factual report?'

Cogitation rendered Mrs Stanhope momentarily cataleptic. 'Dare say she just enjoyed talkin' about it to someone. Chew it over, like. Weird, she is. You never know where you are with her.'

'How long have you been acquainted?'

Mrs Stanhope consulted her father-in-law, who looked sage but remained dumb. 'Five years, Dad, since we moved in? Six? I know it was the year Meg died. How old would she be now? Jimmy was just fifty, so she'd have been—'

'And Miss Kemp,' Miles intervened gently, 'was here when you arrived?'

'Lived here all her life. A fixture, she is. Reckons she owns the district.'

'Friction right from the start, was there?'

'She seemed all right at first. Quite matey. Kept popping round with tinned meat for the dog, stuff for Dad to take—suffers with his asthma, Dad does—and she even put a present through the door at Easter, a box of soap, very nice it was. That's Easter the first year, I'm talkin' about. Then, not long after that . . .'

'Beattie,' grunted old Mr Stanhope, nodding at the Jack Russell.

'Took this sudden dislike to Beattie, she did. Said she was always yapping and getting into her garden. Then it was the cats. Why didn't we keep them in of a night? Always yowling under her window, according to her ladyship. After that . . .'

'Fences.'

'That's right. When was we going to fill in the gaps? I said to her, that one at the end is yours as much as it's ours, I said, why don't *you* stop it up? That did it. Public enemy number one we was, from then on. We've not spoken since.'

'How does she get on,' queried Miles, 'with the other residents around here?'

'Search me.' Mrs Stanhope spoke with indifference. 'We're not ones to go around gossipin'. Personally I've other things to do with me time.'

'Might I ask you something else, Mrs Stanhope?' Miles sought a suitable arrangement of words. 'Are you . . . still on friendly terms with your husband?'

She stared. 'I was, when he left here this mornin'.'

'You've not split up, then?'

'If we have, he's not mentioned it. Is it on account of the Case, you're askin'?'

'Not directly, no. How about your children?' Miles went on recklessly. 'Any problems with them?'

'There might be, if we 'ad any. Never wanted kids, Cyril, did he, Dad?'

'And you haven't a dependent mother?'

'Me? My mum's been dead eleven years. That's why we're able to have 'im.' She nodded towards old Mr Stanhope, who contrived to look simultaneously complacent and anxious, as if half-fearful of the turn the conversation might take.

Shaking off the cat, Miles stood up. 'I'm sorry to have been a nuisance. Just one other thing. If I were to go round and have a word with Miss Kemp, myself, is there anything you'd like me to tell her?'

A hoot came from Mrs Stanhope. 'Got a week or two to spare, have you, love? No, don't you bother. Far as we're concerned, she don't exist no more. Not worth the hassle. Tell her that, if you like. Best of luck.'

The houses in Oak Grove, parallel with those in Lennard Gardens, were a notch or two up on the social ratchet. Most were semi-detached, with Georgian-style windows and integral garages whose vividly-painted up-and-over doors were connected to the street by ribbons of white-speckled asphalt in various states of disrepair. The driveway belonging to The Pines was an exception. It had been resurfaced with immaculately laid pink and grey flagstones, and flanked with conifers. The house itself had recently been touched up with a combination of cream and green paint. The porch tiles were a brilliant red. Treading gingerly so as not to leave footprints, Miles rapped twice with a door-knocker fashioned in the shape of a rampant buffalo. The sound it produced was something of an anticlimax. Before he could launch a second strike, however, the door opened smoothly to reveal a figure in blouse and slacks, with a pair of binoculars on a strap hung about her neck. Her tiny smile was enigmatic.

'I guessed,' she said, 'you might be heading this way. Do come in, won't you?'

Miles entered the thickly-carpeted hall. The wallpaper was floral, and there were multiple mirrors. A contemporary coat-rack and a pair of cane chairs with bright cushions constituted the furniture. There was a faint scent of perfume, but whether it had been sprayed about or came from Miss Kemp herself, Miles couldn't determine. Coming to a halt on the decorative doormat, he turned to face her as she blocked out the street. 'You remember me, then?'

'Of course I do.'

'I wasn't sure if you might. Last time we met, you were Mrs Stanhope.'

She blinked up at him, but said nothing. Swallowing his annoyance, Miles added, 'As you've probably guessed, I'm here for an explanation, Miss Kemp. Why did you pose as your neighbour, opposite?'

'Please come through to the Lounge.' She led the way, as if conducting Royalty to the banqueting hall. 'You've the right to an explanation, of course,' she proclaimed, indicating a chintz-covered armchair by the picture-window, 'since you seem to be still rather in the dark. I assumed you'd have been enlightened by now, but evidently I was wrong. What did the Stanhopes have to say?'

Occupying the armchair, Miles regarded her steadily. 'How did you know I'd been talking to them?'

The tiny smile reappeared as she seated herself on the

tiled window-sill to face him. 'An obvious move, wasn't it, on your part? Besides—' she tapped the binoculars—'with these, I can see most of what goes on over there. I've a clear view from my bedroom window.'

'You spend your time spying on them?'

'Not *all* of it,' she said, taking no offence. 'I have to admit, though, I do like to keep track of events. That's why I keep the glasses handy, as you see. The Stanhopes intrigue me.'

'Obsess you, more likely.' Miles spoke with the candour of total pique.

She replied in a mild key. 'There are two sides, you know, to everything.'

'I'm quite willing to hear yours. But I'd prefer it to be straightforward. Maybe you've forgotten, Miss Kemp, but I'm the guy who had a pretty fantastic yarn spun to him when—'

'I haven't forgotten.' She tilted her head to inspect him kindly.

'But you may not fully realize what you did. You came within a whisker of making us commit an offence.'

'How, may I ask?'

'I'm not sure, to be honest. All I know is, we very nearly published two reports of the same court case, five weeks apart. How it came about I can't guess, but if the second report—'

'Without my intervention,' she agreed, 'the *Gleaner* might well have gone ahead and published a second time.'

Miles shook his head in perplexity. 'I don't get it.'

'Because it's not been explained to you, that's why.' She spoke with the restrained patience of a primary school mistress. 'I expect you're wondering, for instance, where that second report could have sprung from?'

'The thought had occurred to me.'

'There it was, on the desk of that very charming Editor of yours, Mr Hartley. He had it in front of him. All written out in Joe Wilkinson's rather distinctive handwriting. He could so easily have taken it at face value.'

'What stopped him?'

'I did, of course. That's what I came in for.'

'But how could you have known he had it?'

'Because I had it sent in. I wrote it.'

Miles sat forward, staring at her incredulously. 'You did *what?*'

Miss Kemp remained placid. Turning her head a little, she scanned the garden, a small miracle of laundered turf and fresh-leafed foliage, marred only by the decrepit dividing fence at the far end. When she turned back she was expressionless. Miles had the feeling that she had performed the same minor action many times already that morning, as well as on previous occasions too numerous and too unrewarding to recall.

'It's quite simple. I'm a criminologist, you see. Oh, nothing professional. I just like to take an amateur interest. For some while now, I've made a practice of attending the morning sessions at the Magistrates' Court, observing the proceedings. As a result, I've got to know the ropes.'

'Ropes?'

'For example, I've made a study of the Press box. Your Joe Wilkinson, in particular. He has a method of his own. He invariably writes up the cases as he goes along. At the end of each morning he has a finished pile of copy—I believe that's the term?—which he then delivers personally to your office before going off to lunch.'

'You're very observant.'

'It's something I pride myself on,' said Miss Kemp, accepting the compliment and disregarding the irony. 'I'm also fairly deft. It wasn't too difficult for me to purloin a sample of Mr Wilkinson's copy one morning—he often leaves it beside his notepad in the Press box while he goes out for his coffee break. All I had to do then was take it away for half an hour so that I could run off a photocopy.'

'To enable you to study his handwriting?'

'At my leisure. Which I did. I've no special talent as a forger, but I had heaps of time. In the end, I could turn out quite a passable imitation of his style. Luckily he writes very clearly.'

'You faked that report, then?' Miles thrust fingers through his hair. 'It still doesn't explain how it got on to Bob

Hartley's desk, inside a pile of other stories.'

'If I could filch copy from the Press box,' Miss Kemp explained reasonably, 'I could put some back, couldn't I? The court supervision is absurdly lax. I had no trouble returning the piece I took, and still less in planting the phoney item. I simply folded it in the way Mr Wilkinson does, then slipped it into the middle of his stack as I strolled past to the public benches. Nothing to it.'

'It doesn't sound like nothing. It sounds like a lot of trouble to go to for a nil result. If you were going to have the piece kept out anyway . . .'

'Aha!' Miss Kemp wagged an arch finger at him. 'But I might not have. At that stage, I hadn't decided.'

Coming away from the window, she crossed the room to a pinewood dresser on which stood a heavy, orange and purple ceramic vase stuffed with dried flowers. Removing the strap from her neck, she deposited the binoculars carefully alongside the vase and gave them an almost affectionate tap. 'You might say,' she added, turning dramatically, 'I was keeping my editorial options open.'

Miles looked back at her stonily. 'Why?'

Her face closed up. 'I think that's my business, don't you?'

'Mine too, I suggest. You've wasted a good deal of my time, don't forget, with your slightly erratic behaviour. You owe me more than half an explanation.'

'Why can't we just forget it? No harm's been done.'

Turning back to the dresser, she proceeded to dust its surface with a brown paper napkin which she had extracted from a drawer. Collecting a few fallen specks of dried flower, she disposed of them inside a pocket of her slacks, administered a final polish to the woodwork, balled the napkin and stood clutching it while she eyed the display of blue and white china on the shelves at the back. Miles felt that she itched to be giving it all a clean and shine. Presently she peeped across a shoulder.

'I'm afraid I don't know your name . . .'

'Miles Repton.'

'May we leave it at that, Mr Repton? There seems no

point, does there, in your squandering still more of your time? The matter's a trivial one, as far as you're concerned. Why pursue it?'

'Because I'm a reporter, Miss Kemp, and you involved me, and I've rather a dislike of feeling exploited.'

The air between them smoked for a few seconds. Presently she made a part-dismissive, part-resigned movement of her left hand, and supported herself on the dresser with her right elbow.

'To someone like yourself, I suppose it must all seem a little odd. When you've had more experience, you'll begin to appreciate the trials that can be heaped on people, in certain circumstances. The subtle degrees of torture . . .'

A gulp seemed to block her throat. Her eyes closed briefly. When they reopened, they were aimed at the window. Curious, Miles sat motionless, watching her.

'Have you ever,' she resumed on an artificially bright note, 'sat in a train compartment opposite someone gorging himself on chips out of newspaper, resting his feet on the seat next to you, and playing pop music loudly on a cassette? When what you're aching to do, yourself, is sit quietly and look out at the scenery?'

Miles considered. 'I can't say that I have.'

'But you've got imagination. Suppose you did find yourself in such a position. What would you do?'

'If it bothered me, I'd go and find another compartment.'

'There isn't one. The train's packed. What then?'

'I'd have to put up with it.'

'But how would you feel, inwardly? What kind of resentment would be building up inside you?'

'I'm not blind, Miss Kemp, to the analogy you're trying to draw,' Miles said after a pause. 'But you know, lots of people have neighbours they find objectionable. They just have to grin and bear it.'

'Why should they?'

'Or move.'

'It's not always convenient or possible to move. And why should one be forced to? Especially when one has been living quite happily in a place for thirty years or more. Why can't it be the intruders who should have to leave?'

'If it were that easy . . .'

'I'm certainly not saying it's *easy*. What I'm saying is, there's usually an answer if you look for it hard enough.'

'Like playing silly games with the local Press?'

Hoisting himself out of the chintz upholstery, Miles advanced to confront Miss Kemp at close quarters. She shrank a little, but held firm. 'Exactly how,' he demanded, allowing his wrath to gain the upper hand, 'did that performance of yours last Tuesday do anything to achieve what you had in mind? From your point of view, you'd have done better to stick to your original plan—left us to publish the faked report and see what happened. That way, you'd at least have been doing Mrs Stanhope some harm, besides us.'

Miss Kemp bowed her head. She remained silent.

He edged closer. 'Shall I tell you what I think? I think you copped out. Having implemented this crackpot scheme which you hoped would embarrass the Stanhopes—though you were wildly optimistic, I fancy—you then panicked. You realized it might be traced back to you. So what course was left? Just one. You had to retrieve that bogus piece of copy before it got into print.'

Still she said nothing. Her fingertips explored the dresser surface, as if for residual deposits.

'To do that; you had to see the Editor personally, explain the . . .' Miles's voice trailed away. He frowned. 'You could have just come in and asked to speak to him. Why go through that pantomime with me? It doesn't make sense.'

Miss Kemp lifted her face. A blush had risen to her cheeks, and a slight breathlessness was apparent when she spoke.

'It would have been such a let-down.'

'I don't follow.'

'It must be hard for someone else to grasp. I wonder if I can explain? I'd nerved myself, you see, to do this—over a long period. The pressure had been building up, you can't imagine. I felt there had to be some kind of relief. So I did it. But then—you're right, I did have second thoughts: I lost courage. I decided to backtrack.'

She took a quick, nervous breath. 'Even so, the idea of it just tailing off, petering out . . .' Enormous eyes gazed up at him. 'I had to salvage something. Can you understand? It was a kind of therapy. I *enjoyed* my little charade. Somehow it made it all worthwhile.'

'No, Miss Kemp. Sorry. I can't understand.'

'Your Mr Hartley did. He listened, and gave me a cup of tea, and was so kind. Particularly as I believe he wasn't feeling too grand himself, at the time.' Her gaze became more searching. 'Didn't he explain all this to you, afterwards?'

'He went sick. He's been off since Tuesday.'

'I *see*. Poor man. I do hope it's nothing serious.' Miss Kemp reflected. 'This accounts, then, for your coming round here this morning. You wanted to find out . . . I am sorry, Mr Repton.'

In a series of deliberate movements, Miles took a notepad from his hip pocket and a ballpen from his breast pocket, flipped the sheets and began to scrawl. Miss Kemp watched with compressed brows.

'What are you doing?'

'I'm jotting it all down,' he explained, 'before I forget the exact wording you've used. As a journalist, I like my stories to be accurate.'

Her body stiffened. 'You're not intending to write a story?'

'You bet I am.' Miles scribbled industriously. 'How could I pass it up? *Bizarre behaviour by respected resident* . . . If this doesn't sell copies, I'm in the wrong business.'

'I can't see that it's necessary.' Her voice sounded calm, but tension lurked in the syllables.

'Necessary?' He glanced up. 'Your histrionics in our front office were a trifle *un*necessary, wouldn't you agree?'

'Perhaps so.' Miss Kemp fell victim to a touch of breathlessness. 'I feel, Mr Repton, I do owe you an apology for that. The entire thing was uncalled for. Will you please accept my most sincere and humble regrets?'

'Bit late for that, I'm afraid. You should have thought about it sooner.'

Miles wrote on remorselessly. Another thirty seconds of

crucifixion, he estimated, would do Miss Kemp no particular damage, and might help to knock some sense into her. In addition, it was therapeutic for himself. He recorded 'The quick brown fox jumps over the lazy dog' before turning to the next sheet and making a start upon 'Now is the time for all good men . . .'

On the wall facing the dresser hung a gilt-framed mirror. In it, from the corner of an eye, he could see himself reflected, since he had half-turned away as though to concentrate better upon his task. The mirror also showed him Miss Kemp, huge of pupil and open-mouthed, stationed between himself and the pinewood dresser. He noticed that she was clutching the orange and purple vase.

She's about to dust beneath it, he marvelled. In distress, take refuge in routine. Now she was raising it, as if to inspect the underside of the base. Her arms were stretched above her head. Unless she was careful, the vase would slip.

The massive ornament seemed to be hovering directly over him. His brain instructed him to pivot. Before his limbs could respond, he had time to see via the mirror that the vase was commencing a fierce, vertical descent, like a helicopter out of control.

Hard to Live With

'Mrs Kidd?'

'That's me. It's Mr Melrose, right? Come on inside.'

'Sorry I'm late. I had a little trouble finding you.'

'Most people do. But you're nearly on the dot, actually. We did say seven-thirty to eight.'

They faced one another in the oak-raftered hall. In common with the rest of the cottage, it was narrow, which meant that Annabel had had to withdraw a yard or two to make room for him to step over the door-tread of battered copper and arrive gingerly on the royal-blue carpeting. To avoid bumping his head on the nearest beam, he was obliged to stoop. To the welcome in her smile, she added apology.

'We do our best, you'll notice, to make things awkward for visitors. Come through to the lounge, it's taller.'

'Has it ever occurred to you,' he inquired, pursuing her down the hall, 'that the source of your headaches might lie in your choice of habitation?'

Annabel laughed. 'I'm exactly five feet four . . . so that theory takes a dive. The lowest bit of fumed oak around here is five-nine. Quiet, Rudolph. All right, boy. *Friend!* I'll have to let him out of the kitchen, Mr Melrose, so he can get acquainted. Do you mind dogs?'

'Not in the least.'

He crouched to extend a hand, palm uppermost, as Rudolph erupted cautiously and came to a quivering standstill, nose twitching, leg-muscles taut, neck stretched. 'Genetically,' Annabel said disparagingly, 'he's a mess. There's a chunk of Labrador, but mainly he's Alsatian, and our kennel lady in the village thinks a touch of wolfhound almost certainly slipped in as well. Terrific guard-dog. Aren't you, Rudy? Scares the wits out of the postman, when he deigns to call. That's it—say hullo to Mr Melrose. Good boy. There, now you're buddies. Show Mr Melrose into the lounge, Rudy, while I do my imitation of a hostess. Tea or coffee?'

'The latter, if it's no bother.' Straightening up, he regarded her quizzically in the dim light of the hall. 'You're having some yourself?'

'Hah! You don't catch me out that way. Needless to say, I never look at the stuff. But I always keep a supply for callers.'

'Do you get many?'

'The postman,' she said reflectively, 'on rare occasions, when my publisher has something to communicate. The milkman, three times a week. Apart from them . . . It's a touch remote for most people, as you've already found out.'

'But it suits you?'

'Solitude has a lot going for it. Especially for a literary hack.'

Mr Melrose paused at the lounge door. 'You did mention on the phone that you were a writer. Can I ask . . .?'

'Romantic fiction. That's the respectable term for it. The other one is unprintable, even these days. The terminology doesn't worry me, so long as the loot rolls in.'

'Which it does, I hope?'

'We keep afloat. We're getting some payments through from the public libraries now, which helps.'

'Public Lending Right?'

'That's it. Us weavers of soulful tales seem to have done quite nicely out of the scheme, so far.'

'I trust your luck holds.' Mr Melrose coughed. 'I always thought romantic novelists were elderly spinsters, with cats.'

'You'll have to make do with an ageing divorcee, with a dog. Go in and make yourself comfortable. Throw your coat anywhere. Sugar with your coffee?'

'As it comes, thanks.'

In the kitchen, Annabel could hear a succession of soft thuds coming from the lounge. Rudy was introducing the newcomer to his rubber-bone routine: hurl, retrieve, worry, release, hurl, retrieve . . . When she went through with the tray, Mr Melrose was deeply installed in the basket chair by the inglenook with Rudolph sprawled dreamily across his feet. Clicking her tongue at the animal, she set the tray on a low table and lifted the cream-jug.

'You mustn't let him take over, Mr Melrose. If he gets bumptious, heave him off. Cream?'

'A drop, thanks. He's no trouble. You must find it reassuring to have him around.'

'Oh, I wouldn't be without Rudy. Since my divorce, he's the only sort of house companion I could put up with. Though I'm not sure he can't be even more taxing than a husband, when he likes.'

Accepting his coffee, Mr Melrose took a sip, followed by an appreciative mouthful, before resting cup and saucer on the complaining arm of the basket chair and holding it in balance. 'Pardon my asking, but . . . you found your ex-husband heavy going?'

'No more so than he found me, I dare say,' she answered lightly. 'We weren't compatible. Isn't that dreary? Nothing the least thrilling, like third parties or alcohol problems. Plain old mutual can't-stand-it-another-minute syndrome.' Occupying the old-fashioned winged armchair facing his, she shook her head. 'Where I'm concerned, romance has to keep to its appointed place, right there on the printed page. That's the way it is.'

Taking a peck of her milkless, decaffeinated tea, she put it aside on the hearthstone. Mr Melrose gave her a brief, well-mannered scrutiny before turning his face away to scan the room. For an evening visit to a rural lane, his attire was formal: dark suit, striped collar, plain rust-coloured necktie. The sole concession to casualness were his shoes, which were of grey suede, laceless, with crepe soles. His features in repose were clean-cut, agreeable. He looked about fifty. Overhanging a broad forehead and discreet ears was a thatch of dense brown hair, clipped like a bowling green and parted undeviatingly at one side. The faint straining effect at the centre button of his jacket suggested a small, a barely noticeable weight problem. Having completed his assessment of the lounge, he returned to his coffee-cup and made meditative inroads on its contents before glancing back at her.

'How long is it now, Mrs Kidd?'

'I beg your pardon?'

'Forgive me. I meant, since you've been living on your own.'

'Coming up to four years.'

'And how long—'

'My migraine attacks,' she interposed gently, 'began at the age of sixteen. No connection.'

His lips wobbled. 'You've evidently convinced yourself,' he remarked. 'We'll have to see. These attacks—did they get worse after your marriage?'

Annabel considered. 'They certainly didn't improve. Possibly they were more frequent. But I've always been a prey to them,' she added swiftly, 'from adolescence.'

'You've discussed it with your doctor, of course?'

She took a deep breath. 'This condition of mine, Mr Melrose, has bored the ears off more consultants, specialists, quacks and cure-alls than Rudolph there has had dog-biscuits. I've tried the lot. Diet, medicine, nature cures. Self-discipline, self-deprivation. Homeopathy. Long walks. Relaxation in darkened rooms. Aerobics. An active social live. No social life. Tell me something I've missed, and I'll nominate you for the Royal Society.'

'I doubt if they'd look at me. On the question of diet . . .'

'Generally speaking, I behave.' She indicated her cup. 'All beverages pure and harmless: no additives. As for food, I have the complete dossier pinned to my kitchen wall. Cheese, chocolate, bananas . . . You name it, I shun it.'

'And none of this has the slightest effect?'

Annabel shrugged. 'I wouldn't care to say. If I simply gave up and indulged myself, how much worse would I feel? I've no plans to find out.'

Mr Melrose looked down at Rudolph's flaccid ears, gave them an abstracted tweak, glanced up again. 'About how often, on average, do the attacks occur?'

'Again, that's a tricky one.' She frowned. 'Overall, I guess about once every two or three weeks. Occasionally I might go as long as a couple of months. But it always pounces again, sooner or later.'

'Does your work aggravate the condition?'

Annabel gave another shrug. 'I'm always working.'

'Perhaps,' he suggested mildly, 'you should try giving yourself a break.'

'Oddly enough I did, quite recently. I put Rudy into kennels and went on a two-week cruise up the Norwegian coastline.'

'And what did that achieve?'

'A plot for another book. Plus a migraine attack to end all migraine attacks when I got home. Somehow I get the feeling holidays are no answer.'

'Possibly not,' Mr Melrose conceded. He sat running a fingertip down Rudolph's spine. Presently he went on: 'At the risk of seeming intrusive, I'd like to ask you this. How long did your marriage last?'

'Officially, two years. In practice, a week or two.'

'What were the things about your husband that you found intolerable?'

'Oh my God. Where do I start? At the end of the second day, I knew damn well there was nothing about him I cared to investigate. You know how it is. You get this sinking . . . But perhaps I'm jumping the gun. Are you married, Mr Melrose?'

He shook his head.

'Well then, it might be something of a problem for you to—'

'I do know a little,' he interceded seriously, 'about human nature and relationships.'

'Yes, of course.' Annabel beamed at him across the hearthrug. 'I didn't mean to imply . . . All I'm saying is, marriage does things to people. Normally quite harmless specimens of one sex can have the weirdest chemical effects on normally inert specimens of the other, with the result that . . . Here I go again. Shooting my psycho-analytical mouth off. Cut me off if you can't stand it.'

He smiled tolerantly. 'I think I follow your drift.'

'In my own case, virtually everything Lionel did or

omitted to do set up discordant vibrations. I'm not blaming him. No fault of his. The interface between us just didn't mesh, or whatever.'

Mr Melrose pondered. 'But for your marriage,' he suggested, 'do you think it possible you might have shaken off these migraine bouts at an earlier age?'

She made a helpless gesture. 'Once again—no way of knowing, is there?'

Fumbling in a pocket, Mr Melrose drew forth a piece of folded newsprint which he proceeded to unravel. 'Your advertisement,' he said slowly, scanning it, 'had the ring of extreme desperation about it, I felt. "Otherwise healthy female . . . at wits' end . . . tried everything . . . can *anybody* please help?' He peered up. 'In my experience, appeals like that in the Personal column come only from those who feel they've nothing to lose.'

'Right,' she agreed promptly. 'You've hit it.'

'So, although you say you've tried *everything*, you're ready to soldier on and try some more?'

Annabel chuckled. 'You mustn't take small-ads too literally. If someone like yourself were to come along and persuade me he's got some method of treatment that's different, which *works* . . .'

'I doubt if anyone can make a blanket claim of that sort.'

She regarded him for a moment. 'Up to now, I certainly haven't tried hypnotism.'

'Hypnotherapy,' he corrected. 'Do you feel it might be an answer?'

'I'm happy to experiment.'

Releasing his feet from beneath Rudolph's slumbrous weight, Mr Melrose rose and walked reflectively half way across the room, hands clasped behind his back. Coming to a halt under the lowest of the oak beams, he tapped it with a knuckle, peered, gave it another tap followed by the slightest of applauding nods, and transferred his attention to the nearby window. Although darkness had fallen, Annabel had not troubled to draw the curtains. There was nobody to overlook. The diamond-shaped panes in their lead casings seemed to absorb her visitor for a while. Finally, still examining their structure, he said with an air of diffidence, 'I'm a qualified hypnotherapist, Mrs Kidd. I attend people with a variety of complaints . . . nerves, shyness, lack of self-confidence. Physical symptoms, too. Quite often I get results.'

'So you mentioned on the phone.'

'But I do try not to make rash claims. I should emphasize that migraine hardly ranks as one of my specialities. I'm not consulted about it that often.'

'Fair enough.'

'On the other hand . . .' Arriving back at the basket chair, Mr Melrose found it occupied by a recumbent Rudolph, and stood gazing down at the creature as if debating how best to dispossess him with the minimum of fuss. 'I do happen to believe,' he continued, side-stepping the dilemma by perching himself creakingly on the chair-arm, 'that migraines and associated disorders can have their roots in tension. Not food, necessarily; nor drink; nor work-patterns. Any or all of these may aggravate the condition, but the underlying . . .'

Mr Melrose appeared to lose himself in reverie. Annabel said helpfully, 'Stress, you feel, might have a lot to do with it?'

'I'm afraid it gets blamed for an awful lot, nowadays,' he returned with a half-smile. 'What some call stress, others might define as stimulus. It depends largely on the individual. In your case . . .'

'I'm a mass of boiling undercurrents? I wouldn't dispute it for a moment. Shove Rudy off, Mr Melrose, if he's in your way. He shouldn't muscle in like that.'

'Seems a pity to disturb him,' observed the visitor. 'Placid, isn't he? Good-natured, I imagine.'

'Most of the time,' Annabel said wryly. 'Ask the postman . . . Well now. How soon are you proposing to put me into a trance?'

Rising from the basketwork, Mr Melrose adopted a magisterial stance in front of the simulated-log electric fire that palpitated on the hearthstone and devoted some thought to the matter.

'How good a subject are you?'

'Haven't a clue,' Annabel said cheerfully.

'But you genuinely want to have a shot at this, I gather. That's a promising start. You won't object if I ask you some personal questions?'

'During the hypnosis? No, I don't mind. Anything to oblige myself.'

An obscurely troubled expression encroached upon Mr Melrose's face. 'Normally,' he explained, 'as I said on the phone, I prefer to deal with clients at my own premises. More satisfactory, all round. Since you asked for a home consultation . . . Well, I'm willing to make an exception, as long as you're clear on the procedure. What I plan to do, you see, is put you into a fairly light trance; then ask you some questions; and finally, try to implant some fresh . . . considerations in your mind. By this, I don't mean that I shall suggest things to you that in the ordinary way you might find repugnant. You follow?'

'I think so. You want to get me thinking positively about what I, *myself*, can do to combat the causes.'

'You've been reading the softback,' he said drily. 'Of course, it'll take more than one session. That's not sales talk on my part: it's a fact. You're reconciled to follow-ups?'

'I am, but you may get sick of the journey. You did say you don't run a car? How did you get here?'

'Bus to the village, then walked.'

'You must be a keep-fit fanatic. It's close on two miles.'

Unexpectedly he grinned. 'When I was a lad,' he remarked, 'my father made me walk at least eight miles every day—no arguments. Consequently, if I don't get sufficient exercise now, I feel deprived and out of sorts. I enjoyed the stroll here.'

Annabel glanced at the clock. 'You're planning to go back the same way? The last bus leaves from The Plough at nine-forty.'

'Time enough.' Comparing his watch with the clock, he started to unstrap it from his wrist. She watched expectantly.

'Is that what you're going to swing rhythmically in front of me?'

Smilingly he shook his head. 'Just rewinding. It's not like the music hall, Mrs Kidd, or TV. We don't use theatrical props . . . pendulating watches, pulsing lights. All I shall do is this. I'll sit opposite you, quite close, look steadily into your eyes and say certain things: in return, I'd like you to relax completely, put yourself into the most cooperative frame of mind you can achieve, and leave the rest to me. All right? Don't expect to pass out or anything. You'll be fully aware of what's happening. You'll hear your own replies.'

'What a let-down.'

He replaced the watch. 'You were hoping for total oblivion, ending in a dramatic return to reality?'

'One does rather anticipate . . .'

'Most people,' Mr Melrose said briskly, pulling down his shirt-cuff, 'have altogether the wrong idea about hypnosis. There's nothing mystical about it, believe me. May I use this wooden chair? Then we needn't disturb Rudolph. If I place it down here . . . so. Good. Now get yourself comfortable. Rest your head against the cushion, by all means. But keep looking at me. Fine. Unclutter your mind. Make it receptive. Attend to what I say. Listen closely to me. Listen . . .'

His voice had gained an extra dimension of authority. Finding a posture in which her limbs were well supported, Annabel expelled a self-relaxing breath and gazed obediently back at him. His pupils were amber, a shade or two lighter than his hair. After a pause of a few seconds he resumed speaking.

'I think, now, you're feeling perfectly relaxed. You're slipping more into serenity, every moment. This room is warm. Beautifully warm. You can feel the warmth stealing over you. And the peace, and the silence. Absolute silence. Let it all seep in. Yield yourself. There are no problems. Nothing to disturb. Just peace and tranquillity, comfort, repose . . .'

Inclining himself forward, Mr Melrose eyed her intently. She remained as she was, her gaze locked upon his.

'Can you hear me, Mrs Kidd? Answer yes or no.'

'Yes.'

'That's very good. Keep on replying like that. I want you to understand that I'm here to help. Is this how you feel about me?'

'Yes.'

'I'm going to ask you some questions. You've no objection?'

'No.'

Mr Melrose paused briefly. 'Do you dislike what you can recall of your ex-husband?'

'It was more than dislike. I despised him.'

'Why?'

'Because he was contemptible. He'd no guts. He'd rant away about things, but he'd never take action.'

'How did this make you feel?'

'Balked. Frustrated.'

'You wanted him to assert himself, but he wouldn't?'

'I wanted him to act like a man. Take the initiative.'

'But since he refused, you were forced to assume the dominant role?'

'With him, I never assumed any particular role. It wasn't worth it.'

Mr Melrose studied her. 'What did your husband do, Mrs Kidd? What was his profession?'

'Architecture.'

'Was he in practice, with a firm?'

'No. He worked freelance, from home.'

'So he was around, most of the time?'

'He was always under my feet.'

'How did you manage about your writing?'

'For the few months we actually lived together, I don't think I produced anything at all.'

Mr Melrose pondered for several moments. From the basket chair came a creak as Rudolph rose, stretched himself front and rear, lowered himself to the hearthrug, rotated twice, and flopped back into instant coma. The clock, an eight-day relic of a vanished age, proclaimed the half-hour by gonging once, musically, from its perch on the sideboard.

'Now I'd like, if I may, to go back somewhat further.

What kind of a childhood did you have?'

'Mixed.'

'Were you close to your parents?'

'I felt affection for my mother. We weren't close.'

'And your father?'

'He was a bully and a sadist. He put both of us through Hell.'

'In what way?'

'He was violent. We were terrified of him.'

'Couldn't your mother have taken you and walked out?'

'She wasn't the type. No mind of her own. He'd knocked it out of her.'

'And yet she knew you were being abused as well. What did your father do? Hit you?'

'Quite often. When I got to the age of twelve or thirteen, he started assaulting me too.'

'You mean sexually?'

'A few times. Until I learned to take care of myself.'

'Did your mother know about this?'

'I expect so. She wouldn't have dared to interfere. I don't blame her. She was a weak, ineffectual person, out of her depth. He'd demolished her. If I'd had only myself to consider, I'd have left home sooner.'

'When did you leave, finally?'

'The day after she died. I was seventeen.'

'What caused her death?'

'Asthma, it said on the death certificate.'

'You've reason to query that?'

'I'm no expert. She was always nervy. But if the doctor had said it was the outcome of mental and physical torture over a period of years, I couldn't have quibbled.'

Another interval elapsed. Leaning back, Mr Melrose gazed at the raftered ceiling. Presently, in a decisive movement, he returned to his former posture.

'Let me ask you this. What prompted you, later in life, to marry Lionel?'

'I suppose . . . I thought I should be settling down. Proving to myself I could live with a man.'

'Did the fact that he was unassertive—timid, even—tip the scales for you?'

'I doubt if I saw it as a drawback.'

'But in practice, the venture wasn't a success.'

'I was deeply miserable. I couldn't write.'

'Writing is vital to you?'

'I'm not sure. Without it, I don't feel . . . settled. As a girl, I used to take refuge in paper and ink. The habit's probably stuck.'

'You're happy, now, with what you produce?'

'To the extent that it gives me independence.'

'Which also you regard as essential?'

'Most people do, I imagine.'

'If I were to put to you,' Mr Melrose said on a measured note, 'that what you really crave is to be dominated, controlled by someone . . . how would you react?'

'With amusement.'

'If I, myself, were to attempt to take on this dominant role . . . what would be your response?'

'Incredulity.'

'Would you feel animosity towards me?'

'I don't think so. Not particularly.'

'But suppose I were a woman. Then would you feel resentment?'

'If you tried to boss me around.'

'You haven't a high regard for your own sex?'

'I do think some women can be extremely stupid.'

'Are they the ones you write for?'

'Whatever readership I have is bound to include some.'

'Perhaps it might be truer to say, you're writing for yourself?'

'Chiefly, I write to earn money.'

Mr Melrose hitched his chair a little closer. In the gleam from the artificial logs, his face had a dense colour. His eyes were animated.

'Which brings us back to independence. Would I be right in thinking, Mrs Kidd, that the mere possibility of being in thrall to someone is enough to fill you with terror?'

'I do like my freedom.'

'That doesn't quite answer the question. May I try a small experiment?'

'Certainly, if you want to.'

'I'd like you to get up from your chair, walk outside to the kitchen and fry me some bacon and eggs.'

'Now?'

'Right this minute. I'll wait here. When it's ready, put it on a tray and bring it to me, with a knife and fork and some bread.'

He watched intently as she rose, smoothing down the pink sweater zipped over her cream cotton trousers, and made for the lounge door. Rudolph lifted his head from the hearthrug to chart her progress. 'Stay, Rudy,' she told him. 'Good boy.' Opening the door, she went through to the kitchen.

With a soft release of breath, Mr Melrose sat back. Casting him a whimsical look, the dog replaced its head upon the interwoven wool and became still, but its eyes remained open.

Clattering sounds became audible. A low 'Woof?' caused a spasm of Rudolph's body. Mr Melrose glanced down. 'Easy, old chap. It's just a little task I've assigned to your mistress.' Stretching his legs, he smiled introspectively at his shoes.

In the kitchen, Annabel broke an egg into a cup and slid it from there into the pan. Three back rashers were left in the refrigerator. Peeling off two of them, she arranged one on each side of the egg-white and switched on the burner. As the food started to splutter, she took half a white loaf from its bin and sawed off a couple of slices.

Adding the cutlery and a butter dish to the tray, she stationed herself by the cooker, giving the pan an occasional shake. With her other hand, she carried out unnecessary smoothing operations upon her crisply cropped raven hair. She hummed under her breath. The bacon started to curl. She flipped the pieces over.

When the egg stabilized she scooped it out, planted it on a waiting plate, added the rashers, poured a little of the hot cooking oil over the meal, eyed the result critically. Picking up the tray, she carried it through to the lounge.

From her armchair, which he had occupied, Mr Melrose said, 'Put it down there.'

She placed the tray carefully on the glass-topped cane table which he had pulled up alongside. He gave it an inspection. 'You've forgotten the mustard.'

'I'm afraid I haven't any.'

Taking up the knife, Mr Melrose reduced the crisped rashers to fragments. 'The bacon's overdone. I don't think I feel hungry, after all.' He thrust the plate away. 'Perhaps I'll have a Scotch, instead. You keep whisky?'

With a nod, Annabel headed for the sideboard. He watched her produce a half-bottle. 'What about this rigid diet of yours?'

She looked uncertainly at the label. 'I only keep it for occasions.'

'The eggs, too? Surely you don't eat them yourself?'

'Rudolph has a raw one every morning, for his breakfast.'

'How about the bacon?'

'I find that an occasional rasher—'

'Not good, you know. Fried in oil.'

'Sunflower seed. According to my doctor—'

'But you're finished with doctors, Mrs Kidd. Done you no good at all, have they? What possible trust can you place in their opinions?'

From the sideboard, Annabel stood looking at him. He beckoned. Approaching submissively to within a yard of the armchair, she stopped and waited. Reaching across the table, Mr Melrose picked up a slice of the white bread on the tray, took a bite, chewed, swallowed, grimaced. He tossed the slice back. 'Anti-nutritional pap. How long have you been on this junk?'

'I only have half a slice at—'

'Gluten free, steam-baked—that's what you'll eat from now on.' He squinted up at her. 'How does your head feel now?'

'It aches quite a bit.'

'On one side?'

'More at the top. A dull throb.'

Mr Melrose turned his attention to the basket chair, which in the course of their exchange had been reoccupied by Rudolph. Having balled itself into the available space, the dog had subsided into a heavy doze. 'You'd better sit down again,' advised the hypnotherapist. 'Turn the creature off. You mustn't allow it to dictate your movements inside the home.'

'Rudy gets upset if I—'

'That animal is trying to take over your powers of decision. Is this what you want?'

After a moment's hesitation, Annabel went over to the basket chair and placed a tentative hand on the dog's crown. 'Shift aside a little, Rudy, there's a love . . .'

'Be firm. Don't stand for any nonsense.'

Rudolph, awake now, was showing the whites of his eyes. His tail gave an interrogative flap. Annabel poked him. 'Down, boy! Lie on the rug. You'll be quite comfortable.'

'You'll have to help him along.'

She gave the dog a lateral heave. Rudolph uttered a faint snarl, showed some teeth. Mr Melrose said, 'Go on. All the way.'

Without awaiting a further push, Rudolph came upright and jumped to the floor. Immediately on touchdown he slumped once more into the watchful coil, paws crossed. 'You see?' remarked Mr Melrose. 'He knows who's really in charge. Now take his place.'

In a minor fusillade of creaks, Annabel sat.

'Charming place you've got here,' Mr Melrose observed presently, looking around. 'A real touch of gracious country living. Just what I've always hankered after. I think I'll stay.'

His appraisal took in the entire room: furniture, fittings, the prints and watercolours between the timbering, the cut-glass vases with their spring flowers on rustic shelves in the alcoves. Annabel's gaze followed his as it roamed.

'It is perfect,' she agreed. 'But I prefer living alone. Rudy's the only one I want to share it with.'

'You'll make an exception, in my case.'

He said it without variation of tone, unhurriedly, as a

statement. From the hearthrug, the dog maintained its watch with unblinking eyes. Its tail, curved gracefully over the pile, was pinned down by a hind leg. The charcoal coat threw off a sheen.

Annabel said, 'There's hardly enough room . . .'

'Ample for the two of us.'

'I'm not sure I could cope—'

'Between us, we'll manage.'

She glanced towards the window. Rain was starting to tinkle against the glass. 'You'll get wet, walking back. Shouldn't you be off? The bus leaves in less than—'

'I'm not going.' Mr Melrose resettled himself luxuriously. 'Had you forgotten? I've decided to stop on. I like it here.'

'I have to work.'

'We'll come to some arrangement. A spot of give and take, that's all it needs. How's the headache?'

'Getting worse.' Putting a hand on her scalp, she kept it there. After a pause, she added, 'When I get an attack, I can be hard to live with.'

He smiled. 'That won't bother me.'

The rain beat harder. Extending a foot, Mr Melrose hooked a low footstool closer to his chair and rested a leg. Elbows on the side-rests, he sat contentedly surveying the vast bookcase of carved oak that formed virtually the whole of the opposite wall. 'Cosy in here. How far did you say your nearest neighbours are?'

'I'm afraid,' said Annabel, 'I shall have to ask you to leave.'

Mild surprise shone from him. 'You haven't quite cottoned on, Mrs Kidd. I did say, if you recall, that I'm not planning an early departure. I've fallen in love with the place. It cries out for a partnership.'

'I'm sorry. The only person I want as a partner is Rudy.'

Mr Melrose looked down inscrutably at the dog. 'Rudolph,' he said, 'is not a person. From here on, either you must come to terms with that fact or the animal must go. Is that understood?'

'He's my companion. I could never—'

' "Could" and "never" are relative terms, Mrs Kidd.

Rational people don't employ them loosely. A dog is a pet — no more. To set one of its kind on a pedestal is to invite trouble. I'm not going to allow you to continue in that way.'

'You can't take over my life.'

'No one's taking it over,' he said in gentle rebuke.

'Leave me alone, then. Get out of here.'

'That's different. You need help. I'm here to give it, and I've no intention of ducking my responsibility.'

'Unless you agree to go, I shall call the police.'

'That would be rather silly and unnecessary, don't you think?'

'Are you leaving?'

Bringing his other leg alongside the one already planted on the stool, Mr Melrose leaned back and rested his head. He continued to study her with some interest, as though estimating the likely storage capacity and output potential of a new-generation computer. After a short silence, Annabel rose from the basket chair. Walking across the room to the window-sill, she lifted the telephone.

'I do regret,' she told him across a shoulder, 'having to do something like this. But the situation . . .'

Breaking off, she stood staring at the instrument. Behind her, Mr Melrose observed her thoughtfully. 'Something the matter?'

'The phone's dead.'

'Dear me.'

'I've never known it to . . .' She rattled the receiver-rest. Biting her lip, she threw a backward glance before stooping abruptly to examine the floor. When she straightened up, her eyes bulged a little. 'The wire's been cut.'

'That sounds a shade theatrical.'

'But it *has*. I can't imagine . . .'

She turned. Mr Melrose was eyeing her equably from his armchair. The instrument made no sound as she replaced the receiver. Edging away from the window, Annabel circled the room to come to a halt behind the basket chair, gripping its backrest with the fingers of both hands.

She said slowly, 'It must have happened while I was outside, cooking the meal.'

'It sounds a little as though you're accusing me of something.'

'Rudolph couldn't have done it.'

'He might have bitten it through.'

'He's never done a thing like that.'

'Or you did it yourself. While you were Hoovering.'

'That's absurd.'

He dipped his head in assent. 'Mind you,' he said, glancing up again, 'peculiar things are apt to happen when one's living alone.'

Annabel's fingers squeezed the basketwork. 'I want you to go now, Mr Melrose. I'm asking you to.'

'Shall I tell you something? I don't believe it's what you really want, at all.'

'What do I have to say to convince you?'

'Headache getting bad? I can tell, just by looking at you.'

'It won't improve until you're out of here.'

'That,' he said informatively, 'is only what you've persuaded yourself to imagine. In reality, you're on tenterhooks in case I change my mind, decide to leave. You're getting strung up.'

Her nails dug into the chair. 'If I am, it's you who are . . . Listen. Let me tell you something. If you're still nursing the notion that I'm under your hypnotic spell—I'm not. I never was. I wanted to cooperate, so I pretended to be, that's all. I hoped it might help. But I've got all my faculties about me, make no mistake about that.'

Again Mr Melrose inclined his head. 'I never doubted it.'

'So you admit you're a charlatan?'

'I admit nothing of the kind.' He beamed up at her. 'It's a perfectly usual state of affairs. Ninety percent of my clients probably achieve no more than the very shallowest of trances—comprehensive relaxation would be a better description—so naturally they remain in full mental control and know just what's going on. It doesn't mean to say I can't help them in that condition. As I mean to help you.'

'The way you can help is by clearing off.'

His head wagged. 'You need me here. You may not

consciously appreciate it, but you do. I wouldn't dream of leaving now.'

Annabel stood staring at him. On the rug, Rudolph reclined in an attitude of calm alertness, ears half-pricked. He seemed to be listening to the dialogue, making judgments on syntax. Mr Melrose twisted in the armchair to peer at the sideboard.

'I think maybe I'll have that drink now. Not Scotch. A good sherry, if you keep it. Medium-dry. Have a tiny one yourself.'

'I'll drink when I want to, thanks.'

'Suit yourself,' he said peacefully. 'I'm sure you're wise to stay off alcohol. We'll work out a regimen. With me around, it'll be easier for you to stick to it.'

'Mr Melrose, you're not going to be around. I hoped I'd made that clear.'

His gaze slid towards the telephone. 'What exactly do you intend doing about it?'

A crack came from the basketwork. Annabel glanced down blankly at her fingernails. Those on the index and middle fingers of her left hand were split at the top where they had dragged the wicker away from the frame. Mr Melrose clicked his tongue.

'You see? Hypertension. First we must see about reducing that: then we'll go to work on the fundamentals.'

She enunciated slowly and distinctly. 'Unless you're out of here in thirty seconds, I shall be off to fetch help.'

'From the neighbours?' He chuckled. 'The police, perhaps? Only two miles into the village, through slashing rain.'

'To be rid of you, I'd swim.'

'*Rid* of me? My dear lady. Suppose a policeman came back with you . . . what would he find? An empty cottage. Ten minutes after he'd left, here I'd be back again, bright as a button. You won't see the last of me that easily.'

'You can't keep it up indefinitely.'

'Nor, I suggest, can you. Women who continually call in, complaining of persecution, soon outstay their welcome at police stations.'

Stepping back a pace, Annabel folded her arms. 'You won't agree to leave, then?'

'The matter,' he said dismissively, 'doesn't arise on the agenda. Next item: immediate arrangements. There's a spare bedroom, I assume? And somewhere for a wash. Meals: I'll cook for both of us. Give you more time for your work, won't it? Once we establish a routine, I can get down to organizing some proper treatment. You'll be—'

'Rudolph,' said Annabel. 'Come here, boy.'

Rising in an almost feline movement, the dog loped around the basket chair to stand beside her. Its deep-brown, gleaming eyes kept a check on her face. From the armchair, Mr Melrose looked questioning. Crouching, Annabel rumpled the curved hair about the animal's right ear.

'On guard, Rudolph. Stay. Keep under.'

The dog froze. Jaws slightly ajar, it stood looking across the hearthrug at the hypnotherapist. The hair along its back was raised.

Mr Melrose appeared unruffled. 'I understand dogs,' he informed her. 'You don't alarm me that way.'

'I'm not trying to. Rudolph. Circle.'

The dog swept forward, effortlessly, like a trolleybus under peak power. Clockwise, it commenced a silent reconnaissance of the armchair, circling ceaselessly, never straying from an orbit which kept it within a yard at all points. For a few rotations Mr Melrose tracked its course. 'Is this,' he inquired, 'strictly necessary?'

'It needn't have been.'

'Call him off, would you? He's making me dizzy.'

Attempting to push himself out of the armchair, Mr Melrose sank back hastily as Rudolph braked in front of him and exposed some fangs. When he was immobile again, the dog resumed its circumnavigation. Annabel backed towards the lounge door.

'Perhaps I should have warned you,' she said. 'Rudolph can keep it up all night, if need be.'

She vanished into the hall.

On her return, some while later, the man in the armchair was seated bolt upright, clutching the armrests, staring ahead. The dog's activity continued unabated. The hue of Mr Melrose's facial skin had undergone a marked alteration: amid its new-found pallor, blotches were visible.

'He seems to be turning a bit vicious,' he said tightly. 'Make him stop.'

Annabel surveyed the scene pensively. 'I only came back to tell you, I'll be gone for half an hour or so. I shan't be far. See you later.'

'Wait!'

She paused inquiringly at the door. Mr Melrose forced a smile. 'You win,' he said. 'You were absolutely right. I'm no hypnotist. I was just putting on an act.'

'Amaze me again,' she said indifferently, turning.

'Please don't go! It was all done with the best possible motives. I'm a genuine practising counsellor, you know. Broad experience. Quite often I can help people get to the . . . the root of their disorders, simply by making them see how they originated. It's a mental thing.'

'Really?'

'Don't misunderstand me. That charade just now,' he said, a note of desperation stealing into his voice, 'had a specific purpose, Mrs Kidd. It was designed to make you admit to yourself what your subconscious has been trying to hide: namely, that ever since childhood you've disliked and feared male company of any kind and so you've ordered your life accordingly. At the same time, basically you long to be loved and cherished. Incessant conflict. Hence the headaches.'

'How interesting.'

'In all the circumstances,' gabbled Mr Melrose, retracting his feet from the flight-path of Rudolph as the dog came round again, 'your problem's not in the least baffling. It's all down to the male parent. By subjecting an immature child—'

'You're most perceptive. Circle, Rudolph.'

'Can't you please call him off? I'll leave immediately.'

'I'll see you again,' she told him. 'About half an hour.'

Twenty-five minutes later, she was back. This time she was wearing a waterproof jacket and rain-hat, both garments dripping moisture; her face and hands were mud-streaked. Her shoes squelched. Coming to a standstill in the doorway, she looked across the room at Mr Melrose. Indisputably, his face was now chalk-white. Except for an area just below his left jaw, which was raw crimson. Limply he returned her gaze.

'He went for me.'

'So I see.' Annabel went forward, eyed the wound estimatingly. 'You shouldn't have tried to move.'

'Wouldn't you?'

'Not if I'd been told to stay put.'

'All right. You've made your point, Mrs Kidd, very resoundingly. I'm sorry if I alarmed you. Perhaps I went too far. I apologize. Now will you take this creature of yours out of circulation and let me go?'

'You're asking me to release you?'

'I'm imploring you,' he said eagerly. 'You've turned the tables quite beautifully—I must give you that. You're more than evens. Now, surely, you can afford to be charitable. Let me bathe my neck.'

'You are in a bit of a mess,' Annabel said consideringly. 'Leave, Rudolph. Over here.'

Breaking away at a tangent, the dog came to rejoin her. It stood docilely next to her right calf, its coat pressed against her.

Mr Melrose came shakily to his feet. Finding a handkerchief, he mopped at the blood meandering down into his shirt-collar. Catching her eye, he engineered a travesty of a short laugh.

'I suppose,' he acknowledged, 'I asked for that.'

'You did, rather,' Annabel told him. 'And now you're going to get the rest of it. Rudolph. Attack!'

She stood watching. It was over in seconds. Mr Melrose expired chokingly, an expression of bemusement struggling to the last with its rival grimace of pure horror. When the outcome was no longer in question, Annabel said sharply, 'Leave, Rudolph! Come away.'

Abandoning with reluctance the heap on the carpet, Rudolph trotted back. She crouched to stroke and embrace him. Accepting her attentions, the animal stood rigid, licking its jaws.

She crooned into its ear. 'Oh Rudy . . . that's better. My headache's gone.'

Presently she stirred, rose from her knees. Rudolph cocked his head. She smiled down at him.

'When I've switched telephones,' she whispered, 'we'll get him out into the garden. The hole's dug. But you'll have to help me, boy, this time. He's a lot heavier than the last one. Feeling strong, are we?'

The dog wagged its tail.

The Lesson

The gear-change on the Renault required a different touch, Felicity discovered, from that on her father's Ford Fiesta. 'Takes getting used to,' she apologized, jolting the car almost to a standstill on the gradient leading up to the War Memorial. 'Sorry about your cogs.'

'They're designed to take punishment,' Mr Wigthorpe assured her. 'Handbrake on, back into neutral and try again.'

After some abortive motor-crescendo, Felicity regained momentum at eight miles an hour towards the brow of the hill. At her side, Mr Wigthorpe remained impassive. Only when she had achieved third gear and a modest canter did he issue a further instruction.

'Before you reach the Memorial, bear left. Follow the road leading down to the Park. Watch out for the lights.'

Activating the indicator, Felicity wobbled into the left-hand prong of the fork, veered for the kerb, swung violently away, headed for the centre-line. Her instructor said nothing. Teeth clenched, she struggled back on to course. Now travelling downhill, but held back by the lower gear, the car delivered a protest via a roaring note from the engine. Staring fixedly ahead, she said, 'Should I change into top?'

'Stay in third,' Mr Wigthorpe advised calmly.

Moments later they were on the level ground of the Park, their pace reduced to an amble for which qualified drivers showed their contempt by zooming past the Renault like a swarm of demented wasps. Mr Wigthorpe pointed a finger. 'Time for a respite. Turn in there.'

When they were parked in the lay-by and the engine was silent, Felicity allowed herself to sag inside her seat-harness. 'Don't want to wait, do they?' she complained, scowling at the fast-receding hatchbacks in pursuit of each other. 'They forget they were learners themselves, once.'

'Human nature,' Mr Wigthorpe said tolerantly.

He was built on a large scale, with a bull neck and a rugged but gentle face. As though conscious of his bulk, he sat laterally on the passenger seat, pressed to the nearside door with his arms folded tidily away, so that there was a space of a couple of feet between himself and his pupil. He smelt faintly of tobacco. Felicity took no exception to that. So did her father and so, to a greater degree, did Geoff, who contrived to smoke a good deal even though he was on the dole. Maybe because he was on the dole. A warm-hearted girl, Felicity took the view that life's hardships justified a little consolation. Mr Wigthorpe she assessed as being a pipe man.

'I've only had a few goes,' she excused herself, 'in my dad's car. Just up and down a private road. It's different in traffic.'

'Of course it is. I thought you coped well.' He spoke like a psychiatrist charged with the task of restoring morale in an emotional wreck. His rather deepset eyes twinkled remotely. 'Perhaps you'd rather have learned on an automatic?'

Firmly she shook her head. 'I want to be qualified for a manual. I'm going to share an old Mini with someone.'

'That'll be nice. Planning to motor around quite a bit?'

'I'll use it to get to work.'

'Good,' he said solemnly. 'What do you do, may I ask?'

Privately amused at the quaintness of his phraseology, she kept a straight face. 'I'm a dress designer,' she announced. 'With Fulton's. You know? The big place on the Coventry road.'

'I know of it. A niece of mine was in the accounts department there. Good crowd to work for, I understand.'

'They're okay. I'd like to branch out on my own.'

'Design and sell your own creations? Why not?' Mr Wigthorpe sounded judiciously applauding. 'I'm sure you'd make a go of it. If you'll excuse my asking . . . did you make the one you're wearing.?'

'This?' She glanced down at herself. 'I did, actually. Does it show?'

'Only in the sense that you can see it's something a bit special.' He spoke hurriedly, as if trying to erase a bad impression. 'Nice colours. You've obviously got a flair.' On a note of faint wistfulness he added, 'It must be satisfying to be artistic.'

Frowning at the controls, trying to sort out the cigar-lighter from the hazard warning signal, Felicity said idly, 'Most people are creative, in their way.'

'Some of us just plod through life.'

'You probably achieve more than you realize. Dozens of new drivers, for a start, every year.'

'I'm not sure that's altogether a laudable accomplishment.' A chuckle shook him briefly. Falling silent, he pondered for a moment. 'A spot of verse,' he said suddenly, 'now and then.'

'Pardon?'

'I have a stab at poetry. Find it relaxing.'

'Poetry,' she repeated, impressed though dubious. 'Have you had anything published?'

'My goodness. What d'you take me for? Tennyson? I just write for my own pleasure, that's all. Well now. Feel like braving the mainstream again? Gear-lever in neutral, switch on . . .'

Describing her first lesson that evening, Felicity laid stress upon the avuncular and supportive qualities of Mr Wigthorpe. 'I'd sooner have him,' she explained, nursing her glass of white wine for which she had paid herself, 'than some bigheaded know-all who just wants to be macho the whole time. He's a bit old-fashioned, but he's sweet.'

'How old,' Geoff asked jealously, 'did you say he was?'

'How should I know? Forty to fifty. Pushing it, anyway. Who cares how old he is? Getting me through the test, that's what counts.'

'I could have done that. I told you.'

She gazed at him lovingly. He was looking thinner than usual. Job-hunting took it out of you, they said. She hoped he hadn't worn his tatty zip-jacket and jeans for any interviews he might have had. Diplomatically she had refrained from asking. If he'd had any luck, he'd have told her.

'We've been into all that,' she reminded him. 'Husbands can't teach their wives to drive. Common knowledge.'

'We're not husband and wife,' Geoff retorted.

From the shelter of the wineglass she gave him a wide smile. 'Not far off, are we?'

'Watch it, Lissy. You'll have me on the boil.'

'So what's wrong with that?'

Their fingers interlocked under the table. 'Sink the rest of that,' he muttered, 'and let's blow.'

'My, aren't we impatient? I'm not sure,' she said teasingly, 'I feel like it tonight. What with a hard day's work, then an hour with Mr Wigthorpe, not to mention the back seat of that Mini which is hardly—'

'You put up with it last time.' Standing up, he hauled her with him. 'When I make my first half-million,' he murmured in her ear, 'I'll get a Rolls with a fold-down king-size bed. That suit you?'

'Why only *half* a million?'

An hour later, Felicity subsided gaspingly in Geoff's embrace. 'Maybe you were right,' she mumbled presently, nibbling his earlobe. 'We should aim for a nine-seater. I think I've twisted my spine.' She lay silently for a while. Eventually she giggled.

'What's up?' One-handed, Geoff was igniting a cigarette.

'I was just thinking. If Mr Wigthorpe could see me now, he'd go spastic.'

'Why?'

'Let's just say he obviously holds traditional views on things.'

'You don't know. Behind it all, he could be a sex maniac. Is he married?'

'I never asked him.'

During her second lesson, Mr Wigthorpe directed Felicity into a residential estate with unadopted roads, the surfaces of which had evidently been laid down by gangs from an establishment for psychologically-disturbed sedentary workers as part of a therapy programme which had been prematurely called off. After her head had touched the roof for the third time, she applied the brake. 'Mr Wigthorpe,' she said severely, 'I do believe you're trying to turn me off motoring.'

He looked startled, a little confused. 'I'm afraid the potholes have got deeper since I last came along here. I do apologize, Miss Cox. We'll have to go on now—quicker than turning back. I'm so sorry.'

'Don't worry about it.' Her smile was designed to tell him she had spoken partly in fun. 'I was really thinking of the car. Surely it can't be good for it?'

Mr Wigthorpe peered ahead. 'If you take the next on the right, I think it's smoother. We can practise some three-point turns.'

He was right, and for the next fifteen minutes Felicity wrestled with the complexities of reverse gear and backward glances. Finally, at his bidding she immobilized the car on a wide grass verge shielded by shrubs from the nearest house, and switched off. 'My arms,' she puffed, flexing them. 'They're nearly out of their sockets.'

'You've done very well.' He consulted his watch. 'After you've rested, we'll potter back and try just one hill-start on the way.' Settling himself against the nearside door, he gave a nervous cough. 'I hope you'll still be able to wield a needle, after this.'

'I have people to do the stitching for me,' she said complacently. 'I work out the patterns.'

'I see. But if you were to launch your own business . . .'

'I'd probably have to do the lot, at first. Couldn't afford staff.'

'I'm sure you'd soon drum up trade.' Mr Wigthorpe glanced along the tree-flanked street, then back at her, as if comparing the two sights. 'A word here, a smile there . . . You'd have customers eating out of your hand.'

'Think so?'

'Not a doubt of it,' he said earnestly.

Deftly she turned the subject. 'How's the verse-writing? Keeping at it?'

His face lit up. Hitching the seat-belt clear of his chest, he groped in an inside pocket. 'I brought a piece along. Thought you might be interested.'

'I don't know much about poetry,' she said, embarrassed.

'No more do I,' he assured her with an uneasy laugh. 'I just let it pour out, sort of. Shall I read you a little?'

'Have we got time?'

'It'll only take a minute. While you're resting. This one's called *Visions of Night*. I'll just read the first couple of verses. *When lying in my lonesome bed, with hope and worry likewise shed . . .*'

Felicity listened in acute discomfort. At the conclusion of the second verse she said quickly, 'I like that. It's got real feeling. Do you find it hard to make up?'

'The ideas come all the time. Expressing them, of course . . . Finding the words. That's the tricky part.'

'Let's hope the ideas don't dry up, eh?'

'No fear of that.' Refolding the sheets of paper carefully, Mr Wigthorpe restored them with manifest reluctance to his pocket. 'In the past few days, I've had what you might call fresh inspiration.'

'Great.' Avoiding his eyes, she felt for the ignition switch and fired the engine. 'Better be getting back, before I start owing you for a second hour.' With a conscientious glare into the rear-view mirror she let in the clutch. 'Is your wife poetic, too?' she asked, steering around a jutting manhole cover.

'I'm not married. I live with an aunt of mine. You wouldn't call her literary, but she puts up with my scribbling.' Releasing a chuckle which sounded a shade less than spontaneous, Mr Wigthorpe settled back and became an instructor again. 'You'll find, if you take the gear-shifting a fraction slower . . .'

'Writes poetry,' commented Geoff, later that evening, 'and shacks up with an aunt. He sounds a Wally.'

'He's not, he's very nice. Ooh, but his poems . . .' Felicity moaned at the memory. 'If I hadn't been so bored, I'd never have kept a straight face. Hope he doesn't want to read me any more, next time.'

'He will,' Geoff said with conviction. 'He's taken a shine to you.'

'Don't be daft. I expect he recites to all his learners.'

'Yeah? He's lusting after you, that's what.'

'So, he might have an eye for the girls. What of it? At least it shows he's normal.'

Felicity wriggled. She sensed that Geoff was right; that Mr Wigthorpe had indeed taken a tumble in her direction. For some reason she felt loath to concede the probability. She knew perfectly well the effect she had upon most men. At twenty, she had been granted boundless opportunities to find out. This time, however, she had gone to some pains to preserve a detached manner towards Mr Wigthorpe, for the sake of Geoff and because she keenly wanted to pass her driving test as soon as possible. If all her efforts had somehow produced the opposite effect, it was both irksome and ironic. But no fault of hers.

Geoff regarded her broodingly. 'Any joy with the workshop?'

'No,' she said dolefully. 'They wanted sixty quid a week rent, *plus* a down-payment of five hundred. Fat chance.'

'Can't your old man help?'

'You know how Dad's placed. His redundancy money won't stretch for ever. It's all he can do to keep running the car and drive Mum to Sainsbury's twice a week. Where would he find that sort of cash? Even if he wanted to,' Felicity added as an afterthought, 'which he doesn't. They both reckon I should stay with Fulton's. Nice and safe.'

'Why don't you, then?'

'Geoff, you know how I feel about it. Striking out on my own . . . it's all I've ever wanted to do.'

'You can get State aid.'

'Only if you've a thousand of your own to put into the business. So far, I've got a hundred and thirty with the Halifax. How about you?' she ventured. 'Any hopes of a job?'

Geoff sniffed into his beer. 'There's a recession on, hadn't you heard?'

'It's all I ever hear. There must be *something* you could be doing.'

'Queueing for the dole is hard enough work, for me. You try it some time.'

'Sooner be at Fulton's, thanks. Listen. You did mean what you said, about sharing the Mini when I've passed my test?'

'No, love. Sorry.' At her look of dismay, his face broke into the smile that sent her weak at the knees. ''Course I meant it. Can't afford to run it by myself, can I?'

'Not on what they give you, I shouldn't think.' Briefly annoyed, Felicity slapped his forearm and then, relenting, transmuted the assault into a caress. 'Honestly though, love. You ought to think about taking anything that's offered. It's not good, kicking your heels like this.'

'It beats pen-shoving, any day.' His smile broadened to a grin. 'I'll tell you this, Lissy. I'm not leaping into the first lousy opening they chuck at me. I've given the bastards my qualifications. If they can't come up with the goods, that's their funeral.'

'You can't expect to walk into—'

'Look, I'm a technician, right? I've got skills. It's up to them to make use of 'em. Or if not, pay me compensation. That's all it is. Recompense.'

Felicity eyed him dubiously. 'You know about amplifiers, stuff like that. But if they can't find you a slot . . .'

'I've told 'em, haven't I? With a few hundred quid, I can get this mobile disco thing on the road with Eddie Sharpe. We'd be coining it. Then I'd be out of their hair, wouldn't I? Cheaper for 'em, in the long run. Just a measly enterprise grant, that's all we're asking for.'

She lifted her arms, let them fall. 'Keep on at them.'

'They don't want to know.'

Finishing his beer, Geoff seized her wineglass and went off to the bar. When he came back, replenished, Felicity was sitting with an unfocused gaze, her slender fingers tapping the table. He snapped his finger and thumb, making her jump.

'I was trying to work something out. If I could start up on my own, you could come in with me and maintain the equipment, couldn't you? The machines, and that. Plus, you could drive around and deliver the goods. Maybe pick up some custom, too.'

'Yeah, I could.' Dumping the drinks, he sat down and regarded her cynically. 'So how do you figure on raising the necessary?'

Her shoulders sagged. 'I can't think of a way. Only by saving up.'

'Take years.'

'I know. And meanwhile you've nothing to occupy you.' She looked mournfully across at the bartender. Presently she added, 'If we did do something like that, we could get married, I suppose.'

Geoff nodded absently. 'I guess we could.'

For her third lesson, Felicity was taken out on to the by-pass and told to travel in the slow lane at forty until they came to the next turn-off. 'Then,' said Mr Wigthorpe, 'I want you to do a couple of circuits of the elevated roundabout and come back by way of Dallingham Village. That'll give you a few sets of lights and a dodgy junction to negotiate. Think you can manage that?'

She took in a breath. 'Here's hoping.'

Things went reasonably well as far as the village, where she took a wrong turning and arrived in a country lane the width of a car and a half, bordered by menacing ditches. 'Keep on,' advised Mr Wigthorpe, 'until we find somewhere to turn.'

Before this occurred they covered nearly a mile. The turn accomplished, Felicity prepared to retrace their route, but stalled in the gateway. The car refused to restart. 'Flooded carb,' pronounced Mr Wigthorpe knowledgeably. 'Give it a few minutes, then try again.'

'I'm an idiot, aren't I?'

'Not a bit of it. Everyone stalls at times.' His voice and manner were soothing. She gave him a grateful smile.

It seemed to jog a switch inside him. Delving into his inner pocket, he said with a touch of breathlessness, 'I've another poem I thought you might care to hear.'

Her heart slumped. 'Great,' she said brightly. 'Is it a recent one?'

'I composed it last night,' Mr Wigthorpe said significantly. 'In the small hours,' he appended, glancing at her and away. 'I couldn't sleep.'

'That's the creative instinct for you.'

'It wasn't that. It was something more . . .' His words began to slur. Breaking off, he studied the lined paper for a moment before starting to declaim.

'The darkness threatens, and I think of you. The darkness topples, and you give me strength. The darkness stays around me, yet despite it all . . .'

This time she let him continue to the appalling end. When his voice tailed off, she allowed a moment of reverence to elapse before remarking, 'That's awfully nice. I do think you're talented, Mr Wigthorpe.'

To her faint alarm, he shook his head with vigour. 'If I were, I'd do it more justice. The situation.'

'The situation?'

The repetition, she knew instantly, was unwise. Although he remained still, gazing ahead at the field opposite, the atmosphere about them became abruptly supercharged. For a second or two he said nothing. Then, chokingly: 'I've been looking forward to this session, all day.'

'Because it's the last?'

Her flippancy was in vain. His further shake of the head was ponderous, introspective. 'I can't tell you, Miss Cox, how much I appreciate your company.'

'I appreciate yours.'

'It's hard for me to explain . . .'

'Don't try. Will the car start now, do you think?'

He blinked, as if someone had flicked him lightly across the face with a rag. 'We might have a bash,' he said, after a moment's delay. 'Clock's ticking on, I suppose. Always gallops, doesn't it, when you're . . . having a good time. Foot off the accelerator, Miss Cox. Two or three turns of the starter. If it doesn't fire . . .'

Once more he was the competent instructor, handing out directions. Complying with them, Felicity succeeded in restoring life to the hunk of metal under her command and navigating it, with a sense of relief, back to the village and the main road. After that she had no difficulty in keeping the dialogue to a strictly business level. Monitoring her progress, Mr Wigthorpe became monosyllabic. She gained the feeling that he felt rebuffed. To counter this impression, she introduced a matier note as they re-entered the fringes of the town. 'Saturday tomorrow. Hooray! I like weekends, don't you?'

'To be honest, I don't find them a lot different. I'm generally working, you see.'

'Yes, I suppose so. Your busiest time, I expect.'

'It's remarkable,' he said solemnly, 'the number of people who want to learn to drive on a Sunday morning.'

'I'd hate that. Don't you get tired?'

'A bit, sometimes. The money comes in useful, of course. We get extra for weekend working, and as I'm saving up for a special holiday . . .'

'Sounds exciting,' she said, as he paused. 'Where are you off to?'

'A cruise. All around the Med. Three weeks.'

'Away from the petrol fumes. Terrific. You should have a great time.'

'I'm hoping so.'

'Going by yourself?' Felicity liked to take a friendly interest in people's activities, especially those involving recreation. She had a secret yearning to go off with Geoff to somewhere like the Algarve. Fat hope, just now.

'That's the plan, at the moment.' Mr Wigthorpe's utterance sounded a little thick. He sat gauging her approach to the driving school's car park. 'Out a little—more to the centre. Now hard round. Good. Mind you, I wouldn't say no to some company.'

'How about your aunt?'

'She's arthritic, I'm afraid. Can't get about. That space over there.' As the car bucked to a halt, Felicity having delayed her de-clutching an instant too long, he began fumbling with the clip of his seat-belt, making something of a job of it. Still manipulating, he added whimsically, 'If you felt like a sea-voyage yourself, after tackling the perils of roadcraft, you'd be more than welcome.'

'It's a thought.' She kept the exchange at banter-level.

'Problem is, I couldn't take three weeks off. Not all at once.'

'It needn't be the Mediterranean,' Mr Wigthorpe returned eagerly, to her consternation. 'Something shorter.'

'Mm. I still couldn't afford it.'

'Anyone who came along,' he said, stuttering a little, 'would travel as my guest.'

'Oh, well then. You should have no trouble finding somebody. Either way, I hope the trip comes up to scratch. Thanks for the lesson, Mr Wigthorpe.' A shade feverishly, she released herself from the car. 'Same time, Monday?'

'I'll be here.'

As she walked from the car park she sensed that he was gazing after her. It was like something out of soap-opera. Heroine quits scene . . . cut in to taut profile of abandoned male . . . feed in violas . . . She had a laugh about it with Geoff, after the cinema.

'You were right, love. He's gone and fallen for me.'

'What did you think?' Geoff snorted. 'A middle-age crush—that's what he's got. Watch out for yourself, next time. He could get serious.'

'I can handle Mr Wigthorpe,' she said confidently.

'Make sure you do. I don't want you getting hurt.'

She gave a small mirthful scream. 'He wouldn't harm a fly. You want to see him.'

'I don't, that much. How many more lessons you got?'

'Three. Then I thought I could practise in this, till I take the test.'

'I don't know about that.'

'We're sharing, aren't we?'

'Sharing, sure. That doesn't mean wrecking.'

'I won't muck it up, silly. Mr Wigthorpe says I change gear very smoothly.'

'I'll bet he does. Let's see you do it now.'

'You've a one-track mind,' she said in mock disgust, starting to peel off her sweater.

Some while later, Geoff adopted his usual procedure after their rear-seat manœuvres: lit up a cigarette and created a fug inside the Mini while she nestled sleepily against him. Felicity liked this companionable aftermath, although she did sometimes wonder where he got the cash to smoke as he did, besides partly running the car and enjoying rather more than the odd pint. She felt it diplomatic not to ask. This evening she felt especially at ease, cosy, protected. At times like this, when they were alone together, Geoff was at his best: manly, desirable, almost tender. In company, he tended at times to ignore her. She understood that. It was just his awkwardness. Mildly hurtful as it could be, she had learned to endure.

Pulling lingeringly on the cigarette, Geoff tapped ash on to the Mini's uncarpeted floor. 'This cruise,' he remarked. 'Reckon he was serious about it?'

'Mr Wigthorpe?' She was briefly startled. Her driving instructor had been some way removed from her thoughts. 'I'd never be surprised. If I'd said yes, he'd probably have whipped out the tickets, then and there.'

'A three-week beanfeast,' Geoff murmured reflectively, 'round the Med. That'll cost him a bomb.'

'Mm. Even for one.'

'He must have enough readies for two,' Geoff pointed out. 'Otherwise he'd not have offered.'

'That's true.'

Geoff relapsed into further musings. Presently he said, 'How respectable would you say he is?'

'You're still on about Mr Wigthorpe? I've no idea.' She frowned. 'What d'you mean, exactly—*respectable*?'

'Conventional, then. Law-abiding.'

'All I know is, he's a gentleman. I mean, you can tell. He'd never overstep the mark. He's just not that sort.'

Geoff nodded as if satisfied. 'It's given me an idea. You listen to this.'

Minutes later, Felicity sat with a feeling of congestion in her chest and stomach. Leaning back into the corner of the seat, she chose her words with care. 'You're joking, Geoff, aren't you? You're not serious about all this?'

'Why not?'

'Because it's . . . immoral. I could never dream of it.'

'No need to dream. Just a case of performing.'

'Don't be daft. Let's change the subject.'

'Can you pick any holes in it?' he demanded, turning to confront her.

'Only about ninety. Main one is, it would never work.'

'But what if it did?'

Numbly she shook her head. 'Don't even talk about it.'

'Okay.' Taking a final puff, he ground the cigarette-end into the flooring with his heel. After a few moments' silence he said, 'I thought you wanted to get married.'

She placed a hand impulsively on his arm. 'I do, love. I'd give anything . . .'

'Go ahead, then. Do this, and we can.'

'I wouldn't be able to live with myself.'

''Course not. You'd be living with me. Properly, all legal and legit. All it takes is a bit of effort.'

'There's more to it than that,' she replied, low-voiced. 'And you know it.'

'I only know you're not the girl I took you for.'

Thrusting away the backrest of the front passenger seat with a foot, Geoff swarmed over it and returned to his place behind the wheel. Hurriedly adjusting her clothing, Felicity joined him, only just in time before he wrenched activity into the nine-year-old motor and reversed violently from the woodland clearing in which they had been concealed. He drove back fast into town. Sitting in unhappy silence, she debated what to say when they stopped.

'Look, Geoff,' she began, as the car grated to a halt outside her parents' house. 'You know I'll do anything in reason, but there's no way—'

'Forget it.' Leaning across her, he shoved open the door. 'See you around.'

'I just don't see myself—'

'I said forget it.' He waited until she was out on the pavement; then got noisily into gear. 'Have a nice weekend.'

Slamming the door shut, he took off. The car vanished around the corner, its elderly cough dwindling into the night. Choking back tears, Felicity ran for the house.

On Monday she was glad to be back at Fulton's. She had spent a wretched two days waiting for the phone to ring, combating the urge to swallow her pride and her scruples and make the call herself; trying to devise other ways of occupying her time. Since she had started knocking around with Geoff, she seemed to have mislaid the knack of independent hustle. At Fulton's, she was at least usefully employed among people who took her as they found her, unlike her own family who knew her too well to be fooled by any attempted camouflaging of mood. She kept herself hard at work all day, sustaining her resistance to the seductive idea of sneaking to the telephone and dialling the number of the rented premises that Geoff shared with five of his mates. The first move, she told herself sternly, must come from him.

Punctually at six-thirty she was back at the driving school. Greeting her with formal courtesy, Mr Wigthorpe announced that they would begin with ten minutes of reversing around corners. He seemed preoccupied. Just her luck, Felicity thought drearily. For once, she stood in urgent need of some friendly chat. At his bidding, she drove to a quiet, broad thoroughfare, a cul-de-sac leading on to the Common, and embarked on the tormenting process of hugging the kerbstones while contorting her neck. Repeatedly, feeling on edge, she made a botch of it. Eventually Mr Wigthorpe signified that enough was enough.

'We'll come back to that,' he said tactfully. 'Let's try a little straight motoring, shall we? Bear left out of here, follow the road through to Remington, then turn right and complete the circle back into town. Got that?'

As they bowled towards Megwitch, a hamlet on the way to Remington, Felicity made an attempt to thaw the atmosphere. 'I'm starting to feel peckish. Didn't have time for any lunch.' In fact, she had been unable to face the meal. She now felt hollow, somewhat light-headed. 'D'you have something midday, Mr Wigthorpe, or just work through?'

'I normally stop for a sandwich. Here . . .' Wrestling something out of his offside pocket, he snapped off a chunk and passed it over. It was two squares of milk chocolate. 'That'll keep you going.'

'Thanks very much.' She chewed energetically until speech was again feasible. 'These your emergency rations?'

'You could say that. Have some more.'

'Better not,' she said regretfully. 'Can't concentrate on the road.'

He pointed ahead. 'Pull in there a minute. We can finish the slab between us.'

A little dubiously, Felicity followed orders and brought the car to a halt parallel with a thorn hedge where the road widened. Breaking the chocolate bar in half, Mr Wigthorpe divided the spoils. 'I'm quite hungry myself,' he confessed, champing discreetly. 'Like you, I had very little at lunch-time, and it'll be an hour or two yet before I get supper.'

'Does your aunt cook for you?'

'When she can. If she's feeling out of sorts, I hash up something for the two of us.'

His existence sounded a barrel of laughs. Trying to formulate an innocuous follow-up, Felicity detached two more chocolate squares from her portion and promptly dropped the remainder into the space between the seats, where it disappeared from view. 'Oh drat!'

'I'll get it.' He felt around the floor with his right hand. 'Must have gone right under your seat,' he said presently. 'I think I might be able to . . .'

What happened next took Felicity off guard. At one moment, Mr Wigthorpe was inclined towards her, his right arm swallowed up: the next, she felt pawing movements against her left thigh. Although her skirt was lined, it had ridden up while she drove, and for a second or two his fingers were in contact with her bare flesh. She froze. Seemingly unaware, her instructor continued his search for the chocolate, his face reddening a little as he probed. She forced herself to utter. 'Don't bother,' she said tightly. 'Leave it.'

He straightened up. 'Must have slid,' he said breathlessly. His right hand was back in his lap, exerting pressure on the remains of the bar. 'Have some of this.'

'No, it's all right, thanks. We'd best get moving.'

Restarting the car, she took it swiftly away. Although Mr Wigthorpe had raised no objection, she sensed that he would have preferred to be the one to resume the lesson. Too bad. He shouldn't have tried it on.

Had he tried it on? The facial flush, the breathlessness . . . Both could have been due to his floor-exploration. But, in retrospect, she could feel the pressure of his fingertips. Was it true, what everyone said? *Men—they're all the same. No exceptions.* She drove in silence, obeying his murmured instructions, impatient to be back. When they reached the car park, instead of finding a spare space she pulled up in the centre, applied the handbrake and climbed out immediately. 'Got an appointment. See you Wednesday, unless I have to cancel.'

Giving him no time to reply, she walked off. In the High Street she found a call-box.

'Geoff?' she said, when one of his house-mates brought him to the phone. 'You're on. I'll do it.'

'That's my girl.'

By Wednesday evening Felicity's nerves felt stretched, as if one stroke of a blade at a central point would have sent them twanging in all directions. The working hours at Fulton's had passed in a haze. At one point, her best friend and colleague, Jo Isaacs, had voiced concern about her. 'Anything the matter, Liss? You're looking all white and pinched.' Felicity explained that she hadn't slept much the previous night (inaccurate: she hadn't slept at all) and was finding it hard to focus. Thereafter she had exerted herself to appear normal, but the inner strain had taken its toll of her resources. A final telephone conversation with Geoff at lunchtime, to tie up loose ends, had done little for her peace of mind. The afternoon had stretched itself to a month. At times she was convinced that someone was going around altering the clocks. Inspecting her keenly during the tea-break, Jo Isaacs opined that she was sickening for something and should go straight home to bed. From then until closing time, Felicity had kept out of her way.

Now it was six-twenty. Fifty yards ahead of her along the street lay the entrance to the driving school, awaiting an approach. Her stomach churned. Her knees felt unreliable, as if contemplating sudden defection to leave her gasping in the gutter. Loitering at a dress shop window, pretending to examine the styles, she took deep desperate breaths and tried to think of ends rather than means. A shop of her own. A new range of designs, *Chez Felicity*, that would capture the nation. Employment for Geoff. A future for both of them. Inducing her muscles to function, she covered the fifty yards and went inside.

As usual, Mr Wigthorpe was ready for her. His greeting was polite. Shining her most brilliant smile at him, Felicity declared, 'I think I'm on form this evening. I feel lucky.'

'That's good,' he responded gravely, holding the car door for her.

'In fact, I'm ready for anything. Can I choose the route this time, Mr Wigthorpe?'

'If you like.' Installing himself alongside, he checked her harness meticulously, as he always did, before buckling himself down and assuming his self-effacing posture against the nearside door. 'Where were you thinking of making for?'

She made a show of pondering. 'The Wickling road?' she suggested. 'It's got a lot of ups and downs, and the traffic's quite thick this time of an evening. Then we could skirt round into Maychester and come back over the Common. How about that?'

He considered the programme. 'A shade on the lengthy side,' he pronounced, 'but let's see how we go.'

'I'll smash the circuit record,' she said breezily.

It was better once they were moving. After an initial tangling of the gears, the product of muscular inhibition, she was able to relax a little by dint of concentrating on roadcraft and mechanical controls. Apart from a word or two of encouragement or guidance, Mr Wigthorpe remained taciturn. Once they had passed through Wickling and were bearing east, Felicity wriggled herself into a more tolerable position inside the seat-straps and said, 'Woof! How am I doing?'

'Quite nicely. Try to slow down at traffic lights a moment sooner.'

'Sorry.' She flipped him an impish grin. 'My headstrong nature. Dad's always telling me I'm too impulsive.'

Mr Wigthorpe made no comment. Frequent glances through his nearside window seemed to imply that he was appreciating the scenery more than her skills as a motorist. After another mile she gave a cough, lowered her voice to a confiding level. 'I've been looking forward to this, all day.'

'You like driving?'

'When it's with you.'

There was a pause. 'It's comforting,' he said on a dry note, 'for an instructor to be told that.'

'Actually, I was talking more on a personal basis.'

Silence. Against the rules, she turned her head to peep at him. 'You're meant to say "And I like you too, Miss Cox." Where did I slip up?'

'I beg your pardon. I hadn't . . . To be honest, I was a little surprised that you showed up this evening.'

'Surprised?' she repeated innocently. 'What ever for?'

'You did say something on Monday,' he reminded her, 'about possibly having to cancel.'

'Did I? I don't remember. Probably just being cautious.'

'Cautious *and* impulsive,' he remarked, a touch of humour sliding into his voice. 'Quite a combination.'

'Well, you know what they say about women.'

'No. What do they say?'

'Never take 'em at face value. Half the time, they don't know what they're after themselves.'

Mr Wigthorpe sat apparently digesting this. A sign marked MAYCHESTER appeared on their left and he became alert, sustaining his vigil until they had cleared the town centre and were heading back south, on course for the Common. 'You were right,' he observed presently. 'You're handling the controls quite dashingly this evening. As long as you don't overdo it. Measured movements—give yourself time. You know, as far as you're concerned, yourself, I don't really believe it.'

'Pardon?'

'What you were saying just now. I imagine you've a very good idea of what you're after.'

Felicity's fingers tightened on the wheel. She said brightly, 'Okay—tell me. I'd like to know.'

'I can't tell you, exactly. What I meant was, you've a

schedule for life mapped out and you're the type who'll stick to it. Or am I mistaken?'

'Golly. You're a mind-reader. That's just how I've always seen myself.'

Between them and the Common lay a Forestry Commission area, planted with larch and spruce, into which the road now dived. Although the trees were shielded from the highway by mesh fencing, the gateways to the access tracks lay well back, fronted by gravelled expanses. After elaborate signalling, Felicity drove the car on to one of these and pulled up, facing the gate. Another car, unoccupied, was parked at the further end of the inlet, some distance away. Mr Wigthorpe looked at her inquiringly.

'I can't talk properly,' she explained, 'while we're belting along. There's just something I'd like to mention.'

Her heart hammered. She was having supreme difficulty in preventing her voice from skidding between keys. To hide the trembling of her hands she occupied them with the seat-belt release, finally thrusting the harness clear and leaning back with a sigh. '*That*'s better. Must relax for five minutes. I hate being strapped in the whole time, don't you?'

'It's reckoned to be for our own good,' he replied non-committally. 'What was it you wanted to say?'

'It's about Monday. I'm afraid you might have thought I was a bit offhand when I took off. I don't like to give a wrong impression.'

'Monday.' Mr Wigthorpe looked thoughtful. He seemed to be playing for time. 'You did leave a little . . . rapidly, perhaps. I took it that you were in a hurry to keep your next appointment. No offence taken, I assure you.'

'That's good.' In her own ears, her squeal of laughter rang near-hysterical. 'I'd still like to explain, though. The point is . . .' She hesitated confusedly. 'This is going to sound dreadful. You know when you were looking for the chocolate?'

He nodded. 'Under the seat. I found it afterwards.'

'Oh. Well, it seems silly now, but . . . You were poking around, weren't you, and having to lean over? And I thought at one stage your other hand was doing a spot of investigating by itself. On me, that is. D'you get what I mean?'

She looked at him full-face. Deepset though they were, his eyes were bulging and his colour had risen, beet-red. He blinked several times.

Before he could speak, she went on swiftly. 'Of course, I realize now how wrong I was. You're not the sort, Mr Wigthorpe, are you? I was just being fanciful. But that's the reason I went off in a bit of a huff. Can you forgive me?'

He swallowed, twice. Then cleared his throat. 'Miss Cox, you're putting me in a rather awkward position. A driving instructor—'

'I know, I understand.' With a small deft movement she tapped the catch of his seat-belt, releasing it. He seemed unaware of what she had done. He looked dazed. Regenerating her widest smile, she added roguishly, 'I'm not saying I'd have blamed you, anyhow. I mean, two people packed close together in a car . . . A lot of temptation, isn't there? That's why you instructors have to be extra careful. I appreciate that.'

'But the point is—'

'I was annoyed with myself, mainly. For over-reacting.'

'Not at all. If you had reason to suppose—'

'That's just it. There wasn't any reason. And that choked me a bit, too, when I came to look back.'

Glancing away, Mr Wigthorpe scanned the surrounding woodland as if seeking inspiration. He remained mute. Softly she said, 'The truth is, you see, I'm not really the type of girl you might have taken me for. I'm no shrinking violet. I've got modern ideas.'

Once more he cleared his throat. 'There's no necessity for you to—'

'If a man appeals to me, I can't see the sense of smothering the feeling . . . on either side. It's just natural. Why get all uptight about it?'

'But there have to be limits, boundaries. When you're older—'

She turned herself sideways in the seat. 'What does age

have to do with it? Mutual attraction. Isn't this what it's all about?'

She coiled an arm lightly around his neck. He felt rigid. With a slight tug she drew him closer, went halfway to meet him. Her hair brushed his left cheek. Twisted at the waist, he sat with his face towards the rear window of the car. Neither resisting not cooperating, he remained stiffly immobile as she nuzzled his jawline with the tip of her nose. With her free right hand she was pulling at the zip of her sweater. In the ordinary way it ran easily: tonight it had snagged. Overcoming the obstacle with an extra wrench, she took the zip all the way down, parted the sweater. Beneath it she was wearing nothing.

Next, her skirt. The zip-tag eluded her. A moment's panic; then her fingers made contact. She lowered the zip a few inches.

Taking her hand away, she touched the hazard warning lights switch on the panel.

Within seconds, footsteps crunched the gravel outside. Bracing herself against Mr Wigthorpe, careful not to drag herself clear of him, Felicity uttered a scream.

The nearside door was thrown open. 'What's going on?'

Geoff, when he chose, could sound wrathfully authoritative. For a moment, she herself was almost convinced of his anger. Collecting her senses, she started to struggle. 'Please help me,' she gasped. 'I'm being attacked by this man.'

'Out of it, buster. Leave her alone.'

Yanked unceremoniously out of his seat, Mr Wigthorpe landed with both feet on the gravel and the upper part of his body draped around the door-pillar. Geoff peered past him into the car. 'All right, miss? Not hurt? Lucky I was passing. What happened?'

'We were just sitting here, talking, when he made a grab at me.' Felicity made clumsy attempts to zip up the sweater, which was still in disarray. 'He interfered with my clothes.'

'I did nothing of the kind.' Mr Wigthorpe spoke in a throttled way from his half-sprawl. 'I never touched her.'

'Didn't look that way to me.' Geoff made a sign to Felicity with his eyes. Scrambling out by the offside door, she rounded the car to join him, completing the zipping of her sweater in front of Mr Wigthorpe's popping gaze. Shedding his jacket, Geoff placed it prudishly about her shoulders, pulled it across her. 'There you go. Feel a bit shaken up, I dare say. Know this gentleman, do you?'

'Only as an instructor. I wasn't expecting . . .' Burying her face in her hands, Felicity burst theatrically into tears.

'See what you've done?' Geoff demanded of Mr Wigthorpe. 'Scum like you should be locked up. I'll see your employers hear of this.'

'Look, you're under a total misapprehension.' By now the instructor had struggled upright to stand with a hand clutching the car roof while he gazed disbelievingly at the sobbing girl. 'I didn't assault her. On the contrary, she—'

'Try telling that to the magistrates. They'll believe you —oh sure. I'll get you fired for this.'

'Don't be absurd. It's her word against mine.'

'Oh no it's not, squire. I saw what was happening through the window. You'd got her sweater half off.'

'It's not true. If her clothes were disarranged . . .' Mr Wigthorpe groped for words. He looked shell-shocked. 'Who are you, anyway? What right have you got to interfere?'

'I'm a witness, mate,' Geoff said pleasantly. 'Heard of them, have you? Witnesses? I'll be speaking up for this lady in court—count on it. After I've had a word with your firm's management.' He turned righteously to Felicity. 'Like a lift home, miss?'

'Please.' Mopping her eyes with the handkerchief he proffered, she avoided Mr Wigthorpe's gaze.

'The Mini, over there. Door's open, you'll find.'

She began walking slowly towards it. Behind her, Geoff's voice continued its tirade. 'Now then, squire. Let's just sort out a few details, shall we? Aside from your name, which I can find out, no problem, I want to know . . .'

Opening the door of the Mini, Felicity subsided into the front passenger seat and stared numbly ahead at the trees. From the gateway the two male voices were faintly audible, but even with the window down the words escaped her. She felt sick. A van went past at speed. It was the first vehicle along since they had stopped. Geoff had been right. At this time of day, the road to the Common drew little traffic, and such as there was had attention only for its own affairs.

Presently she remembered her skirt. Raising herself in the seat, she reinstated the zip and adjusted the garment until it sat once more comfortably on her hips. Geoff's jacket she removed and hung on the neck-restraint of the adjoining seat. She felt an insistent desire to rinse her hands in ice-cold water.

A renewed scrunching of the gravel announced Geoff's return. Apathetically she looked up as he swung himself into the driver's seat. He bared his teeth at her.

'Okay, partner. Let's fade.'

As he reversed into the road, she saw that Mr Wigthorpe had his head and shoulders inside the Renault, performing movements which indicated that he was brushing the front seats and floor. For some reason the sight brought back her sensation of nausea. She sat in silence, fighting it. Wasting no time in achieving his customary reckless speed, Geoff carolled a few unmusical notes at tenor pitch and biffed the wheel twice with his right palm. 'Lissy, you were great! What a performance! You should be on TV.'

She took a breath: the first, it seemed, for an hour or more. 'What did he . . . ?'

'Two hundred.'

'*How* much?'

'A hundred apiece. Not bad, huh?'

Felicity stared out at the forest. After a moment she said, 'Not as much as we hoped.'

Geoff chortled. 'That's just for starters. Wait till he's coughed up the first instalment. Then he'll be up for grabs.'

'What if he doesn't have the money?'

'Taking a cruise, wasn't he? You don't do the Med on a couple of lousy hundred.' Extracting a cigarette from a packet lying open on the panel shelf, Geoff handed it to her to light. 'Relax, Lissy. If we don't at least double the score by this time next week, I'm losing my touch. The guy's petrified.'

'What did you say to him?'

'Just suggested he might want to keep his job. And I mentioned his aunt. That scared him paralytic. The idea of her getting to hear . . .'

Felicity said lifelessly, 'A few hundred quid isn't going to solve our problems.'

'Won't exactly add to 'em, will it?'

'Won't it?'

Geoff gave her a sharp glance. 'What's got into you? He's a groper—you said so yourself. He deserves to pay for his fun.'

'I don't know. I'm not positive about him touching me. On purpose, I mean. He might've thought it was the seat-plastic.'

A sardonic laugh exploded from Geoff. 'Sure he did.'

She sat silently for half a mile. 'When is he paying up?'

'Tomorrow night, same place. You needn't come. I'll meet you afterwards and we'll celebrate.'

'That'll be nice.'

At Fulton's the next morning, Jo Isaacs studied her with real concern. 'You look worse than ever. Great dark rings under your eyes . . . Sure it's not gastric 'flu or something?'

'I'm all right,' said Felicity. 'Had another bad night, that's all.'

'Something on your mind?'

'Nothing special.'

'Bust-up with Geoff?'

Felicity shook her head. 'Saw him yesterday evening. We went to a disco.'

'That's it, then.' Jo nodded wisely. 'You were too keyed-up to sleep.'

'You might be right.'

At eight o'clock that evening she sat waiting for Geoff in the lounge bar of The Crown and Anchor. A few early-evening male imbibers had eyed her speculatively, but by keeping her face interred in the evening paper she had contrived to preserve her isolation at the corner table, while absorbing not a syllable of the newsprint's contents. Although she felt empty and shaky inside, she couldn't eat. The packet of bacon-flavoured crisps she had purchased with her vodka-and-tonic sat untouched at her elbow. Breakfast had been a cup of strong coffee, and she hadn't bothered with lunch. She knew she needed nourishment, yet the bare thought of it turned her stomach. The vodka was going to her head. Regardless, she ordered a refill.

The bartender raised his eyebrows. 'On a bender tonight?'

'Celebrating,' she told him.

As she paid for the fresh drink, Geoff arrived, wordless and poker-faced. She got him a beer. When she joined him at the table, she could tell from his breath that he had been drinking already. She inspected him anxiously. He seemed in no hurry to talk. Bracing herself with sips from her glass, she took the initiative.

'Well? How did it go?'

He felt inside his hip-pocket. Producing a small buff envelope, he slid it across the table. She placed a hand upon it, but left it lying there. 'A hundred?'

'Fifty.'

'But you said—'

'A hundred. That's all he showed up with. That's your cut. There'll be more to come, don't you worry.'

She stared down at the envelope. 'He's already halved what you agreed. What makes you so sure he'll come up with extra?'

'I told you. He's scared.'

'Then why has he fobbed you off with less?'

'He's not fobbed me off,' Geoff said irritably. 'I'm touching him again next week.'

'What for? Another hundred?'

'Better than peanuts, isn't it?'

'It's got us nowhere,' she said slowly, after an interval. 'We needed at least a thousand between us, just to have a hope of getting started. We've done all this for nothing.'

Geoff shrugged. 'If you don't want it, I'll have it back.' He drew the envelope away. She made no attempt to stop him.

'Try and do something constructive with the money,' she said dully.

'You bet. Pay for new brake-linings, for a start.'

His tetchiness had evaporated. She forced herself to smile at him. 'Well,' she said, 'that's that. Cheerio, Mr Wigthorpe. Have to find a different driving school now, won't I?'

'Lots to choose from.' His grin was vulpine. 'Plenty more Mr Wigthorpes too, I dare say.'

Felicity leaned back. 'Never again. Once is too often.'

In the course of the ensuing week she saw little of Geoff. He was busy, he told her on the phone, chasing up job prospects and taking the Mini in for repairs. His natural bounce was unimpaired. Manifestly he enjoyed having cash to spend. On one topic he was evasive: that of the proposed follow-up meeting with Mr Wigthorpe. Felicity suspected that he had no real intention of further pursuit. She was glad. The entire sordid business was best forgotten.

She continued to have difficulty in sleeping.

On the Friday morning of the following week she came down to breakfast to find her mother seated at the kitchen table, intent upon an item in the local newspaper. At Felicity's appearance she looked up. 'Arthur Wigthorpe,' she announced. 'Wasn't that the name of your bloke? The one teaching you to drive?'

Felicity's vitals gave a lurch. 'Right,' she agreed, with outward calm. 'What's he in the news for? Instructor of the Year Award?'

'Far from it. He's been found dead, poor beggar. Aspirin overdose. Killed himself, they reckon.' Mrs Cox passed her daughter the newspaper. 'Too many dealings with the likes of you, I shouldn't wonder. Shot his nerves.'

The rest of the day slipped by in a fog. The one distinct recollection to stay with Felicity up to late afternoon was a mid-morning telephone conversation with Geoff: she had a notion that she had tried his number half a dozen times before finally reaching him, but the important thing was that they had spoken and agreed to meet. Through the shroud, she clung to that. At lunchtime, instead of going to the canteen with Jo she wandered out to the shops, but bought nothing; simply drifted amid the crowds, searching for something she couldn't pin down. Later, without conscious effort, she found herself back at her workbench. From extremely close range, Jo was addressing her earnestly and incomprehensibly. Some while later, the staff welfare officer was asking questions while feeling her forehead and peering into her eyes.

Later still, she was in a car. The driver was vaguely known to her. From another department, he sometimes gave her outline designs to develop. He, too, was asking questions.

'You're sure I can't take you right to your door?'

'No, thanks. This'll be fine.'

'Get straight to bed, won't you?'

She promised to go to bed.

When the car was out of sight she turned away from the mouth of her own street and caught a bus back into town. Since there was an hour to kill, she had a black coffee in a bar and took two more codeine tablets, making six in the day . . . or was it eight? She couldn't recall, and anyhow they seemed to make no difference to the headache. It wasn't a genuine headache. More a sensation of pressure, as if the skull were being asked to accommodate more than it could.

The Mini was five minutes late. When it finally arrived at the agreed corner she got inside with barely a glance. 'Drive up to the Common.'

Geoff complied inscrutably. Neither of them spoke until the car was wedged into their favourite spot, between clumps of gorse on the side of the Common farthest from the town, remote from the nearest through road. It was amazingly quiet. Felicity could hear the beating of tiny mallets inside her bruised head. She turned to face him.

'When did you see him again?'

'Tuesday.' Geoff answered with a kind of sullen airiness.

'And I suppose you put the screws on?'

'What we agreed, wasn't it?'

'How much did you get out of him, that time?'

'Another hundred.' Tilting himself, Geoff produced an envelope. 'Here's your fifty.'

She averted her face. 'I don't want it.'

'Suit yourself.' The envelope crackled as he stuffed it away. 'Bit late in the day, isn't it, to get sensitive?'

'You wouldn't understand.'

'Look. I didn't ask the bloke to take it so hard. He shouldn't have tried to get fresh with you.'

'He never did.'

'He what?'

'I don't believe he'd any intention . . . What's the use? He's gone now.' She staredly bleakly out at the Common. 'When you left him on Tuesday, did you say you'd be back?'

'I left him to figure it out for himself.'

She said bitterly, 'Well, he did that all right, didn't he?'

Raindrops spotted the Mini's windscreen. It was the end of a dry spell. Felicity sat tracing the progress of the droplets as they crawled down to the lower edge of the frame. Beside her, Geoff stretched and yawned.

'Snivelling about it won't fetch him back. He'd only himself to blame, for Christ's sake. If he didn't want to pay, he needn't have. He could have taken us on. Only he didn't. I know what that suggests to me.'

Her mind raced in useless circles. While she was striving to bring it to heel, she felt a hand and arm slide around her waist, tighten slightly. Geoff's voice crooned into her right ear. 'You think it through, Lissy. You'll find I'm right. So in the meantime, why eat your heart out? Serves no purpose. Come on.'

Unwillingly she let herself be impelled against the front of his leather jacket. Their lips made contact. Light contact. Geoff knew when not to rush her. As the magic started to flow, she relaxed a little, sagged towards him. The position was excruciating. Her body was twisted and the contents of the zip-pockets near his lapels pressed painfully into her. She drew back. 'Take that thing off.'

Responding with alacrity, he threw the jacket on to the rear seat.

By the time they had quietened and the car had stopped rocking, the rainfall had increased to a torrent. Geoff lit up the inevitable cigarette. Limp against the door, she watched him smoke it to the end, saw his languor slip away, the restlessness return. Sure enough, he sat up. 'Told Bob I'd help out at the disco tonight. Let's shift.'

He gave the ignition key a wrench. The starter whirred, without result. Repeated attempts ended in failure. Finally the battery signalled exhaustion. Geoff swore.

'This sodding rain. Leads must be drenched.' Opening the door, he climbed out and raised the bonnet.

Felicity sat up. The sense of melancholy was creeping back: to take her mind off it she exposed the visor-mirror and used it in patting her hair into place, then found her lipstick. While applying some, she spotted the jacket on the rear seat. She called out, 'Don't get wet.'

Half-buried in the engine, Geoff failed to hear. Retrieving the jacket, she was about to get out of the car with it when the extreme bulkiness of one of the zip-pockets proclaimed itself to her knuckles. She frowned. At this rate, the entire cut of the garment would be distorted. Unzipping the pocket, she inserted her fingers.

Out came a bundle of banknotes, doubled inside an elastic band.

A clink of metal from the front of the Mini jerked her back to an awareness of her surroundings. How long had she sat there, staring out unseeingly at the saturated gorse? The cramp in her limbs rivalled that in her brain. Fumbling open the door, she crawled out on the squelching turf. At her approach, Geoff glanced up. Rat-tailed hair hung about his eyes. He said brusquely, 'Get back in, you little idiot. No sense two of us getting soaked.'

She held up the bundle. 'Did you get this from him?'

Under the moisture, his face turned a dull red. 'You been snooping in my belongings?'

'*Your* belongings? There must be a couple of thousand quid here. Where did it come from, Geoffrey?'

'Sold some disco gear.' Snatching the bundle, he pocketed it in his trousers. 'I was keeping it as a surprise.'

'What gear? You don't have any. You got it from *him*. I'm right, aren't I?'

'If you say so.' A sneer disfigured his voice. 'Never wrong, are you? Self-righteous little tart. You and your precious Mr Wigthorpe deserved each other, I reckon.' He tugged viciously at a lead. 'What you got to complain of, anyhow?

I offered you some, but you wouldn't take it. You look after your conscience, doll, I'll take care of mine.'

Turning his back on her, he set to work on the lead with a dry cloth.

Across the wing of the car lay a heavy box-spanner. It fitted snugly into Felicity's palm. Raising her arm high, she brought the tool down with as much force as she could muster, felt the jarring of muscle as it connected. Geoff, she observed cloudily, was lying sprawled rather untidily across the engine. There was a job that needed finishing; a pattern to complete. Lifting the spanner again, she took careful aim.

Dispersed by the downpour, the trickling crimson made a vivid contrast, she noticed, with the lemon-yellow bodywork of the Mini. In its way, it was quite appealing. For her next design, she would have to bear it in mind.